JEEVES AGAIN

JEEVES AGAIN

Twelve New Stories from the World of

P. G. Wodehouse

ALAN TITCHMARSH • ANDREW HUNTER MURRAY
DEBORAH FRANCES-WHITE • DOMINIC SANDBROOK
FERGUS CRAIG • FRANK SKINNER • IAN MOORE
JASPER FFORDE • JOHN FINNEMORE • RODDY DOYLE
SCARLETT CURTIS • WILLIAM RAYFET HUNTER

HUTCHINSON
HEINEMANN

HUTCHINSON HEINEMANN

UK | USA | Canada | Ireland | Australia
India | New Zealand | South Africa

Hutchinson Heinemann is part of the Penguin Random House group of companies whose addresses can be found at global.penguinrandomhouse.com

Penguin Random House UK,
One Embassy Gardens, 8 Viaduct Gardens, London SW11 7BW

penguin.co.uk

First published 2025

002

Copyright © Fergus Craig, Scarlett Curtis, Roddy Doyle, Jasper Fforde, John Finnemore, Deborah Frances-White, Andrew Hunter Murray, Ian Moore, William Rayfet Hunter, Dominic Sandbrook, Frank Skinner, Alan Titchmarsh, 2025

The moral right of the authors has been asserted

This work is published with the permission of the Estate of P. G. Wodehouse. The rights of the Estate and its copyright in the works and characters of P. G. Wodehouse are reserved throughout the world.

Penguin Random House values and supports copyright. Copyright fuels creativity, encourages diverse voices, promotes freedom of expression and supports a vibrant culture. Thank you for purchasing an authorised edition of this book and for respecting intellectual property laws by not reproducing, scanning or distributing any part of it by any means without permission. You are supporting authors and enabling Penguin Random House to continue to publish books for everyone. No part of this book may be used or reproduced in any manner for the purpose of training artificial intelligence technologies or systems. In accordance with Article 4(3) of the DSM Directive 2019/790, Penguin Random House expressly reserves this work from the text and data mining exception.

Set in Garamond MT Pro 15.5/18.4
Typeset by Six Red Marbles UK, Thetford, Norfolk

Printed and bound in Great Britain by Clays Ltd, Elcograf S.p.A.

The authorised representative in the EEA is Penguin Random House Ireland, Morrison Chambers, 32 Nassau Street, Dublin D02 YH68

A CIP catalogue record for this book is available from the British Library

ISBN: 978–1–529–15421–4

Penguin Random House is committed to a sustainable future for our business, our readers and our planet. This book is made from Forest Stewardship Council® certified paper.

Contents

1. The Icebreaker
   by Frank Skinner — 1
2. Jeeves and the Forbidden Fruit
   by John Finnemore — 29
3. Ah Jaysis, Jeeves
   by Roddy Doyle — 62
4. The Age of Spode
   by Dominic Sandbrook — 94
5. Mixed Doubles
   by Deborah Frances-White — 118
6. Drive On, Jeeves
   by Andrew Hunter Murray — 149
7. On Becoming Aunt Agatha
   by Scarlett Curtis — 196
8. Dead Body in My Hotel Room
   by Fergus Craig — 210
9. Just Ask Jeeves
   by William Rayfet Hunter — 234
10. Jeeves and Wooster II
    by Alan Titchmarsh — 269
11. Jeeves Out-Jeeved
    by Jasper Fforde — 291
12. Jeeves by a Nose!
    by Ian Moore — 340

The Icebreaker

Frank Skinner

I have never made a secret of the fact that, ever since I chose Jeeves to serve at my right hand, he has been, in all matters, barring his rather terse opinions on my appetite for speculative daywear, an absolute brick. Consequently, it shook me somewhat to see him down on all fours, looking up at me like a hound who couldn't nose the old aniseed. 'I say, Jeeves, are you pursuing a collar-stud?' I asked, trying to conceal my burgeoning concern for his good health.

'No, sir,' he gasped. 'I'm afraid being suddenly belched forth by a block of ice caught me somewhat unbraced. Perhaps I could trouble you for some assistance?'

'I'd be more than happy to muck in, Jeeves, but I'm afraid that, in my case, the old frozen vault hasn't quite relinquished its grip.' I raised my left arm to point at my right, still encased in the cold stuff, like a Finnan haddock in a crate.

'Perhaps you could take the arm and leave the sleeve, sir?' Jeeves was always a dashed creative cove when it came to extricating oneself from insistent bother. I tensed my shoulder and rotated my arm in a manoeuvre not dissimilar to the one that produced the much-feared googly which once brought me 6 for 54 when I was first change for the Malvern House Second XI. In a flash, I was helping Jeeves back to *Homo erectus*.

'Well, I suppose I'd better give Professor Mayhew his five pounds,' I muttered, with some rue.

'Are you in the professor's debt, sir?' Jeeves asked, always, it seemed to me, slightly affronted at the suggestion that I might live some part of my life free as the feathery ones and temporarily disengaged from his close captaincy.

'The thing is, Jeeves, I bet the professor five pounds that he couldn't freeze me in a block of ice for a whole hour without me perishing in the first twelfth. He insisted that I'd emerge, as the clock marked sixty minutes, fresh as a daisy. And, blast it all, he was spot on.'

'If the experiment had caused you to expire, sir, how did you intend to receive your winnings?'

'Well, in cash, obviously,' I rejoined. 'I wouldn't risk a cheque from that scoundrel.'

Jeeves was generally as sharp as a tack, but it seemed the big freeze had somewhat hampered his reasoning. 'I fail to see why I was also frozen,' he said, in a tone that had much in common with indignation.

'Yes. I wasn't expecting us both to get the shove,' I confessed. 'Dashed tight squeeze in that freezer thing. He'll probably claim double-bubble, but we shook hands on a fiver and I'm d—'

'Does it seem odd to you, sir, that the room has changed so considerably in the course of that frozen hour?' Jeeves suddenly enquired.

'Well, that's because it's a different room altogether,' I explained. 'Anyone can see that. Mayhew must have shoved us in a storeroom or the like. Probably keen to get me out of the way so he could continue flirting with Millicent. The old goat was positively salivating. I thought I was going to have to take a chamois leather to the poor girl.'

'I could be mistaken, sir,' he said with a tone of disbelief that rather undermined that suggestion, 'but if one might ignore the dust, the cobwebs, the peeling paint and other signs of neglect, magnified, it seems, by the passage of time, the room is just as it was when we were bundled into the ice-chamber. There is the professor's desk, with its test tubes and jars. Here, the framed reproduction of the Periodic Table. There, the ashtray where you and the other gentlemen rested your cigars.' Jeeves was waving his arms around as though he was communicating the prices for a twelve-horse handicap in fluent tic-tac. 'And there, the door where I entered the scene, enticed by the roar of motors and the loud crackle of electricity.'

'Bally awful, that cheroot,' I said. 'Scientific types, they're all the same, Jeeves. They get awfully feverish about cobalts and calciums but spend no time at all on choosing a decent smoke.'

'My contention, sir—' Jeeves continued, with some increase in volume, stubbing out my cigar talk with an abruptness prompted, I felt, by simmering impatience.

Look, at this point, I feel I must interject and declare, with the greatest respect, and all that rot, that Jeeves could be quite curt if he felt I wasn't totally buying into one of his brainwaves. He was usually right, of course, but being 'usually right' was the cross that Jeeves had been fated to bear and I, on occasions such as this, often found myself cast as his Simon of Cyrene.

'My contention,' he repeated, with the underlying frustration of someone forced to call their dog to heel for a second time, 'is that we have been in the ice for a good deal longer than sixty minutes.'

My response featured a small stagger. 'Oh, Jeeves! I hope you're not saying what I think you're saying.'

'I fear I am, sir.'

'But surely I'll be back on the clock for lunch with Freddie at the Withington?' His nose-wrinkling suggested that my prompt arrival for that appointment was far from certain. 'I mean, there's no real need to change the old togs. If anything, the icy interlude has spruced up the whole ensemble. I wouldn't be the first gentleman to arrive for lunch at the Withington in his evening wear. I could, at least, cross the finishing line in time for a *tarte Tatin*?'

Completely ignoring my plea for reassurance, Jeeves said, 'Might you help me with this door, sir? We seem to have been incarcerated.' He rattled an uncooperative handle.

'Oh, that's bad form,' I exclaimed, as I offered Jeeves an extra shoulder. 'We'd best be brisk or poor Millicent will be in danger of losing her good name. That old test tube twiddler has probably already swooped to swaddle her in swan's wing, as, I think, the Greek expressed it.' I'm not totally sure what the Greek meant, in that instance, but it conjures up the sort of behaviour a decent chap might think rather forward. Jeeves is often compelled to put me right on my poetic allusions but the sudden bursting open of the door provided a helpful distraction. We stepped through it, Jeeves struck a lucifer, and we inched our way through timber and rubble 'amid the encircling gloom' as the cardinal so neatly put it. The papist writers are dashed good when it comes to gloom and the like. We scrambled about in the old 'encircling' for what seemed like an absolute age. We climbed unreliable stairs, we tiptoed over absent floorboards. The prof didn't mind risking five pounds on a reckless wager, but he clearly drew the line at paying seven shillings a week for a diligent maid.

Jeeves pulled and prodded at various sections of wall but the black-bat night had definitely not flown and didn't seem to be in any hurry to do so. Then, at last, he tore at a whole section of boards and rails that eventually fell away to reveal a high window. Light didn't exactly stream in, but it did its very best to illuminate the grime. To my surprise, Jeeves scurried up the wall like a marmoset and came to rest on an elevated ledge. He wiped a pane of the window with his fingers, peered out in silence and then, after a pause in which he seemed to be deliberately gathering himself, he beckoned me to share his shelf and have an observatory ogle.

When, with some help from my sturdy valet, I finally reached the perch, I gazed outward and audibly gasped. Jeeves, I felt, would have gasped in a similar fashion but by now he was on an I-told-you-so mission that was too urgent to be interrupted by an expulsion of air.

'As I said, sir,' he almost purred, 'a good deal longer than sixty minutes.'

In my youth, I travelled to Italy. My Latin master, the Reverend Nantwich, had long trumpeted the merits of the Roman poets. Such was the persuasive nature of his blah-blah-blah that a classmate, Porky Ellwood-Smythe, and I set off to breathe the air they breathed, if you'll forgive the intimate nature of my metaphor. Turned out the modern blighters had ditched Latin and replaced it with a language with which we were not familiar. The second revelation was that the Eternal City was quite different from Mayfair and its environs. We anticipated the odd pagoda to add a dash of local colour but we certainly weren't anticipating anything quite so, well, foreign.

But now I looked upon a scene even stranger, even more alien and, in some inexplicable way, one made particularly unsettling by the odd flash of the familiar. There were many automobiles of various colours, with chassis much less interrupted by horns and levers than was the usual. For all that, they didn't seem to be moving any faster than the ones I was used to. The inhabitants of the scene were certainly a strange lot. There was a young man whose trousers were worn so low that, even at this distance, I could see the upper part of his underthings. I couldn't decide whether aforesaid trousers were falling down or he was rising up out of them. There was a woman carrying a dog and pulling a suitcase behind her, in a complete reversal of the norm. But, at the same time, just across the street was the local branch of my bank that I regularly frequented to top up the lolly for some jaunt or other and, some fifty yards to my left, the dear old Church of St Boniface, where I'd joined the congregation for Binky Baxter's memorial service. Poor chap had mistaken some fearsome fungus for a scarlet elf cup. Thus he died of ignorance, a merciless killer that has done for so many of my social group.

The shops seemed more colourful, the windows much larger. There were sausages and newspapers, pretty much the staples of life, but there were also things that left me startled. One grocery shop boasted, on its frontage, that it sold cider for three pounds a bottle. Three pounds! I should scarcely spend that on a demi of Château Lafite. Strangely, the architecture above the shops seemed as before. It was as if the buildings had risen up out of the pavement, like that young chappie had risen up out of his slacks, to reveal retail-driven underthings that had been previously hidden below.

The positioning of the bank and the proximity of the church showed that Jeeves was, as per usual, quite right. The evidence did indeed suggest that the room we had woken in was the same one in which Professor Mayhew pulled that joystick, sending poor Jeeves and I off on our frosty whatevers. 'Earth stood hard as iron / Water like a stone,' as the poet says, and we two fellows had pretty much followed suit. But that still didn't explain 'this brave new world that hath such people in it' which we gazed upon, from our dusty vantage point.

'I say, Jeeves,' I piped up, gesturing towards the street, 'how do you explain this brave new world that has such people in it?'

'I believe, sir, the Bard elides the last two words to "in't".'

'Hard times, price of paper,' I replied. 'Even the greats must sometimes economise. Sobering thought but there you have it. Thing is, Jeeves, I'm less concerned with Shakespeare's stationery cupboard than I am with our current state of affairs. What on earth has happened to the high street? Where are the parasols, where are the boaters and, as for the emporia, please tell me,' I said, now pointing at a nearby shop sign, 'what level of moral observance and old-fashioned piety is required to guarantee a pilgrim his place in Vape Heaven?'

Jeeves, at first, seemed reticent to reply but soon recovered his natural assurance. 'I cannot answer your theological question, sir, but as to the disappearance of familiar items of fashion, I believe that parasols, boaters and a good many other accoutrements are no longer *en vogue*.'

'Dash it all, Jeeves! I ask for clarity and what do you give me? French!'

'Forgive me, sir. My theory is that parasols and boaters have simply gone out of fashion'.

'Out of fashion?' I said, my incredulity unhidden by my tone. 'In sixty minutes?'

'Perhaps you could help me with this window, sir?' he said, rather pointedly changing the subject.

I was becoming uneasy about this new trend, i.e. Jeeves asking me to help him with things.

Getting him to his feet, forcing various locks and handles: our relationship was beginning to veer towards democracy. That simply wouldn't do. Jeeves may well be cleverer than me, but the basic social order must not be strained. It seemed to me that if one agrees to carry the dog, one will soon end up leading the suitcase. Even in the midst of all this confusion and strangeness, I was rather pleased with that thought. Again, I wasn't completely sure what I meant by it, but I had the feeling it might qualify as an adage.

Oh, I say! I'd invented an adage. I'd only discovered what one was a few weeks ago. Jeeves had given me a bit of an 'adages for beginners' chat at the Cheltenham racecourse following my confused response to something he'd said about a fool and his money. Now I was in the know on the adage front, it was my intention to jolly well slot one in at every opportunity, even if, as in this instance, it was to remain unspoken. I mean, I had only become aware of the dog/suitcase turnaround two minutes ago and now here I was employing it as wordplay. I should have liked to try it on Jeeves while it was still warm from the pan, so to speak, but I decided the matter of the master becoming the servant was a bit too volatile to air in this current situation. Instead, I followed my valet's instructions and, pretty soon, after much strain and straddling, we were standing outside the house.

'Right,' I said, shortly after our soles hit *terra firma*. 'I'm going to give that scoundrel a piece of my mind and take poor Millicent straight home. I mean, it's daylight, for goodness' sake! Her poor mother will be a fountain of tears.'

'That might prove difficult, sir,' Jeeves said, pointing over my right shoulder. I turned to the wall behind me to find a blue plaque, emblazoned with the following dedication:

PROFESSOR BERNARD MAYHEW 1878–1969
PIONEER OF CRYOGENICS. LIVED AND
WORKED IN THIS BUILDING.

'What a thing!' I muttered, with some confusion. 'I have to admit, Jeeves, I did not notice that when we arrived last night. Some ruse for avoiding debtors, I shouldn't be surprised.' I read it again. 'What the devil is cryogenics?'

'There was an article about it in *The Times*, sir. It seems someone froze a rat in a block of ice for two weeks or so. When the ice was finally melted, the rat emerged unharmed.'

'Well,' I said, supportively, 'that is fascinating, Jeeves, but we must try and stick to matters that are relevant to our current situation.'

'Yes, sir.'

'The thing is, we're too bally smart for him. We weren't born under a mulberry bush, yesterday, and all that. No mocked-up memorial is going to stop me from giving that charlatan a piece of my mind,' I announced, striding towards the prof's front door. Jeeves eyed me like a pretty girl watching an army march towards certain annihilation. I had no idea he was so afraid of the professor. Undeterred, I reached for the front doorbell. Something else I hadn't noticed last night was that the man of science had, in fact, four doorbells. Some harebrained experiment or other, no doubt. Or was it? Each button had a small nameplate next to it. There was a dentist, something called a Wellness

Clinic, a cranial something-or-other – I should not have been surprised to discover another annex of Vape Heaven – but there was no mention of Mayhew. I'm not sure exactly how I looked at Jeeves, at this juncture, but it may well have been pleadingly.

'Perhaps we might sit here, sir,' he said, pointing at a suitable wall. 'I fear you are not altogether grasping our predicament.'

'So, you're seriously telling me we have woken up in 1969?'

'I suspect it is some time even later than that, sir,' Jeeves replied. 'The plaque does not have the look of a recent addition.'

I placed my head in my hands. It was quite a thing to consider. Like when the bridge club finally discovered the truth about the Reverend Harper.

'Of course, there is one sure way of discovering the actual date,' Jeeves said. He patted my back reassuringly as we walked towards the bank.

'But I don't feel any older, Jeeves,' I protested as we walked. 'I mean, I've hardly a bristle. We should both have beards like sages.'

'I believe our entire bodily functions were suspended, sir.'

'Steady on, Jeeves,' I said, slightly affronted. 'Keep the party clean and all that.'

'Forgive me, sir,' he replied. 'It seems time travel has made me somewhat skittish.'

We entered the bank. Jeeves was right. (A phrase I would happily carve on his headstone if I had the chisel skills.) I recognised the large, ornate glass case above the counters, in which the calendar mechanism was held. The case, at least, had not changed a jot. The date, however, had changed considerably: 7 July 2025. We sat, simultaneously, on a convenient wooden bench.

'But Jeeves, we've slept for almost a hundred years. I didn't sleep that long when I was at Eton.' We sat in silence, both, I assumed, giving a good deal of serious thought to the situation. 'Well, that's ta-ta to the *tarte Tatin*,' I eventually concluded.

'Quite, sir,' he sighed. We sat amongst our own thoughts for some further minutes. At last, I gave in.

'So, come on, Jeeves, what's the plan?' I entreated.

'Plan, sir?'

'Yes. The plan. How do we get back to 1929?' He went quite pale. It could only mean one thing. I had to accept the unacceptable. He did not have a plan. It was like getting a wet rugger ball smack in the solar plexus. 'But dash it, Jeeves, you always have a plan,' I protested. He went even paler, like those terrifying portraits of Good Queen Bess, when she looks like a French clown.

'I think I need a little air,' he mumbled, and left the bank. It was, I thought, pretty rum behaviour, leaving a fellow on his lonesome in the wrong century. I was about to snuggle down into a warm blanket of self-pity when someone spoke to me.

'Can I help you, sir?' she said. She was bespectacled and quite lank in the hair department.

'Probably not,' I said, slightly cranking up the tone of despair. Why is it that one's actual, authentic tone of despair never seems quite good enough? It's like when one's ill. I think to myself, well, I am ill but if I just be ill, with no trimmings or performance, no one will believe me. I need to contrive an extra level, for effect. And then I end up doing a regular David Garrick.

'Do you have an account with us?' the lady asked.

'Erm, well, I'm not sure. I certainly used to have an account with you, but I've been . . . er . . . inactive for some time. You see, I met this scientist . . .'

'Well, if you'd like to come to the counter, sir, we can check your balance. If you've been with us for some time, it might be that you've accrued interest on your savings . . .'

'I say, Jeeves. I think we should try and be a tad more positive about this situation,' I said, emerging from the bank like a forty-niner who'd just hit pay dirt. 'The Woosters have always made the best of a bad job, even when things looked hopeless. When my Great-Uncle Walter was challenged to a duel—'

'Perhaps we should read a newspaper, sir,' he said, gesturing towards a fellow standing with a bundle of them, a little further down the road. 'It might help us get a better idea of what kind of world we find ourselves in.'

'Yes, Jeeves. It will probably be a dashed exciting read. You stay there.' His usual skin tone was slowly returning. I marched off towards the newspaper vendor. The fellow thrust one in my hand as soon as I came within reach.

'How much?' I asked.

'Oh, a hundred pounds should cover it,' he replied with a rather over-familiar sparkle. He was a handsome young fellow, very blue eyes, but he seemed to have chosen 'bedraggled' as his signature look. He wore a sort of undershirt, with no collar, which had a large tick across the chest area, as though he had won the approval of some draper.

'Oh, I say,' I protested. 'I could get thirty-three bottles of cider for that and still have change.'

'Well,' he countered, his sparkle evolving into a

positive dazzle, 'they say an apple a day keeps the doctor away. And I don't remember anyone saying that apple couldn't be fermented.' My previous pride at being an exponent of the adage was somewhat reduced. If adages were the stock in trade of mere newspaper sellers, I should have to find something more exclusive. I handed him a hundred pounds from the large wad I had just withdrawn from the bank. It would not, I lamented to myself, last long in a world where even newspapers were so expensive. I had not become as rich as I thought.

The blue-eyed man's dazzle suddenly descended like a basement-bound elevator. It didn't even stop at 'sparkle' on the way down. He too took on the pallor of the Virgin Queen. He seemed to be in shock. I looked about me to discover what had rocked him so, but it was hard for me to discern any particular 'unusual' in an wholly unusual world.

I dashed back to Jeeves who seemed much more like his old self. 'I need to give some thought to accommodation, sir. Berkeley Mansions will certainly have a new resident. Indeed, it may no longer be extant.' I might have found myself suddenly homeless, but I still had enough self-respect to resist asking him the meaning of 'extant'. 'But what about my belongings?' I said. 'I should be sad to think those pink spats have gone for ever.'

'The loss of "those pink spats", sir, is one of the few pools of light in a sea of darkness,' he replied. Personally, I thought that was a bit strong but any risk of estrangement, just at the minute, seemed unwise. I did not wish to find myself, like the beady-eyed mariner, 'alone on an open sea' so to speak.

At that moment, a young woman, clearly in a state of some distress, approached us, pointing and shouting as if the barbarians were at the gate. The first thing that struck one about her was her red hair. I don't mean red hair such as is commonly found spouting from one of our Celtic brethren. I mean red hair as in hair that is the exact shade of a fine claret. I assumed she was some sort of theatrical who'd stepped out for a breath of the fresh stuff during a convenient interval. One could imagine her confidently predicting the next Thane of Cawdor. I will not directly quote what she said to Jeeves and myself because it was interspersed with a good deal of barrack-room language, but her thrust was that the man she pointed out, racing away down the street, was a thief and that we should pursue him with some purpose. I thought she said he had stolen her phone but that seemed highly unlikely unless she lived close by. He was certainly not trailing cable.

Jeeves did not seek further clarification of the man's crime, but set off like a lurcher at the heels of a hare. I had no idea he could move so fast. The young woman, with little regard for her abandoned cauldron, followed close behind. Her surprisingly long stride was unhindered by the usual ladies' apparel. She was wearing some sort of plimsolls and her skirt, if one might call it that, was so short I assumed it to be an undergarment. It was, I supposed, possible that her *actual* skirt was what the man had stolen. Of course, her get-up could have been theatrical togs but surely no sensible witch would approach a blasted heath in such scant covering.

All this pontification had left me at rather a disadvantage so far as catching the crook was concerned. I hadn't really run since school but the alternative – turning on my heels to seek a nice pavement café and a pot of Bohea – didn't seem quite the gentlemanly thing to do, so off I shot.

I managed to catch up with my fellow-hounds just in time to see the hare board a departing omnibus. He soon appeared at the upper rear window of the vehicle, waving some illuminated rectangular object and grinning triumphantly. She of the red hair turned on me with some venom. Her coarse language was now almost completely uninterrupted by acceptable utterance. It seemed that I had unintentionally put the tin hat on her already awful afternoon when, as the man's laughing face had disappeared into the distance, I'd instinctively waved. I argued that he began the waving process, but she countered with a stream of unpleasantness. Again, it seemed to include the word 'phone' but I would be loath to report any other details.

'Taxi,' I heard Jeeves call and turned to find he had brought a hackney carriage to a kerbside halt. Having recovered from his initial shock, he now seemed less disturbed by the twenty-first century than he was by my pink spats.

Jeeves asked the cabbie if he would be so kind as to pursue the omnibus until it came to a designated halt, so that we might change the proverbial horses in midstream. I sat as far away from the turbulent theatrical as the cab's seating would allow, only then to disturb the waters further by asking if she was acquainted with the fellow on the bus. In short, she felt him unworthy of her friendship and fully intended to gouge out his eyes when we had him in our grip. I had imagined her involved in the Scottish play but now I pictured her prising the blinkers out of poor old Gloucester. And I did not like the way her thumbs were flexing and unflexing in rabid anticipation.

'So, the object waved from the bus window was your telephone?' Jeeves enquired. His now-recovered composure 'rebuked the winds and the sea and all was calm' or something of that sort. At the mention of her phone, her left thumb suddenly fell lifeless but her right gained considerable speed and vigour. I was beginning to hope that the thief might make a getaway. I did not wish to get 'vile jelly' on what was currently my only outfit.

'I was calling my mum,' she explained, finally uttering something that could be related in direct speech. 'She'll be worried to death,' she continued. 'I was telling her about . . .' She seemed to question whether candour was advisable in this instance and then cast caution, if not quite to the winds, then certainly in their general direction. 'My relationship has recently ended, well, been ended, and my mum is very supportive.' I think I felt less discomfort when she was screaming at me. This was hardly a conversation for mixed company. But then, to my surprise, nay, to my horror, Jeeves chimed in.

'I was once what one might call "close" to a seamstress in Kennington,' he began. 'We would walk in the park, arm-in-arm. I don't know that I've ever been prouder or happier to be seen out in public with someone.'

I must admit I was genuinely hurt by that latter remark. Luckily, the intense heat being generated by my current embarrassment served to cauterise the wound.

'We spoke of marriage, of children even,' he continued.

I began to consider the risks of leaping from a moving vehicle.

'But then,' Jeeves said, with a slight tremble in his voice, 'I received a letter which . . .' He faltered and fell silent. The woman took his hand in hers. He looked into her eyes. 'It was a long time ago,' he murmured.

'It certainly was,' I interjected. Jeeves looked anxiously across as if I was about to reveal all but even I could see that a yarn about being frozen in a block of ice for a hundred years would do little to reduce the already gargantuan awkwardness of the current conversation. Instead, I decided to go in from the top diving board.

'The only female who really broke my heart came second in the St Leger,' I said, with a wistful look through the cab window. The thespian glowered at me as if I was joking. The confessional thing, it transpired, wasn't really my forte. Once again, my authentic tone of despair had let me down. If only I'd had the courage to attempt a trembling voice.

Happily, the cabbie chipped in with some old-fashioned lower-class practicality. 'Here's the bus,' he announced. 'That'll be thirteen quid.' I handed him twenty as I scrambled onto the pavement.

THE ICEBREAKER

Jeeves and his new friend raced towards the bus, and, to my great dismay, they were still holding hands. I'm not a person who gets flustered about an age difference – my Great-Uncle Morty, a notorious philanderer, married a chambermaid who was young enough to be his granddaughter, only to eventually discover that she was precisely that – but this was really pushing it. Jeeves must've been only a few scampered singles away from one hundred and fifty.

The thief clearly saw us coming because he suddenly emerged from the stationary vehicle and bounded down a nearby alley. This passageway was so narrow that Jeeves and the actress had to abandon their impromptu hand-holding and switch to single file in order to continue the pursuit. I tagged on behind, happy to let Jeeves get all the glory. The alley terminated in a small, closed-off courtyard. As we came to a halt at its centre, we realised our quarry had stopped just inside the entrance. That entrance had now become an exit and one that was blocked by the thief. He had pocketed the twenty-first-century telephone and was holding, instead, a large knife.

'I'm going to walk out of this alley and wait at the end,' he said with a snarl. 'The first one to come out gets sliced.'

I was transfixed by the knife's sizeable blade.

This was partly due to its obvious menace but also because, along its length, letters had been cut out to spell a word: P-I-Z-Z-A. It looked like Italian to me. He was probably one of Mussolini's lot. He even wore a black shirt. It had two awful skulls pictured on its lower half and more Italian lingo – 'Metallica' – emblazoned across the chest.

'It wouldn't be the first time I've used—' Our fascist assailant broke off abruptly, mid-sentence, and dropped suddenly to his knees. His swagger sank like a badly managed sponge cake. A second man had appeared in the alley and now had the black-shirted criminal in a very restrictive-looking headlock. I couldn't make out the new arrival's face at first – it was somewhat concealed behind the Italian's black curls – but soon I saw a familiar pair of very blue eyes. He called to me, through the tresses, 'I've been following you since you paid for that newspaper.'

'Should I have tipped?' I asked, wondering if the fascist, currently becoming a little blue from lack of oxygen, had committed the same *faux pas*. Oh, now I was talking French. It had been a very trying day.

'Can one of you phone the police?' the newspaper vendor asked. The red-headed one looked at Jeeves and me in some anticipation. 'Neither I nor Mr Wooster have a "phone",' Jeeves said. The actress and the blue-eyed man stared at us, dumb-founded. I cannot speak for my valet but it would not be an overstatement to say that I experienced, for some unfathomable reason, genuine shame. At this point, the crook, now lavender in hue, reached into his pocket and offered the stolen phone to his restrainer. I knew it to be the stolen phone because, as it appeared, our female associate whimpered like a mother who'd seen her child climbing from a newly moored lifeboat to the safety of the dock. She leaped forward and clutched it, passionately, to her breast.

'I need to call my mum first,' she said. We four watched in silence as she fired out her story. It was a relief to realise that, when speaking to her mother, her vocabulary, unlike the poor phone thief, became considerably less blue. 'I chased him with two posh blokes I met,' she explained. Jeeves and I exchanged a look. We could not prevent the upward movement of our collective eyebrows. 'No, Mum, they're not all stupid. It seems to be about fifty per cent.' At this point, I thought it best to stop listening.

'I'm Richard,' said, well, Richard. He of the newspaper industry. 'I would shake your hand but . . .'

'You need both of them for strangling,' I interjected, helpfully.

'You gave me a hundred pounds for the newspaper. I couldn't believe it. I thought it might be fake money but when I realised it wasn't I jumped on my bike and followed you.'

'If only I could follow you,' I said. 'I have no idea what you mean.'

'The newspaper is free,' he explained. 'The hundred pounds thing was just a stupid joke'.

'Free?' I said, aghast. I turned to Jeeves. He shook his head.

'We have much to discuss, sir.'

'Yes. Quite,' I said, the realisation of our predicament suddenly vivid again. 'Look,' I said to Richard, 'keep the ton. I rather admire your honesty and, by jingo, you got us out of a pretty awful scrape with this chappie.'

'Oh, thank you. That's amazing,' he beamed. I was, it has to be said, expecting a bit more of the old 'No, I couldn't possibly' but the fellow had earned it and, truth be told, a hundred years of interest had left me pretty flush. If we were living in a world where newspapers were free, I probably wouldn't need much cash, anyway.

By now, she of the red hair was introducing herself to Richard. 'I'm Andrea,' she said. Richard was twinkling again.

'She's an actress,' I explained.

'No, I'm not. I'm a tattooist,' she snapped. Good

Lord! I'd assumed all those snakes and serpents were part of her make-up.

'Oh, I was thinking of getting some tats,' Richard, now on full dazzle, said to her. Good idea, I thought. I was starting to feel pretty hungry, myself. 'Do you fancy a coffee or something?' he continued. She mirrored his zeal. Jeeves and I bowed and left the scene.

'Do you think young love is blossoming, Jeeves?' I queried as we moved out of their earshot.

'I think it not out of the question, sir.' We looked back down the alley. The courtyard was bathed in sunlight. 'I must say,' he went on, 'the suffocating felon provides an unlikely chaperon.'

'I thought you were falling for inky Andrea yourself, at one point,' I said, with what, I'm ashamed to admit, could probably be described as a leer.

'No, sir,' he said, firmly. 'In truth, I found her to be something of a wildcat – albeit a broken-hearted one. However, I was prepared to use empathy in order to prevent a public blinding.'

'Ah, I see,' I said, to the loud accompaniment of a penny dropping. 'So the seamstress—'

'To return to the subject of accommodation, sir,' he said, with a sudden practicality of tone, 'I believe I might be able to guide us to the Savoy hotel from here.' We walked on in the sunshine, remarking on all the wonders of this new world. 'Of course, there is the small matter of back-pay,' he casually remarked, at one point.

'There is also the small matter of sleeping on the job,' I rejoined. We walked on.

'As I said, sir, we have much to discuss.'

Jeeves and the Forbidden Fruit

John Finnemore

'A telegram for you, sir.'

Pausing only to emit a strangled yowl, I leaped from my packing case, executed a couple of impromptu dance steps on the planking, and that, as near as a toucher, was the end of the last of the Woosters.

'I beg your pardon, sir.'

'And so you jolly well might, Jeeves! I do wish you'd sound your horn! Particularly when only a half-dozen warped boards lie between the young master and eternity!'

'I must apologise once again, sir. I made the assumption that you had perceived my ascent of the various ladders.'

Well, this, of course, was just the very thing I hadn't perceived. I've spoken elsewhere of the uncanny ability of Jeeves – my man, you know – to materialise and dematerialise at will. This speciality act, unnerving enough even when performed in the home, becomes fraught with peril when executed in the upper echelons, if echelons is the word I want, of St Paul's Cathedral. Had it not been for the cat-like dexterity of the Woosters I should assuredly have ended my career as a fine mist on the floor of the north transept, removable only by mop.

'But half a mo,' I seem to hear the outraged customer baying. 'What's all this rot about Bertie Wooster infesting the belfries of cathedrals?'

The question is a fair one. From Quasimodo, of course, one takes this sort of behaviour in one's stride. One expects it. Ditto in the cases of the pipistrelle, brown long-eared or Natterer's bat. Bats will be bats, one remarks good-naturedly, and passes on. But confronted with the same tendency in Bertram one looks askance, and seeks explanation. Such I shall now provide.

The thing to bear squarely in mind regarding the knotty affair of my Aunt Dahlia, Brigadier Ridley's port, the cryptic verse on the blotter and the shoal of queer fish – to which the above-mentioned telegram was to serve as the starting gun – is that it took place in the early winter of the year Galatea won the Thousand

Guineas. A year also notable for being the one in which that ghastly little tick with the Chaplin 'tache finally made himself so objectionable to one and all that the authorities were compelled to step in. The subsequent imbroglio led, as you doubtless recall, to a good many chaps finding themselves in unlikely places, and an early example of same was the presence of Wooster, B., in the upper portions of a cathedral, St P.'s.

Not that this had been my first choice of billet. I trust I need hardly assure my public that once the binge was finally announced as being on, I lost no time in surging round to the recruitment office and laying the Wooster services at the feet of the British Army. Rather a nasty jar, then, to be asked by what looked like a prefect in fancy dress to kindly pick them back up again.

'We are at present only calling up men between the ages of eighteen and forty-one,' the prefect had said, and this undeniably did rather let me out. However, I did not despair, as I so often don't. A fundamental misunderstanding seemed to me to have arisen between the pride of the school and myself, and I hastened to adjust it.

'Oh, rather, absolutely. But, you know, I wasn't so much thinking of mucking in with the rank and file. Jolly good chaps though they no doubt are,' I added hastily, in case he'd started that way himself. 'No, I rather saw myself trickling in somewhere round about the Col level. Or a notch higher, if poss, because Chuffy Chuffnell has swindled his way into a colonelship, and I'm dashed if I'm going to salute an ass like old Chuffy.'

I don't know if you've ever seen the face of a high priest when an unbeliever blasphemes their sacred idol? I haven't myself, come to that, but now I don't need to.

'Lieutenant Colonel Lord Chuffnell was at Eton, Oxford and the Guards!' the stripling eventually spluttered.

'So was I too at Eton, Oxford and the Guards!' I retorted, stung. 'Except the Guards.'

Well, it turns out that whilst the British Army certainly appreciates the spadework put in by Eton and Oxford, the establishment to which it particularly looks when it wishes to stock up on colonels is the Guards.

These facts established, the boy wonder took down my vital statistics, and promised to notify me if any duties came up for which I was fitted, but he did so with a nasty supercilious smirk which seemed to indicate he felt that these were likely to amount to tucking a rug over my knees, and blowing the froth off my cocoa. Accordingly, I trickled home in disconsolate mood.

'You find me in disconsolate mood,' I informed Jeeves, as the honest fellow relieved me of hat and plied the syphon.

'I am grieved to hear it, sir.'

'Disconsolate to the very gills. It's a little thick, after all, in this time of national travail, that a perfectly fit specimen like myself, ready and eager to do my little all, is given the elbow by an elongated child in epaulettes, purely and simply because his forty-first birthday is a year or two in the rear-view mirror.'

'Most exasperating, sir. If you recall, I took the liberty of mentioning to you that, after my own experience—'

'Yes, yes, yes, yes, yes,' I said, a little snappishly. Jeeves had attempted, the week before, to sign back up with his old regiment from the first show, and they had shown a similar tendency to shuffle the feet and look the other way. I was aware he felt this as keenly as I did, but you know how it is – when one's troubles are fresh one wants to wallow in them a spot rather than hear all about the other fellow's. 'Well, we shall just have to see if the Royal Navy are any better at spotting a good thing when it's served up on a plate with watercress round it.'

'Yes, sir. But in the unhappy event that they are not, might I suggest you consider the role of fire watcher?'

I started like a mustang touched on some tender

spot. 'If by that remark, Jeeves, you intend a nasty crack at my supposed dotage, then I—'

'You misapprehend me, sir. The post of fire watcher is a vital and I may say dynamic one, sir.'

'Oh, it is, is it? And what do they do, these fire watchers?'

'They watch, sir, for fire.'

'Oh, ah? Where?'

'A variety of locales, sir, but perhaps most notably the great cathedrals.'

I remained lightly fogged. 'Are there often fires in the great cathedrals?'

'No, sir.'

'Then, whilst one applauds the safety-first spirit, perhaps an excess of caution, what?'

'It is felt probable, sir, that at some early date hostile forces will seek to encourage such conflagrations by means of the interpolation of incendiary devices.'

There was a time when this would have whizzed straight past me, but practice tells.

'All but the last two words, Jeeves. Once again?'

'Incendiary devices, sir. Or in common parlance, bombs.'

'Oh, I see!' I said, for I saw. 'First the bombs, then the fire?'

'Quite so, sir.'

'Where there's smoke, there's fire, as they say, but

also, where there's bombs, there's dashed well soon going to be fire too, likely as not?'

'In a nutshell, sir.'

'And the fire once under way, these watchers . . . watch it, do they? Observe its movements keenly?'

'No, sir. At that point it becomes their duty to attempt to extinguish the conflagration.'

'Oh! Put it out, you mean?'

'Precisely, sir.'

'With water, and so forth?'

'Water is a valuable tool in the arsenal. Also sand.'

'. . . Sand? Sand, you mean? Stuff you get at Le Touquet, I mean to say? Or Margate?'

'The very material, sir.'

'I wouldn't know what to do with the stuff. I tell you frankly, Jeeves: give Bertram Wooster a pile of sand and a roaring fire, and tell him to do the latter a bit of no good by means of the former, and you have him snookered. He stares at you nonplussed.'

'Training, sir, will be provided.'

Which it dashed well was. And so it came to pass that when this telegram I was going to tell you all about arrived, it found me in my usual roost in St Paul's, as liberally supplied with both sand and water as a young beach. The only things for which I lacked were fires. I don't know if you remember, but this recent contretemps kicked off with something in the nature of a lull or lacuna, if things can kick off with a lacuna, which Jeeves tells me they can't. Things hotted up all right later, I grant you, but for those first few months, proceedings reminded me of nothing so much as that ghastly moment in a country house party when the hostess claps her hands together and states that we simply *must* play charades, and whilst everyone grimly admits that we must, no one actually does.

After weeks of sitting in a chilly cathedral not putting out fires, then, conceive of my excitement upon reading the telegram Jeeves had carried aloft:

Come at once Brinkley Court. Bring Jeeves. Gravest matters of national honour hang upon your presence. At once means now. Do I make myself clear, fathead? PS if London has bananas bring bananas. Also chocolate, worsted, and Tom says pipe cleaners. Travers.

This Travers, I was instantly able to discern, was my Aunt Dahlia. In the past, I have had cause to deprecate the aged relative for a tendency to indulge in the cryptic when composing a telegram. But in the present case I had no such complaint. The recent communication had, I considered, been judged to a nicety. Where clarity was called for, the aunt had been limpid. Where discretion had been indicated, what with Goebbels standing with ears flapping in every telegraph office – I speak metaphorically – she had prudently resorted to the code book.

'Well, Jeeves! Stirring, what?'

'Mrs Travers certainly seems intensely desirous of your presence, sir.'

'Indeed she does. An attitude, if I may say so, from which the British Army could learn not a little. But what the devil can she mean by matters of national honour? Market Snodsbury's a charming spot, but it would be a very dark night on which one would mistake it for the crossroads of Europe.'

'Under usual circumstances, certainly, sir. But one recollects that a platoon of the administrative and logistical corps has just been billeted at Brinkley Court.'

For the second time in this chronicle, I started like a mustang. The same mustang, possibly, or else a colleague.

'By George, that's just what one does recollect! The old shack is positively a nerve centre!'

In this matter of the billeting of the flotsam and jetsam of wartime, you see, the different natures of the two most prominent of my coven of aunts had sharply displayed themselves. My Aunt Agatha, the boa constrictor, had swiftly registered her country seat of Woollam Chertsey with the authorities as being possessed of two bedrooms. In doing this, she neglected to mention that this unusual shortfall in a stately home of England was counter-balanced by its twenty-seven libraries; thanks to a recent and strategic redistribution of the volumes of an *Encyclopaedia Britannica*. My good and deserving Aunt Dahlia, on the other hand, had flung wide the gates of Brinkley Court, and immediately succeeded in bagging these administrators of war.

'Well, Jeeves! Our course seems clear. Perching in the tops of cathedrals watching fires that aren't there is all very well; but there comes a tide in the affairs of men which, well, I forget the rest, but the gist is, it's time for the right element to hustle, forty-three or no bally forty-three.'

'Indeed, sir.'

'Right ho! Then there remains only the coded portion of the *communiqué* to decipher. Slip round to the War Office, Jeeves, and obtain the key.'

'I fancy that will not be necessary, sir.'

'Not necessary? Of course it's necessary! How

else are we to know what she means by bananas and worsted and pipe cleaners?'

'I cannot be sure, sir, but it is my intuition that by "bananas" Mrs Travers wishes to indicate bananas, by "worsted" she means worsted, and by "pipe cleaners", pipe cleaners. Mrs Travers, I surmise, is laying down supplies.'

'Something in that, possibly. Very well, then. Scratch War Office in the recent programme and substitute Selfridges. Then ho for Brinkley Court!'

I don't know if you've ever been to Brinkley Court – and nor do you, come to that, because I've changed its name – but in usual circs it is a tolerably idyllic sort of spot. As Jeeves and self tooled up the drive in the old two-seater later that p.m., however, I noted with regret various innovations which diminished its idyllic qualities not a little. The first was that every window in the place was gummed up with brown paper and packing tape, giving the poor old pile the appearance of being blindfolded. The second, I'm sorry to say, was the appearance of these military administrators, as they loafed about the grounds.

One does not like to Talk Britain Down and all that, but still it must be said that as a fighting force they did not instil confidence. Nor even, for that matter, as an administrative force. Distinctly queer fish, they seemed to me. The ones that weren't tubby were scrawny. Uniforms were worn haphazardly, if at all, and it was hard to escape the conclusion that if this was what the British Army had chosen to recruit in preference to self and Jeeves, then the British Army needed its various heads examining.

But the final, foulest, and least explicable of these innovations was the presence of one of those ghastly topiary bushes in the large flower bed in front of the hall, trimmed to resemble either a snowman or a cottage loaf. I was about to wonder aloud to Jeeves how in the world this excrescence was intended to help the war effort, when the bush revolved on its axis, waved a pleased trowel, and revealed itself as an aunt.

'Ah, Bertie! You got my telegram! Have you bananas?'

In the course of our long association, I had never until that moment seen Jeeves staggered. Deeply moved, yes. Gravely dismayed, by all means. But never staggered. I shouldn't have thought the thing could be done. But it can, and I can now record that what it takes to achieve the feat is the sight of an elderly Englishwoman of gentle birth striding about in broad daylight in an emerald-green romper suit. For such, believe me or believe me not, was the vision that now met our four appalled eyes. Jeeves's two, I mean to say, and my two.

'What's the matter with you, Bertie?' piped the recent bush. 'Don't goggle. Bananas! If you have bananas, prepare to shed them now!'

'Bananas be blowed!' I retorted, once speech returned. 'The upholstery! Why? For what purpose?'

'Oh, this? This is my siren suit. Do you like it?'

Aunt Dahlia was tolerably rich in years by this stage in her career, but age had not withered her. In fact, quite the reverse. You cannot inhale Chef Anatole's fine French cuisine twice a day for twenty years without increasing the tonnage to a certain extent. Take this generous helping of aunt, then, encase it from collarbone to brogues in vivid emerald serge, and the result is something calculated to stagger humanity.

'No, I do not like it. And what's more, nor does Jeeves.'

'What drivel. Of course you like it, don't you, Jeeves?'

The man was by now himself again, though with a certain hard glitter in his eye.

'Since you are so good as to canvass my candid opinion, madam, I do not.'

'Whyever not? Dashed useful garment.'

'No doubt. But distinctly unsuited, if I may say so, to a person of your station.'

'What rot! Why, Winston wears one!'

Jeeves looked at her with quiet reproach.

'Mr Churchill, madam, wears a polka-dot bow tie.'

He had her there, of course. He does.

'Well, I think the pair of you are talking through your hats. It's a perfectly splendid thing. But listen,' she continued, extricating herself from the flower bed, and leading the way into the house like something out of Birnam Wood. 'I didn't bring you here because I wanted your sartorial advice.'

'Then what do you want? Your telegram was long on atmosphere but short on specifics.'

'What I want,' she said, producing a fairly ripe glitter in her own eye, 'is Brigadier Ridley's port.'

'. . . His port?'

'His port.'

'Don't you have your own port?'

'Of course I do. Quarts of the stuff.'

'But you want this Ridley's?'

'I do.'

'And he won't let you have it?'

'Yes, he will! That's just it, drat the man! He's

extended an open invitation for all comers to help themselves!'

'Then I'm not sure I quite see your dilemma.'

'Of course you don't bally well see my dilemma, because you won't stop yapping for two minutes to let me tell you my dilemma! Or, vastly more to the point, tell Jeeves my dilemma.'

I sensed the aged relative was growing fretful, and gave her the floor.

'This Brigadier Ridley is the commanding officer, or boss of the gang. And being apparently a playful sort of ass, he has set up, in the study I've given over to him, a tantalus.'

I broke my silence to plead for a footnote. 'A what's that?'

'Tantalus. One of those wooden cages you lock your decanters up in if your butler's a dipsomaniac.'

'Oh yes, I know. Proceed.'

'Well, there it sits, plumb spang on the writing desk, with a whacking great padlock on it and an impudent note on the blotter reading, "Help yourself."'

'I see. And you want Jeeves to pick the lock?'

'I do not. There is also a scrap of demented verse on the blotter. Evidently it's some sort of clue as to where to find the key.'

'Aha! And what is the verse?'

'See for yourself.'

For with rather neat timing the above conflab had brought us to the door of the study in question. Aunt Dahlia flung it open, and we oozed in. The scenario within was just as she had sketched it. There was the writing desk, and on it sat the tantalus, a stout wood-and-metal affair inside which decanters of gin, whisky and port, in the order named, were securely padlocked. On the blotter someone had scrawled in red ink, 'Help Yourself.' And below that, in black ink by way of a change, the following specimen of doggerel:

> *Take the skillet from the pantry*
> *And the bridle from therein*
> *Fish the doctor from the drink*
> *Right for port and left for gin.*

Of this, I could make nothing. I turned to my aunt.

'Dashed rummy. What does it mean?'

Aunt Dahlia exhibited symptoms of an aunt rising to the boil.

'I don't know what it means, you priceless chump! If I knew what it meant, I shouldn't have had to send for Jeeves, and therefore endure you!'

One saw her point, of course. I turned to the boy with the brain. 'Well, Jeeves? What does it mean?'

'I couldn't say, sir.'

'No? No early leads?'

'No, sir.'

'I see. Well, dwell on it a spot, will you?'

'Very good, sir.'

The words were all right, so far as they went, but the delivery lacked vim, if you know what I mean. I returned to scrutinising the verse.

'Well, the first bit's clear enough, anyway. "Take the skillet from the pantry and the bridle from therein." Presumably one toddles along to the pantry, locates the skillet, within which one finds a bridle – by which I assume the ass means a rein – and the next clue is attached to that, what?'

Once more the aunt began to froth lightly.

'Do you imagine that in three days of staring at this thing it would take *you* to make me think of checking the pantry? There's no skillet or anything like it in the pantry, nor ever has been! There are pots and pans in the kitchen, of course, but not a sniff of a bridle in any of them. And I've had to let Anatole lock himself in there now, to stop the various weird birds constantly popping in on him!'

'Oh, you consider them weird birds, do you?' I asked, interested. 'I thought them queer fish.'

'Some of each, I should say. Don't mention this to Goering or anyone, but I fear that if this is the best the British Army can do for soldiers nowadays, we're washed up before we begin.'

My own opinion, of course, was that this was very far from the best they could do, if only they weren't so dashed finicky about birthdays, but I kept my own counsel.

'But, I say, in that case presumably this is some sort of test this Ridley chap's set them to try to lick 'em into shape. No doubt he'll tell you all about it if you ask him.'

Aunt Dahlia snorted.

'Not he! I asked him the very first evening. He just gave me a soupy sort of smile, and said it was only a trivial little diversion, but these things were always so much more rewarding when one solved them for oneself, and he'd hate to deprive me of the fun of it. I suspect he thought I was a hireling in the pay of one of his weird birds.'

'Or queer fish.'

'Or queer, as you say, fish. Either way, you see it's now a matter of honour for the home side to work it out first. As I said in my telegram.'

'Actually, you said a matter of *national* honour.'

'Yes, well. I had to make sure you came.'

I should have had a thing or two to say about that, but it was at that moment that I had one of my brainwaves.

'Wait! What about the *butler's* pantry!' I cried. 'Have you checked that?'

'We don't have a butler any more, ass. There's a war on. Seppings is off polishing bayonets in Aldershot.'

'I see. And you immediately had his pantry demolished as a mark of respect, did you?'

An auntly eyelid flickered, and I saw I had scored. 'Very well. Let us trickle round and inspect it, shall we? Coming, Jeeves?'

'I think not, sir, thank you.'

'Well. Just as you like.'

'Whatever's the matter with Jeeves?' asked Aunt Dahlia as we trickled. 'Distinct damp squib he's turning out to be. Is he off his oats?'

Of course, I had the answer to that. 'If you ask me, it looks like he's branching out.'

'Branching out?'

'Into womenswear.'

'Stop blithering, Bertie.'

'Not a blither in me. You recall how, over the years, Jeeves has put the kibosh on divers hats, socks, ties and spats of mine to which he has taken exception?'

'Yes, and he was right every time.'

'Freely admitted. And something you would do well to remember, because now he wants your siren suit.'

'Wants it? What for?'

'In less troubled times, I should say he wanted to burn it. But now, waste not want not and so forth, I imagine he's planning to strain jam with it, or offer it up for chaps to build Spitfires out of.'

'Is he, by Jove? Well, he's dashed well not getting it.'

'That's your affair, of course ... Ah. Does one form a queue, do you think, or take a number and wait for service?'

For we had arrived at the butler's pantry, and although it was indeed as bare of butlers as Aunt Dahlia had prophesied, it was teeming with a positive shoal, or flock, of the queer fish and weird birds. On closer examination, they fell into two main types: the long stringy exhibits, who ran to spectacles and cricket sweaters; and the short tubby specimens, who favoured beards and pipes.

'I say,' I said, addressing them generally, 'hate to intrude and all that sort of rot, but I wonder if any of you chaps happen to have seen such a thing as—'

'Don't say "a skillet",' growled the nearest and perhaps the queerest of the fish.

Well, as this of course was just the thing I *had* been about to say, I felt my guns had been to some extent spiked. Luckily, Aunt Dahlia was on hand to mount a rear-guard action.

'Naturally not. Heavens, we found the skillet days ago. What we seek now is a bridle. What price bridles in these parts?'

'No bridles,' snapped a second fish, from behind flashing spectacles. 'No bridles, no skillets . . . if you ask me, old Ridley's quite simply lost his marbles due to nervous strain. I've been expecting it for some time.'

'Ah,' I said, 'well, we'll be tottering along, then. Oh, but incidentally,' I continued, as a happy thought struck me. 'I don't suppose you have such a thing as a doctor on your strength, do you?'

'I have two doctorates,' said a heavily bearded bird in the corner, from somewhere inside the foliage. 'Mukherjee and Sanders have one apiece, and Lippincott's lost count of his. But before you ask, none of us are in the drink, literally or metaphorically, and no, you can't fish any of us out of it!'

Well, that seemed about sufficient for the pantry. Self and aunt continued to trail dutifully around the grounds, but to little or no avail. The stables were naturally rich with bridles and reins, but none within skillets. The nearest thing to 'the drink' Brinkley Court can provide is the ornamental fish pond in which Aunt Dahlia from time to time invites me to drown myself, but this proved entirely free from swimmers, medically trained or otherwise.

There was one thrilling moment when I thought I'd cracked the 'right for port' bit, by remembering 'port' is what naval johnnies say when they mean right. But then Aunt Dahlia, who has yachted a spot, rather took the shine off this by pointing out that no, it isn't.

Accordingly, by the time we trudged back up to the study in the quiet evenfall, we could only have resembled Inspectors Gregson and Lestrade returning from a hard day's bafflement more closely if Inspector Gregson had been Inspector Lestrade's aunt.

We found Jeeves standing tranquilly by the writing desk, looking for all the world as if he hadn't moved a muscle since we left.

'Ah. There you are, Jeeves.'

'Yes, sir.'

'Not tiring yourself out or anything, I hope?' asked Aunt Dahlia, with a return of the nasty glitter.

'No, madam.'

My aunt now swapped the rapier for the bludgeon with which she is always far more at home.

'I don't know what's got into you today, Jeeves, but whatever it is, I do think you might have put it aside and helped us search.'

'I assure you I would have done so, madam, had I believed your efforts remotely susceptible of success.'

'Oh, it's like that, is it?' retorted Aunt Dahlia. But I quelled her with an upraised hand. For I saw the inward nature of the man's statement.

'Jeeves,' I said, putting the thing to him squarely. 'Do you know where the key is?'

'. . . No, sir.'

'Then all is lost!' cried the febrile aunt.

'I don't know so much about that.'

For before Jeeves's reply, there had been an infinitesimal hesitation and the merest imaginable flicker of an eyebrow. I knew that hesitation, and that flicker, and could read them as plainly as if the man had tapped his nose, winked three times, and slapped his thigh. A contingency that is, as he would say himself, remote.

'If you don't know where the key is, what *do* you know?'

'Sir?'

'You know *something*, Jeeves. You always do.'

'... I have a purely conjectural theory, sir.'

'Let's hear it.'

'To confirm or refute it, sir, I should have to make a practical experiment.'

'Then make it!' howled Aunt Dahlia, in the tones of one for whom the end of the tether is but a fond and distant memory.

'I should not like to do so, madam.'

'Whyever not?'

'... I should not like to.' And his eye came to rest, almost dreamily, upon Aunt Dahlia's siren suit. She looked down. She got it. She yipped.

'No! Absolutely not!'

I must say, it was rather jolly watching it happen to someone else for a change. There was a silence. Aunt glared at valet. Valet gazed at aunt. The whole set-up reminded me of a gag Honoria Glossop once sprang on me concerning irresistible forces and immovable objects. I forget the details but the gist of the thing was, if an irresistible f. tried to move an immovable o., what would the harvest be? If I ever run into Honoria again, which heaven forfend, I am now in a posish to let her in on the answer: the immovable object wins hands down.

First Aunt Dahlia wilted. Then she sighed. And then, in a move that I think surprised us all, she unzipped her siren suit and shrugged it off. It turns out that one wears these foul things on top of one's usual raiment, but I didn't know that then, and I wish I had.

'There you are, blast you!' she said, thrusting the mass of serge at Jeeves.

Jeeves is always magnanimous in victory.

'Thank you very much indeed, madam. It is for the best.'

'Well then? This theory? Produce it!'

'As I say, madam, it will be easiest to test by experiment. If you will permit me?'

'Of course I permit you! Jump to it!'

If I had thought that seeing an elderly countrywoman casually disrobe in mixed company was the most surprising sight I was likely to come across that day – and I dashed well *had* thought that – I was wrong. For it was at this point that Jeeves drank the ink.

I mean, he poured it into a glass and sipped it, he didn't glug the stuff direct from the inkwell, but the effect was still rather more than my shredded nerves could bear.

'Jeeves!' yipped self and aunt in unison. But Jeeves

was performing the minute rearrangement of his face that is the closest he ever comes to smiling.

'As I hoped, sir. A Croft '04, if I am not mistaken. Or just possibly a Dow '07.'

'But . . . the decanters!'

'The locked decanters, madam, I discerned almost immediately to be a species of blind or misdirection. The invitation was to help oneself, and one cannot help oneself from a locked decanter. Besides, the liquids inside the decanters are self-evidently not as advertised.'

'How do you know?'

'There are no lees at the bottom of the port, sir. And the meniscus of the whisky lacks viscosity.'

This last remark sailed over my head by several fathoms, but I got him to write it down for me later so that I could use it to show policemen I was sober.

'But what about the dashed verse?' said Aunt Dahlia.

'Yes, madam. I addressed myself to that matter whilst you were making your . . . investigations. I had a notion that it was more in the nature of a word game than a treasure hunt, and so it proved.'

'Well?'

He coughed. '"Take the skillet from the pantry." A skillet, of course, being a pan. "And the bridle from therein." A bridle, as you pointed out yourself, sir, is a rein. "Fish the doctor from the drink." The customary abbreviation "Dr" seemed indicated. And, if one removes "pan" from pantry, "rein" from therein and 'Dr' from drink, one is left with . . .'

'. . . Try The Ink,' breathed Aunt Dahlia.

'Precisely, madam. The port, as indicated, in the right-hand, red inkwell. The gin in the left-hand, black inkwell. And the whisky, I should be disposed to imagine, in the well reserved for copying fluid.'

We gazed at the man in awe. In recent years, though I shouldn't dream of mentioning it to him, his hair has begun to thin just a spot at the crown. But the circlet of dome thus revealed only adds to his majesty. It's like being allowed a glimpse of the engine of a Bentley Speed Six. I was just opening my mouth to pay due tribute, when we heard someone climbing the staircase without.

'Ridley!' cried Aunt Dahlia. 'I know his step. Quick!'

Well, it was a scramble, but we just made it. By the time Brigadier Ridley entered, self and aunt were carelessly arrayed on sundry bits of furniture, each with a glass in hand.

'Ah, brigadier!' chirruped Aunt Dahlia. 'How nice. I hope you don't mind, but we thought we'd avail ourselves of your very kind invitation.'

Brigadier Ridley, an intelligent-looking fellow built along the lines of Basil Rathbone, flashed a look at the inkstand, which Told Him, as the novelettes say, All.

'... Not at all. Most welcome. And, congratulations.'

'Oh, well . . .' laughed Aunt Dahlia carelessly. 'Naturally, one tumbled to the thing straight away, but we thought it only sporting to let your chaps have a few days to work it out. Did any of them, out of interest?'

'They did not.'

'Oh dear. Well, never mind. We can't all have brains. No doubt they have beautiful souls, or are good at rugger, or something. Now, will you join us for a glass? And Jeeves, you might ring for the Stilton to be sent up. Though I'm afraid, brigadier, before we can let you have any, you'll have to beat Bertie at noughts and crosses.'

And so began what turned into a moderately fruity binge. We had up a few of the more gregarious birds and fish; Brigadier Ridley produced the remainder of the bottles like a sportsman; Aunt Dahlia matched them from her plenty; and in short a distinctly good time was had by all.

At one point, I saw Ridley talking rather intently to Aunt Dahlia, and her indicating Jeeves. Shortly afterwards, I saw Ridley talking rather intently to Jeeves, and him indicating me. I was just trying to decide whom I would indicate when my turn came, when I found it was too late, because it had.

'I say, Wooster. I've just been talking to your man, Jeeves.'

'So I saw. Did he scintillate?'

'Tolerably. Remarkable man, your man.'

'I have often remarked on it,' I replied cordially.

'He happened to mention you were keen to do your bit for the war effort?'

'Yes, dashed keen! But nothing doing. The Wooster stock is down in the cellar with no takers. And where does that leave me? Putting out cathedrals that aren't on fire, that's where!' I spoke with no little vim, for the thing still rankled.

'Well. It so happens that I may have a berth for you, should you be interested.'

I looked at him with what is known as wild surmise.

'No, I say, what? Really? I say, thanks awfully!'

'It's rather a curious job, I'm afraid.'

'No matter! Be it never so rummy, Bertram's your man!'

'Well then. Strictly between ourselves – and as your man appears to have deduced – what we're setting up here is a sort of . . . central military admin centre. Deadly dull, I'm afraid, but at the same time rather important. Deuced irritating if the place got bombed, I mean to say. And what with one thing and another, it's going to involve all sorts of people, from all services and none, popping in to work with us. Which is the sort of thing that might attract attention. What we need, d'y'see, is a cover story. And then . . . here *you* are. Attached to the family that owns the place. Well known for your wide circle of friends. My idea is to draft you immediately into my own regiment, at the rank of, say, captain—'

'Rather! Or, say, colonel?'

'. . . Captain, I think.'

'Right ho.'

'. . . And attach you to our platoon here. And then, what more natural than if, finding yourself somewhat under-worked, you invited various of your friends round for shooting parties, and all that sort of thing? Under cover of which, we can bring in whomever we like to help us out with the admin down in the huts.'

'I see! And of course, I could help out with that too!'

'Oh no. Rather not. Waste of your talents.'

'Oh. Well, just as you like. So . . . then, my job would be to . . . spend the war in my aunt's house, eating Chef Anatole's cooking, and having my pals round for parties?'

'In a nutshell, yes.'

'And this, you feel . . . will help us win the war?'

'I honestly do.'

'Then lead me to it, laddie!'

And so they did. In no time at all, I had signed, not only up, but also the Official Secrets Act, of all things. Though to this day the only deuced official secret I know is the name of Brinkley Court. Oh, don't worry – that's not it. By good luck, way back when I first started producing these spots of memoir, Uncle Tom put his foot down with some force about having the name of his house dragged into them, and obliged me to change it. Not that I changed it all that much. Just made it a Court rather than a Park, and called it Brinkley rather than . . . well, I suppose I oughtn't to say what. They were rather insistent about that.

Anyway, with this all concluded, and Ridley and I on the point of parting with mutual expressions of regard, conscience suddenly smote me a blow. There was something, conscience remarked sternly, that I was rather forgetting.

'Oh, I say! Rather mouldy having to ask you for a favour straight away, don't you know, but . . . I don't suppose, by any chance, you could see your way clear to finding some sort of billet in your admin huts for my man Jeeves? Only I know he's just as pipped about not being in uniform as I am, and he's fearfully brainy and all that sort of thing.'

Ridley looked at me in rather a rummy sort of way, as if I'd said something funny. Couldn't see it myself.

'Yes . . . as a matter of fact, I offered Major Jeeves a post just now.'

'Oh, good egg! What did he say?'

'. . . He asked me to speak to you.'

'Oh! Which, of course, you were just on the point of doing anyway! How splendidly these things work out. Hang on, though . . .' For something had just caught up with me. 'Did you say "*Major* Jeeves"?'

'Yes. That was the rank he achieved by the end of the last war. Didn't you know?'

'I did not! But I say . . . if I'm a captain . . . will I have to salute him?

'Naturally.'

Well. It was a bit of a facer, just at first, but then, when one thought about it . . . I mean to say, why not? If there's a chap more deserving of a salute, I should bally well like to know who it is.

'Right ho, then! Jolly good. Oh . . . but just one more thing.'

'Yes?'

'What *is* your regiment? I mean, my regiment. Our regiment.'

'The Royal Worcestershire. Any objection?'

'None at all,' I said, and nor had I. I mean to say. 'Captain Wooster of the Worcesters.' It has the jolly old ring to it, what? Absolutely!

Ah Jaysis, Jeeves

Roddy Doyle

So I woke up rich.
 I fell into the scratcher the night before, knowing I was rich. Well-oiled and rich. But waking up sober and still rich – it's different. Lying back in the bed, luxuriating – if that's the word – and remembering that you've become a multi-millionaire. Well, it's nice.

You've guessed it. I'd won the Lotto. But come here, it wasn't the ordinary Lotto, the Irish one, where you only win a couple of million. The way things are these days with the inflation and that, you'd buy a few pints and a takeaway, a house in Malahide and a flight across to Manchester to see United being bet, and you'd be back to square one. Sober and skint.

It was the EuroMillions I was after winning.

I remember Lanky McNally from the football club telling me once that his cousin had sued a doctor because his leg had gone septic after 'a routine procedure' – Lanky's words – and that the cousin had been awarded 'a figure north of a hundred grand' – Lanky's words again. It took me a while to figure out what 'north of' meant. Most of the lads I hang around with would just tell you the exact figure, how much the man was after getting. Not Lanky, though. Why say 'rain' when you can say 'deluge'? That's Lanky. Anyway, I asked him what the routine procedure was. 'Amputation,' he said. 'It was the other leg that went septic.'

So fair enough, I wouldn't begrudge the cousin his few quid. But back to 'north of'. My figure – my 'amassed wealth', Lanky would probably call it – was now north of thirty million euros. I swear to God. It was only a few kilometres south of forty million. Absolute mad money.

I told no one – I'm no sap. I went down to my local, the Bag of Spuds, and bought a pint, everything as per the usual. Except I knew I had enough money to pay for another six and a half million pints. But I kept it all – the news, the money, the fact that my heart was head-butting my chest – under my hat. Although I don't have a hat.

Come here, though – I'm not mean. No one could ever accuse Bertie McDevitt – that's yours truly, by the way – of being tight-fisted. I've never been careful with the spondulix and when it comes to doling out the cash to the nieces and nephews, I've never hidden behind the door. Uncle Revolut is what they call me.

But the day I won the millions – well, I was confused. I should have been over the moon – or over the natural satellite that orbits the earth once a month, if Lanky was telling the story. But you're lucky – he's not. I am, and I wasn't feeling as over the satellite as I thought I should have been. And that was why I was telling no one.

I hate admitting it, but I was happy enough with my life before I won the gazillions. My life has – *had* – very few complications. I live in the house I was born in. Actually, I was born in the front garden, two minutes after my ma told my da that she was going into labour and a minute after my da copped on that she wasn't talking about her voting preferences.

Anyway, I still live in that house. I bought it off my brothers and my sister. Lanky would call them siblings, but all I see when I hear that word is little ducks – ducklings, like. And although one of the brothers, Eddie, quacks a bit when he's laughing, none of the rest look anything like ducks, myself included. So anyway – where was I? Oh yeah, I bought the gaff off the ducklings after our ma died and that's where I live. Alone. By myself. Solo.

But come here – I'm not Billy-No-Mates. Far from. My social calendar is up there with the Beckhams' and I've had my fair share of, eh, romantic interludes – hello, Lanky – with the women. There's one girl – and before you start objecting to a middle-aged man calling a middle-aged woman a girl, I went to school with her. I've known her since she *was* a girl and I was a boy and I asked her for a quick look at her maths homework and she said she would but only if I went behind the bike shed and kissed her. So I did, and I got ninety per cent – for the homework, like, not the smooch. It was the only time I ever got ninety per cent for anything and the teacher had a nosebleed when he was adding up the total. Mandy Montgomery her name is, and it's been on and off between us ever since. More off than on, to be honest. But even when she was married it was on a bit, and off, and on again, if you get my drift. And by the way, it was called the bike shed even though there were never any bikes in it.

Anyway, I lived on my own and I liked it that way. And something told me that if the rest of them found out that Bertie Mc the house painter was also a multi-gazillionaire – well, I wouldn't be left on my own for long.

And I was right.

And I was wrong.

Here's what happened – what transpired, in Lanky-speak.

I gave a lot of thought to what I could do with the readies. I thought about buying a new car. I thought about buying a new van. I thought about buying one of those little robot lawnmowers that never stop cutting the grass. I thought about getting one of those little robot hoovers that never stop— You get my drift.

I began to feel a bit desperate. A life of luxury was waiting for me and all I'd managed to buy was one of those air fryers and a Crunchie. Was I really that miserable? The air fryer was brilliant, by the way. It's out the back, in the shed now, beside my Nespresso. But I'm jumping the gun here – forget I mentioned those yokes. I will say this, though – put a Crunchie in an air fryer for a few minutes. Unbelievable.

Anyway.

I was scooting through the channels one night because there was no football on and the only films seemed to be those superhero ones and I can never follow what's going on in those films, so I always end up feeling a bit thick. It was too early for the boozer, so I kept surfing the channels and I stopped at *Downton Abbey*.

Come here – I hate *Downton Abbey*. Posh Brits

talking drivel in a big house? No, thanks. All of my family fought in the War of Independence back in the day, both sides – I mean both sides of the family, not both sides of the war – for the right of the Irish people not to watch *Downton Abbey*. But you know your woman from *The Commitments* who plays the butler's evil wife? She's brilliant. And there she was, so I stopped the surfing. Just for a minute, like. I didn't become – give us a hand here, Lanky – engrossed. But somewhere before the ads the thought popped into the head – I wouldn't mind having a butler. Maybe I thought he'd bring his evil wife with him – I don't know. There'd be a ring on the bell and there he'd be on the step with his suitcase, the new butler, and there'd be herself standing beside him. 'We'll bury him in the back garden,' she'd whisper into my ear as they were going past me into the kitchen.

By the way, remember to take the Crunchie out of the wrapper first.

Anyway, back to me in front of the telly. I did a quick google. 'Butlers for rent in Ireland,' I tapped. But before I even looked at what the phone coughed up, I knew I didn't want an Irish butler, with or without an evil missis. I just knew I'd know him or he'd be related to someone I knew, or he'd be useless and I wouldn't be able to sack him and I'd end up bringing him his full Irish in bed every morning. The possibilities, the things that could go wrong, were endless. Come here, though – I love my country. I'm a proud Irishman. I cried when Johnny Logan won the Eurovision. But an Irish butler? It would never work. He'd just be too – well – Irish. Picture it, yourself. You're reclining in front of the telly, waiting for *Match of the Day*, with your butler, O'Leary, standing beside you at the ready. 'Stick the kettle on, O'Leary, before *Match of the Day* starts,' you say. And you know exactly where O'Leary will tell you to stick the kettle before *Match of the Day* starts. It's inevitable – no bookie would take your bet.

He had to be English or nothing. So I deleted 'in Ireland' and gave the phone another tap. 'Now we're talking,' I said – to myself, like – as I scrolled down. The words that tipped me over the edge – 'Gentleman's gentleman'. I have to admit, I liked the sound of that and before I could give it too much thought – any thought, really – I'd paid the deposit and my gentleman's gentleman's air fare to Dublin. And before I could think, What in the name of Jaysis am I after doing?, I got an email confirming that Jeeves, my gentleman, would be arriving on Wednesday.

AH JAYSIS, JEEVES

I spent all day Tuesday cleaning the gaff. The house was already clean. I'm no slob. 'Cleanliness is next to godliness' is tattooed across the back of my neck. But there was no way I was letting a Brit into the house with even a dirty cup in the sink. I slept on the floor on the Tuesday night so I wouldn't wrinkle the duvet. And first thing Wednesday morning I was standing in Terminal 2, holding up a piece of cardboard with 'JEEVES' painted on it in Parisian Red. But there was no sign of anything that looked remotely like a gentleman's gentleman coming through the sliding doors. The cardboard was wilting and the Parisian Red was starting to look more like Mullingar Grey. I was beginning to wonder if I'd turned up on the wrong day. It wouldn't have been the first time. I once turned up for a date two weeks late which, I accept, was bad form and even a bit weird. Weirder still, though – your woman was still waiting for me.

Anyway, I was taking out my phone to double-check the email.

'Sir.'

The shock – Jesus. The phone flew out of my grip and, before I could make a grab for it, a gloved hand came over my shoulder and caught it.

I turned.

'Jeeves?'

'Yes, sir.'

'Good catch.'

'The iPhone Eleven lends itself to ready capture, sir.'

I looked at him.

That has to be the most pointless sentence ever written. Of course, I looked at him. But the point is, I can't really describe him. He was wearing a black overcoat and a bowler hat so, in the airport – the land of leisurewear – he stood out. When was the last time you saw a man wearing a bowler hat? I'm betting 'never' is the answer. In all sorts of ways this was an unusual meeting. But I can't remember what he looked like. We lived under the same roof for months but I never really got the hang of his appearance.

Nondescript.

That's the word I'd use. I know what you're thinking, especially if you're a woman – that describes virtually every man you've ever met. But this was different. Most men would never want to be thought of as nondescript. The Jeeves fella, though, I could tell – he was professionally nondescript.

There was one thing about him that stood out, though – he had an eyebrow. One of those eyebrows that speaks louder than words, if you get my drift. The slightest lift could do more work than twenty pages of Shakespeare, and he lifted it high when I made a move to pick up his suitcase.

'Fair enough,' I said, and I stepped back, hands in the air.

It *was* a suitcase, by the way, no straps or wheels.

I tried to get him chatting as we strolled across to the car park.

'Was the flight okay, yeah?'

'Perfectly satisfactory, sir.'

'No problems, no?'

'None, sir.'

Ask the average Irish person if their flight was okay and you might as well write off the rest of the day. Before you know it, it's a ten-part series on Netflix. This guy was a dead loss, though. But I kept reminding myself that he was the butler, not one of the lads. I was getting what I'd forked out for.

The van, I admit, has seen better days. Mandy Montgomery, who's been in it once or twice, calls it my rescue van. Jeeves hesitated before he pulled himself up onto the passenger seat.

'Shove those cups and cartons out the door if you need the legroom,' I told him.

'The footwell is quite commodious, sir.'

If this fella and Lanky ever met up, it was going to be some game of Scrabble.

Anyway, I'll fast-forward to the next morning. He'd seemed happy enough with the box room when I'd shown it to him the night before, and there were no complaints when he saw the Thomas the Tank Engine duvet cover.

'The nephews and the nieces,' I explained.

'Yes, sir.'

'Goes well with the My Little Pony wallpaper, but, doesn't it?'

'A feast for the eyes, sir.'

But yeah – the following morning.

I opened my eyes and the first thing I saw was a man standing beside the bed. I was halfway out the window before I remembered that it was Jeeves and he was only doing his job. I tried to make it look like I'd been opening the curtains.

'Grand looking day out there, Jeeves.'

'Exceptionally clement, sir.'

'That means grand, does it?'

'Indeed, sir.'

He stood there holding a tray.

Just to be clear – I don't have a tray. Nevertheless, the man had a tray and there was a teapot parked on it.

'English tea, sir?' he said.

I sat up. I was back in the bed, by the way.

'Sorry – wha'?'

'English tea.'

I let him have it. I gave him the full history, the eight hundred years of oppression, Cromwell, King

Billy, 1916, Italia 90 — the works. It was dark outside by the time I shut up.

'The tea isn't English, Jeeves.'

'No, sir.'

'It's Barry's tea and it grows in Cork.'

'Yes, sir.'

'And Cork's in Ireland,' I told him. 'Just about.'

'I stand educated, sir,' he said.

'Good man.'

'Irish tea, sir?"

'Pour away there, Jeeves.'

And there I was, sitting up in the bed, drinking tea that I hadn't had to make myself. I was living the dream. But I didn't like it. It wasn't exactly a nightmare but as dreams go I'd had much better ones.

First of all, I prefer coffee. Second of all, I've never been that fussed about drinking tea in bed. The bed is great for loads of things but drinking tea isn't one of them — not in my opinion. Third of all, I could hear your man below me, making the breakfast. Any minute now he was going to come back in with his tray and the full Irish — the rashers and sausages and what-have-you, the stuff that made this country great. I just hoped to God he didn't call it the full English and I'd have to get the blackboard out and give him another history lesson. The thing was, I wasn't a hundred per cent comfortable with it, him down there doing what I should have been doing for myself. Fourth of all, I'd been a bit cruel. I know, I'd been defending the national heritage and that, but I'd gone over the ball. Was it not possible to be filthy rich without being obnoxious?

I got up and threw on the jeans.

'D'you need a hand there, Jeeves?' I asked, as I bounced into the kitchen.

'Thank you, sir,' he said. 'That won't be necessary.'

'I'm making the coffee,' I said. 'D'you want one?'

That was when I realised that I wouldn't be making the coffee. The Nespresso was gone. It should have been beside the— Where was my air fryer? You already know the answer to that question, but I didn't.

Where was anything? The window and door were exactly where I'd left them but everything else had changed. The cups were where the plates should have been. The plates were where the biscuit tin with nothing in it used to be. The mugs – the mugs were just gone. My Man United mug, my Up the Dubs mug, my Dennis the Menace mug – there was no sign of any of them. And – ah, here – where was the bloody fridge?

'Behind you, sir,' said Jeeves.

He'd just answered a question I hadn't asked him.

I turned – and it was there, waiting for me. I think it even went, 'Boo.'

I got it – I understood. I was in the way. The kitchen was no longer mine. I was starring in *Upstairs, Downstairs* and my place was upstairs. But it wasn't a country estate or a big gaff in a posh part of London. It was a terraced house built by the council in 1969. There were three bedrooms upstairs, and the bathroom and the landing. There was no library or smoking room. Was I going to spend the rest of my life sitting in the bath? I stood out in the hall, feeling – give us a dig-out here, Lanky – befuddled and forlorn.

Jeeves rescued me. He took me into the lounge. It was the exact same, even though he kept calling it the drawing room. He sat me down.

'Your eggs, sir,' he said.
'What about them?'
'Poached or scrambled?'
'Fried.'
'Poached or scrambled, sir?'
'Scrambled, so.'
'Very good, sir.'
'Like my brain.'
'Very droll, sir.'

It wasn't all bad. He ironed my shirts. Actually, he ironed everything. My socks had a crease in them.

And he was always a step ahead of me. Like, just the way I held the remote control, he knew I was getting ready to stand up and go down to the Bag for my nightly pint.

'I laid out your exercise suit, sir.'

He must have seen something in my face. He must've seen something *missing* in my face.

'Your tracksuit, sir.'

'Ah— Gotcha. Thanks.'

'Thank *you*, sir.'

So yeah, it was weird having a servant. There was always that distance. And keeping that distance in a house like mine was a challenge. There was one day, I stood at the top of the stairs and he stood at the bottom, and the both of us were going, 'No, you go first, no, you go first', for an hour and a half. I was the one who had to surrender, even though I was the boss and it was my house.

One night, he delivered a cup of Irish tea to me, and a few Irish Jaffa Cakes, when I was watching the news.

'The state of the world, Jeeves,' I said. 'It's in rag order, isn't it?'

'"Things fall apart,"' he replied. '"The centre cannot hold. Mere anarchy is loosed upon the world."'

'Coldplay?'

'Yeats, sir,' he said. 'W. B. Recipient of the Nobel Prize in Literature in the year 1923—'

'Thanks very much, Jeeves.'

It never felt right, calling him by his surname.

'What's your first name, Jeeves?'

The pause between the question and the answer went on for just south of an eternity. I deliberately didn't look at his eyebrow.

'Reginald, sir.'

'Ah well,' I said.

The next time I needed tea I pulled back my head and roared.

'Reggie!'

There was no sign of your man. I knew he was in the kitchen.

'Reg!'

Maybe he'd gone to the shops. Maybe he was out the back, sunning himself or hanging up the washing.

'Jeeves!'

'Sir.'

I'm not a fan of gasping but I gasped. He was right behind me.

'Ah Jaysis, Jeeves – me heart.'

'My apologies, sir.'

It takes a lot to rattle a McDevitt, so I was back to my normal self in slightly north of no time.

JEEVES AGAIN

'You're too efficient, Reg.'

He said nothing.

'You're too efficient, Jeeves.'

'Thank you, sir.'

The eyebrow slid back into its parking space.

I was a total eejit. I thought I could get away with having a butler without anyone finding out about it. But, like, the man had to go out now and again. I couldn't do my own shopping – he wouldn't let me. And a man wandering the aisles of SuperValu wearing a bowler hat and carrying a net bag like the one your granny used to have – well, he's going to stand out, isn't he? Even before he opens his mouth and calls Bernie on the till 'madam'. And when the same man is coming in and out of your gaff with his own key, well, all sorts of stories start pinging off the walls.

The texts came first.

R u ok? X

Is dere sumtin u need to tell us? Do u want a famly meetin?

Who's your man with the hat?

And, to be fair, I answered all of them.

Yeah. X

No.

Me cousin.

The visitors were harder to bat away.

I've an auntie, Agatha, my da's last surviving sister, who's always hammering on the door, usually with her forehead. She's not the worst. No, hang on, she is. She *is* the worst. And I'm the family disappointment, because I'm not married. She barges past me, hoping to catch a woman in the house. Mandy Montgomery once had to spend hours hiding in the attic while Auntie Agatha occupied the kitchen and refused to leave. I heard a noise that could only have been one thing – Mandy sitting on a mousetrap. Two things, actually – the snap and the scream. But luckily Agatha had left her hearing aids at home, along with her teeth and her heart, so she didn't hear Mandy trying to dislodge herself from the trap.

But come here – Agatha is no homophobe. She hates everyone – she doesn't care which side they play for. So she'd have been delighted to find Jeeves in the kitchen, as long as I promised to marry him. She'd have forced me to get down on a knee and propose to him. Jeeves hadn't met Agatha but I knew one thing for sure – he wouldn't have turned me down. He wouldn't have dared.

Anyway, she was bound to have heard about Jeeves, so I was constantly gawking out the window to see if she was launching herself at my front door. And early one morning – is that a line from a song? – I was only out of the hay when I opened the curtains and there was, not Agatha, but a different woman, an entirely different challenge, heading straight for the doorbell.

I was down the stairs in three strides and a groin strain and I'd pulled the door open before Mandy Montgomery had the opportunity to lean on the bell.

Come here – nine times out of ten, ninety-nine times out of – hang on – yeah, a hundred, I'm over the satellite to see Mandy Montgomery. Ever since my voice broke and I suddenly noticed her, I've always thought that Mandy was a fine thing. And more than forty years on, I still do. There's more of her these days but, let's be honest, there's more of me as well.

The thing is, Mandy and me get on. We like a kiss and a cuddle but we're pals as well, and – I'm consulting my inner Lanky – confidants. I've told Mandy things that I'd never tell anyone else and she's told me things that I wouldn't be able to explain without a few pints and a box of crayons. And we both agreed – years ago, this is – that if we ever got married we'd wreck it. Mandy's been married twice, I think, maybe three times, but never to me.

Anyway, there she was.

'Howyeh,' I greeted her.

She stared at me.

Normally, being stared at by Mandy adds a bit of

zest to life but this time she wasn't staring at me so much as she was staring at what I was wearing. I forgot to mention, Jeeves had bought me pyjamas. He wouldn't let me go to bed in my jocks and my old Cantona T-shirt.

'Why are you dressed like a Christian Brother, Bertram?' she asked.

She moved me aside and before I could say, 'They're Ralph Lauren and they cost well north of four hundred euros,' she'd marched into the kitchen and met the man who was making me wear them.

Remember I told you that Jeeves had an eyebrow? Well, so does Mandy. So it would be more accurate to say that their eyebrows met. It was *High Noon*, although I wasn't sure which of them was Gary Cooper.

Mandy was the first to move. She fired over her shoulder – at me.

'Who's your friend, Bertram?'

But I didn't get the chance to tell her because a voice behind me announced the end of the world.

'Got yis!'

It was my Auntie Agatha. I'd forgotten to shut the front door.

I said something I've said seven times before, unless I'm mistaken and I've forgotten one or two.

'It's not what you think, Auntie Aggie.'

And then I said something that I'm almost certain I never said before.

'He's me butler.'

'Your wha'?' said Auntie Agatha at the exact time that Mandy Montgomery said it.

'Your wha'?'

There was a big difference between them, though. Auntie Agatha shouted her 'Your wha'?' but Mandy said it silently, if you get my drift. She turned to me as she mouthed the words and she kind of looked me up and down, like it was the first time she'd ever seen me.

I've made a few mistakes in my life. Remind me to tell you about the time I went for a pint and woke up on the banks of the Zambezi in a sleeping bag with the Dalai Lama. But the biggest mistake came much closer to home – there in the kitchen. I decided that Mandy, because of the way she was looking at me, had changed her mind about marriage – marriage to me, that is. Because of the gazillions.

I'm cringing as I write this, by the way. I'm hiding under the table even though I'm the only one in the house.

Anyway.

There's only one person in Dublin who isn't afraid of my Auntie Agatha and that's Mandy Montgomery. And there was only one person in the kitchen that day brainier than Jeeves and that was also Mandy Montgomery.

She took a step closer to Jeeves and she kissed him. On both of his lips.

'See yeh later, pet,' she said – to Jeeves, like. 'I've to go and get meself measured for the wedding dress.'

Then she walked slowly around my Auntie Agatha and she stopped in front of me. She straightened the collar of my Ralph Laurens.

'Bye bye now, Bertram,' she said.

Then she gave me a wink and strolled out of the kitchen.

Those of us still in the kitchen – in case you're a bit lost, that was me, Jeeves and my Auntie Agatha – heard the front door closing softly. Auntie Agatha had her hearing aids with her, and her teeth. But not her heart.

'You gobdaw!' she hissed.

She was looking at me, by the way.

'Wha'?'

'Don't "wha'" me,' she said. 'You had a queue of marriage candidates waiting for you. But you took so long to make up your mind, they've decided to marry each other!'

She growled as she passed me and she was still growling when she slammed the front door – twice.

I started breathing again.

'We ducked a bullet there, Jeeves,' I said.

'Indeed, sir?'

'She'd have made the pair of us get married,' I told him. 'And no offence, Jeeves, but I don't really want to marry you or any other man.'

'I would concur, sir.'

'She'd have had us walking up the aisle and – no exaggeration now – if we'd said no, she'd have buttered us over the front garden.'

'A most unfortunate outcome, sir.'

'Absolutely,' I said. 'But Mandy Montgomery saved the day when she pretended the two of yis were already engaged.'

'Ms Montgomery was the young lady, sir?'

'She's not that young, Jeeves,' I said. 'In fairness.'

'"Age cannot wither her nor custom stale her infinite variety."'

'Yeats?'

'The Bard, sir.'

'Christy Moore?'

'Shakespeare.'

'Grand,' I said. 'My Auntie Agatha would have insisted that two men who weren't brothers living under the same roof would have to do the decent thing and get married. She'd be a stickler for that. Especially if one of them is me.'

'An arrangement that would, I fear, go beyond the terms of my contract, sir.'

'Well, there go you, Jeeves – I'm with you. But fair play to Mandy, when she pretended you'd be marrying her instead, when she kissed you, like.'

'A most impressive stratagem, sir.'

'Brilliant. But come here, Jeeves.'

'Sir?'

'We're not out of the woods yet.'

'Indeed, sir?'

'Not by a long chalk,' I said. 'It is "chalk", yeah?'

'I believe so, sir. It is, by most accounts, a nineteenth-century expression which originated in Canada but first became commonplace in Great Britain. The chalk referred to is—'

'Ah Jaysis, Jeeves.'

'Sir?'

'I don't want to hear the history of chalk. Just listen.'

And I told him. I revealed my fears about Mandy, how I thought she'd want to marry me after years of avoiding it, because of the money, and she knew I had the money because I had a butler.

'She winked at me, Jeeves.'

'Indeed, sir?'

'I don't know the story where you come from, Jeeves. But around here – yeah? – the wink is every woman's weapon of choice.'

'I wasn't aware of that, sir.'

'They learn it on their mammies' laps,' I told him. 'What am I going to do, but?'

'To deter Ms Montgomery from the conviction that her future happiness depends on a formal union between you and Ms Montgomery?'

'Yeah— I think.'

He held up a scarf. It was one of those silky, colourdy ones that women like to wear – grand to look at but useless on a cold morning.

I pointed at it.

'That's Mandy's scarf.'

'And our Trojan horse, sir.'

'Sorry – wha'?'

He held an elbow – one of mine – and guided me to one of the chairs. I felt weak and a bit helpless but I have to admit, it was nice to be sitting in my own kitchen again.

He had a plan – of course, he did – and he outlined it for me without Powerpoint or even a stick of long chalk. Churchill couldn't have done a better job.

'So,' I said when he'd finished. 'We just tell her that I'm already engaged to another woman.'

'Precisely, sir.'

'But I'm not.'

'No, sir.'

'She'll know.'

'Not if the young woman doesn't exist, sir.'

'I still don't get you.'

'A lady from outside the immediate locality, sir,' he said. 'Not of Ms Montgomery's social sphere.'

'Posh.'

'Who came to your acquaintance as a consequence of your recent good fortune.'

'And all I have to do is—'

'Anything you wish, sir. Attend a game of association football. Or simply go to a different locale and have what I have heard you refer to as "a few pints".'

'And I tell everyone — but Mandy really, like — that I'm going to meet — what's my fiancée's name again?'

'Ms St John-O'Halloran, sir.'

'Jaysis — I just hope I can remember it. What's her first name?'

'Béibhínn, sir.'

'Bay-veen.'

'I believe that is the correct pronunciation, sir, although my knowledge of Gaelic is, as yet, quite rudimentary.'

'Hang on — you're learning Irish?'

'When in Rome, sir.'

'Béibhínn St John-O'Halloran,' I said.

I was beginning to see her.

'She sounds like the real deal.'
'She is, sir.'
He was still holding the scarf.
'What's the scarf for?'
'Our Trojan horse.'

The scarf – or giving it back – would be Jeeves's excuse to go around to Mandy's, get invited in and, while he was there, let Mandy know that Mr McDevitt – me, like – already had a—

'What's the word again, Jeeves?'
'Betrothed, sir.'
'And that's the Béibhínn one, yeah?'
'Precisely, sir.'

So that's what happened. Jeeves went off with your woman, Béibhínn Sin Gin O'Halloran. He was gone about two hours – a hundred and twenty-three minutes to be exact. I heard him coming back in. He stuck his head in the drawing room – sorry, the lounge – door. Crisis averted, he said, and he headed straight up to his bed.

And that was it, really. Crisis averted, as the man said.

But I'll be honest. I was miserable. I saw Mandy coming out of the dry cleaner's one day, with a pile of clothes on hangers over her shoulder – she was drowning in dresses – and I was on my way over to give her a hand. But she saw me and crossed the road and kept walking. I was tempted to shout after her, 'She doesn't exist, Mandy! He made her up!' But that would have been blaming Jeeves. And there was only one eejit worth blaming. Yours truly.

You know that saying they have about the Normans who invaded Ireland back in the day, 'They became more Irish than the Irish themselves'? Well, I wouldn't go that far if I was describing the changes I began to see in Jeeves. He was never *more* Irish but he definitely became a bit more Irish, if you get my drift.

'All good, sir?' he said one morning when he was bringing me my Irish tea. And there was another time, I wanted to know if he'd ironed a shirt for me because I was – officially – heading across to Ranelagh to meet my fiancée Béibhínn but – unofficially – going for a few scoops with some lads I knew in Ringsend.

'Jeeves!'

'I'll be there in a minute!' he shouted.

No 'sir' or apology. And – come here – he wasn't there in a minute, or two minutes, or even ten. He strolled in after half an hour. Fair enough, he had the shirt with him but it looked so stiff I was half-afraid to put it on.

Then there were the days off. Listen – I've had my

own company, Acme Painting and Decorating, for years. It was supposed to be 'Acme' but another fella got there ahead of me. Anyway, I've employed men and boys and a few women and they'll line up to tell you the same thing – that I was fair. Tough but fair. So I didn't begrudge Jeeves his time off.

'Where are you off to, Jeeves?'

'There is a painting by the Italian master, Caravaggio, sir, in the National Gallery—'

'Good man.'

He was always in grand form when he came home from his sightseeing. I'd even hear him whistling as he was performing his duties around the gaff. 'The Aul' Triangle' and 'What's Another Year' seemed to be his favourites.

There was another morning – a Saturday – I came down to watch the early match on Sky. Jeeves came out of the kitchen, dressed for the great outdoors.

'You're taking both days off this week, Jeeves?'

'Yes, sir.'

'Where are you off to this time?'

'I am informed, sir, that the Zoological Gardens are the business at this time of year.'

'You're going to the zoo?'

'Yes, sir.'

'I've to make my own tea so you can visit the monkeys?'

'I have a particular interest in the suricates, sir.'
'The wha'?'
'Meerkats, sir.'
'Fair enough – don't let me stop you.'
'*Slán leat*, sir.'

I didn't have my butler but I had the house to myself. What you lose on the swings, and that.

But.

It wasn't working out. I'd grown fond of the man but I didn't want a butler. And I told him.

'Would you be cheesed off if I sacked you, Jeeves?' I asked him.

He was silent for exactly three seconds.

'If by "cheesed off" you mean upset or angry, sir, no, I don't think I would be.'

'It's kind of mad, this, isn't it, Jeeves? Like, me having a butler.'

'Unusual, sir. Not mad. I shall be sad departing but ready to embrace fresh experience.'

'You're all right with it, so?'

'Quite all right, sir.'

'Thanks.'

'No bother, sir.'

He was downstairs bright and early the next morning, with his case and his bowler, standing at the door, waiting for me to emerge from the master bedroom.

'I'll give you a lift to the airport,' I told him.

'That won't be necessary, sir.'

'No, fair's fair – I'll give you a lift.'

'I won't require conveyance to the airport, thank you, sir. I can complete my expedition on foot.'

'You're walking to England?'

'No, sir,' he corrected me. 'I am walking around the corner. To my betrothed's residence, in fact.'

'Hang on – your betrothed?'

'Ms Montgomery, sir.'

'Ah Jaysis, Jeeves – Mandy?'

'Yes, sir.'

'Come here – did you bring her to the zoo?'

'Ms Montgomery's enthusiasm for suricates is quite infectious, sir.'

'Hang on – Mandy likes meerkats?'

'Yes, sir.'

'I never knew that.'

'Ms Montgomery is currently the honorary treasurer of the Irish Suricates Appreciation Society, sir.'

'She never said anything about the meerkats to me.'

'You may have noticed the collage on the south-facing wall of Ms Montgomery's hallway, sir?'

'Meerkats?'

'Yes, sir.'

I shook my head.

'Never noticed it,' I said. 'Is it big?'

'It is substantial, yes, sir. It features all the subspecies, including one which, sadly, is now extinct.'

I sat on the stairs. I was feeling extinct, myself.

'And really, like – you're marrying Mandy?'

'Yes, sir,' he said. 'We have come to an understanding. "Through chaos as it swirls, it's us against the world."'

'Yeats?'

'Coldplay, sir.'

And he winked at me.

A thought hit me as he turned to open the door. It – the thought, like – made me sit up and it had nothing to do with meerkats. If Mandy got married again, she'd be knocking on my door in no time.

'Good luck now, Jeeves,' I said.

'You're grand, sir,' he said back.

The Age of Spode: Britain 1896–1988

Dominic Sandbrook

MARKET SNODSBURY UNIVERSITY

DEPARTMENT OF HISTORY

Spring Semester Examinations 2025

You have **three hours** to answer this paper. You should expect to spend the first two hours on Part 1 and the final hour on Part 2. You should not use substantially the same information in more than one of your answers.

PART 1
Answer **two** of the following questions.

1. 'Roderick Spode's Saviours of Britain offered the most plausible and intellectually coherent answer to the Depression of any mainstream British party' (LORD SKIDELSKY). Do you agree?

THE AGE OF SPODE: BRITAIN 1896–1988

2. What role did the seventh Lord Sidcup play in the Munich agreement of 1938, and how far can one blame him for Chamberlain's 'piece of paper'?
3. Why was Lord Sidcup's Stand Up for the Empire tour in the late 1950s such an unmitigated disaster?
4. To what extent did the Redlands controversy of 1967 turn on the relationship between Lord Sidcup, Mick Jagger and Marianne Faithfull?
5. 'If Sidcup had played his cards more cleverly, the world would never have heard of Enoch Powell' (SIMON HEFFER). Do you agree?
6. What does the rise, fall and rebirth of the Eulalie lingerie label tell us about the objectification of women in the post-war years?
7. 'The day Roderick Spode appeared on *Multi-Coloured Swap Shop* was the day that British culture died' (POLLY TOYNBEE). Is this fair?
8. How do you explain the success of the Spode Must Fall movement?

PART 2

Comment on **three** of the following source extracts. What do they tell us about British culture and politics during the life of Roderick Spode, seventh Earl of Sidcup?

(a) A 20-year-old student left Oxford Magistrates' Court in disgrace yesterday, having been fined ten shillings after stealing a police constable's helmet.

Roderick Spode, a geography undergraduate at St Edmund Hall, hung his head in shame as the magistrate pronounced sentence. Earlier, Mr Spode had admitted stealing the constable's helmet as a wager with a college friend, who has not been identified.

In mitigation, Mr Spode explained that he had been drinking heavily throughout the day, having returned from watching the University Boat Race. When asked why he was not serving his country in Flanders, he explained that he had been exempted because of bone spurs in his feet.

He promised that he would never interfere with the constabulary again, and assured the court that he had learned a harsh lesson.

'In the Courts', *Oxford Times*, 4 May 1918

(b) He was, as I had already been able to perceive, a breath-taking cove. About seven feet in height, and swathed in a plaid ulster which made him look about six feet across, he caught the eye and arrested it. It was as if Nature had intended to make a gorilla, and had changed its mind at the last moment.

But it wasn't merely the sheer expanse of the bird that impressed. Close to, what you noticed more was his face, which was square and powerful and slightly moustached towards the centre. His gaze was keen and piercing. I don't know if you have ever seen those pictures in the papers of Dictators with tilted chins and blazing eyes, inflaming the populace with fiery words on the occasion of the opening of a new skittle alley, but that was what he reminded me of.

'Roderick,' said old Bassett, 'I want you to meet this fellow. Here is a case which illustrates exactly what I have so often maintained – that prison life does not degrade, that it does not warp the character and prevent a man rising on stepping stones of his dead self to higher things.'

Bertie Wooster, *The Code of the Woosters* (privately published, late 1930s)

(c) Last night to hear Spode speak at the Public Hall, which is in structure a theatre. It was more than half empty – about fifty people, I should say, most of them sheltering from the rain. About a dozen Black Shorts on duty, all of them weedy-looking specimens, and a couple of girls selling his magazine, *The British Thrust*.

Spode spoke for about an hour and a half and completely failed to take the meeting with him. He was clapped at the start but loudly booed at the end. Several men tried at the beginning to interject questions. The Black Shorts attempted to throw them out, but the men had no trouble in fending them off.

Spode is a dreadful speaker. His speech was the usual claptrap – Empire Free Trade, down with the Foreigner, higher wages and shorter hours all round, etc. But he was completely thrown when one of the men at the back shouted a word I didn't quite catch.

The odd thing is that the man was dressed in the most old-fashioned way, like an Edwardian domestic servant, and only spoke once. Whatever he said, Spode seemed completely taken aback by it. He went bright crimson and jabbered meaninglessly for a few moments, and never managed to recover his poise.

Afterwards I went out to look for the man who had spoken up. He was just striding off when I came outside. I called out to him, but he merely raised his hat and disappeared into the shadows.

George Orwell's diary, 16 March 1936

(d) I feel extraordinarily fit, gay and silly . . . had no luncheon, but a Turkish bath instead. Evening at the Dorchester. I found a motley crew, including Sir Watkyn Bassett and his daughter Madeline, rather a pretty little thing. She has got herself married to Roderick Sidcup, of all people.

I can't think what she sees in him. I knew him quite well at Oxford: he is a great mad fellow, not entirely unattractive, animated by an urge for power. Lady Colefax told me that he changed his ways after succeeding to the earldom, but I struggle to believe it.

P. told me that Roderick went around town for months begging for a commission, but Winston could never forgive him for the Black Shorts business. In the end they found him a place in the Home Guard.

I saw him a few days ago, as P. and I were walking in the park. A little platoon of old men and boys, some of them rather appealing, and poor Roderick at the front, barking orders. I was amused to see that he was wearing those dreadful shorts again: khaki this time, of course.

As we passed, I gave him a little wave, and he just glared at me. There were a couple of other people standing there, laughing at him. I thought I recognised one of them from Bobbie Wickham's parties, a grinning, vacant-looking man, but I couldn't remember his name.

P. said afterwards that we should tell the world about that extraordinary evening when we ran into Roderick in Paris. I said it would hardly be fair to Madeline; and in any case, nobody would believe us.

Henry 'Chips' Channon's diary, 10 April 1941

(e) As regular readers will know, I have long been concerned about the rapid and visible degradation – not merely moral, but intellectual and physical – of the state of Britain's youth.

Today the fine young men who relieved Mafeking and Ladysmith, the strapping boys who went over the top at the Somme, the splendid specimens who put the Japanese in their place, are nothing but a distant memory.

And when I turned on my television last Saturday evening, I was horrified to see that our national degeneracy has reached a chilling new nadir.

JEEVES AGAIN

What a bottomless chasm of vacuity! The huge faces, bloated with cheap confectionery and smeared with chain-store make-up, the open, sagging mouths and glazed eyes, the broken stiletto heels!

What a fearful indictment of our education system, which corrals our children into gimcrack classrooms and fills their pitiful, stunted minds with unashamedly Left-wing delusions!

Worst of all was the figure at the centre of this dreadful cult: a little jester, strutting across the stage and imploring his audience to 'move it' – whatever on earth that means.

At the root of all this, says my friend Sir Roderick Glossop, one of Britain's most eminent brain doctors, is that sickest and most modern obsession – SEX!

I don't doubt it. And when, one day, historians list the reasons why we lost our Empire, I strongly suspect that programmes like *The Cliff Richard Show* will be at the top of the list.

Lord Sidcup, 'Isn't it time we drove these prancing pygmies off our television screens?', *Sunday Express*, 28 March 1960

(f) There is a great deal of evidence which satisfied me that there is a group of people who hold parties in private of a perverted nature. At some of these parties, the man who serves the dinner is nearly naked except for a small square lace apron round his waist such as a waitress might wear. He wears a black mask over his head with slits for eye-holes. He cannot therefore be recognised by any of the guests.

Some reports stop there and say that nothing evil takes place. It is done as a comic turn and no more. This may well be so at some of the parties. But at others I am satisfied that it is followed by perverted orgies: that the man in the mask is a 'slave' who is whipped: that the guests undress and indulge in activities of a vile and revolting nature.

Apart from hearsay, there was not a shred of evidence adduced before me that the man in the mask was Lord Sidcup, as some newspapers claimed. I reject the rumour therefore as utterly unfounded.

I cannot leave this rumour, however, without mentioning that some of the newspapers believed it because of an earlier rumour they had heard about Lord Sidcup. It was rumoured that some years earlier he had been involved in an improper incident in Shepherd's Market, about a man who, being chased by a policeman, hurriedly left a house by foot, having stolen the constable's helmet.

If there had been any such notification of a stolen policeman's helmet (such as the rumour suggests) a record would have been made of it. There is none. There is therefore not a shred of evidence to support this additional rumour.

Lord Denning's Report on the Inquiry into the Security Aspects leading to the Resignation of the former Secretary of State for War, John Profumo (1963)

(g) I asked the four Beatles for a list [for the *Sgt. Pepper* album cover] and I did one myself.

John gave me a list and so did Paul. George suggested only Indian gurus, about six of them, and Ringo said, 'Whatever the others say is fine by me,' and didn't suggest anyone.

All kinds of people were suggested. Hitler was there; he is actually in the set-up, but he is covered by the Beatles themselves as we felt he was too controversial. The same applied to Jesus.

Of course the biggest controversy was about Roderick Spode – Lord Sidcup, as he had become. For some reason he was the first name on John's list. But it turned out that he belonged to the same club as Sir Joseph Lockwood, the head of EMI, and it soon became obvious that we had a problem.

Sir Joseph organised a meeting at the EMI offices. It was awful. Spode was there when I arrived, an enormous man, steam coming out of his ears. He was quite old at that point but absolutely terrifying.

Suddenly John said, 'You're an ape! You're a fascist ape!' and Spode just went for him. Before anybody could stop him, he grabbed

John by the collar and threw him against the wall. 'I'm going to turn you into a jelly, I'm going to rip out your spine and make you eat it for breakfast!', all that sort of thing.

It was total chaos. John was kicking and screaming. Paul was trying to drag Spode away. George started chanting a kind of Indian mantra, which somehow made everything worse. And I can still see Ringo just sitting there, laughing at the whole thing.

In the end, of course, we had to leave him out. We put in Marlene Dietrich instead.

The really odd thing is that years later Spode and John became such great friends. You'd never have believed it, but Yoko thought he was absolutely wonderful. I just couldn't understand it.

Interview with Peter Blake, in Spencer Leigh, *Love Me Do to Love Me Don't: The Beatles on Record* (2016)

(h) To Bristol. The train was almost full, but for one first-class compartment. There was a man in there reading the *Telegraph*, and when he lowered the paper, who should I see but Roderick Spode, larger and redder than ever. So I took the seat opposite him, and we talked all the way back to London. It was great fun.

I said, 'The last time we met, you were asking me about disclaiming your peerage. Whatever happened to that?'

He said, 'Oh, Madeline talked me out of it. She has always liked being Lady Sidcup. It meant a lot to Sir Watkyn.'

We talked about the strikes. He said all the usual things about the shop stewards being Communist, Britain turning into East Germany, foreign substances in our precious bodily fluids, all the rubbish that he puts in that awful column in the *Express*.

I asked him about his daughter. She used to know Stephen at university a bit.

At that he had a great coughing fit and his face went absolutely scarlet, then he said,

'She married a chap called Wooster. Madeline set it up, you know. She was great friends with his father.'

He started coughing again and for a moment his face seemed to turn black. I could just make out the words 'miserable worm'.

I asked him about the Tory leadership contest. 'Ted has got to go,' he said. 'It's time to let the ladies have a turn.'

'Do you really think the MPs want Thatcher?' I asked.

His eyes went positively misty. 'Oh yes,' he said. 'She's just what the country needs. And besides, Madeline adores her.'

After that I told him about my plans for the National Enterprise Board and some of my ideas about the workers taking control of industry. He went very quiet and closed his eyes in thought, and for the next hour or two he barely said a word. I could tell I was really making him think.

When we arrived at Paddington, blow me down, he said, 'I'll take you home.' He told me his driver was waiting and he could drop me at Notting Hill Gate. As we walked off the train together, the engine driver leaned across and called out, 'I wish I could get a picture of you two buggers for the newspapers!'

It was really such a lovely chat, and I didn't expect it at all. I used to think he was a dreadful gorilla, but the way he talks about his wife is really very sweet. He's a bright guy. I am sure history will be much kinder to him than people think.

Tony Benn's diary, 10 January 1975, in *Against the Tide: Diaries 1973–76* (1989)

(i) The long-running saga of the Eulalie Soeurs retail chain came to an end yesterday with the news that the remaining stores have been bought by an American investor.

At its peak in the mid-1960s, Eulalie was one of the fashionable brands on the British high street. Models and film stars such as Jean Shrimpton, Julie Christie and Vanessa

Redgrave were photographed wearing its plastic underwear, and the brand became famous across the world after striking a lucrative deal with the James Bond films.

However, the firm's image suffered after the collapse of Lord Sidcup's libel action against the humorous magazine *Private Eye* in 1967, in which it emerged that he had been behind the original shop, Eulalie Soeurs, which opened in Bond Street more than three decades ago.

Despite the campaign against 'Black Short brassieres', few retail experts predicted Eulalie's fall from grace. Unfortunately, Lord Sidcup's controversial views on the Vietnam War, not least his suggestion that unemployed British youngsters should be rounded up and sent to fight, proved an insuperable obstacle to the firm's recovery.

The kiss of death came in 1973, when the board gambled on the so-called 'Big Eulalie' department store in Kensington High Street. But the art deco interwar stylings only revived memories of the association with Lord

Sidcup, and the Kensington store closed with heavy losses a mere three years later.

A spokesman for the new owners said they were confident they could revive the brand's fortunes, especially in the United States. 'Nobody over here has heard of this Spode guy,' he said. 'We just think the name sounds classy.'

Guardian, 30 August 1977

(j) A celebrated English nobleman was arrested by Palm Beach police officers Tuesday, after reports of an affray at the Bella Grande Plaza Resort and Spa Hotel.

Earl Roderick R. Spode, 85, was briefly detained after a scuffle broke out by the swimming pool. A police spokesman said they had responded to a number of calls from hotel staff, following an altercation by the diving board.

Sources at the hotel told the *Commercial-Scimitar* that the fight broke out when the English holidaymaker – who carries the ancient title of Duke of Sidcup – accused other residents of making indecent approaches to him. After an argument lasting several minutes, Earl Spode, who was wearing only a pair of black swim trunks, allegedly lashed out at the men, who were several decades his junior.

Eyewitnesses reported that the elderly aristocrat, a respected confidant of British prime ministers from wartime hero Winston S. Churchill to modern-day premier Margaret Thatcher, was led away while shouting about 'democracy manifest'. The hotel's executive vice-manager told reporters that Earl Spode had been asked to leave and would not be welcome at the Bella Grande Plaza again.

This is not the first time that Earl Spode, a regular visitor to Palm Beach, has found himself at the center of controversy.

In 1978 he was barred from the Hi-Stakes Resort and Casino after punching a croupier. On that occasion police accepted his explanation that he had become overwrought following the sad death of his wife two months earlier.

The Palm Beach Chamber of Commerce, where the nobleman was due to speak Wednesday on the 'Death of Olde England', said that his appearance would be postponed pending a review.

But Earl Spode's friends insisted that he was not a violent man.

'Earl is a very, very smart guy, a fantastic businessman,' said Donald J. Trump, a visiting real estate investor, who told the *Commercial-Scimitar* that he had known the Englishman for 'many, many years'.

'They were going to put him in as their prime minister,' Mr. Trump said, 'but he didn't want it. He's a very humble man, a good man. I think he has been treated horribly.'

'English Aristocrat Held After Hotel Affray', *Palm Beach Commercial-Scimitar*, September 17, 1981

(k) The Prime Minister joined peers, parliamentarians and well-known names from the worlds of business and the media at Westminster Abbey yesterday to pay tribute to Lord Sidcup, described as 'very much a man of his time'.

The seventh Earl of Sidcup, formerly Roderick Spode, died on 17 July aged 92, after a short illness. His wife Madeline predeceased him.

Lord Sidcup first came to public attention in the late 1930s, when he founded a group known as the Saviours of Britain, nicknamed the Black Shorts. At first his movement seemed a serious rival to the better-known British Union of Fascists, led by his former schoolboy fencing adversary Sir Oswald Mosley.

But Lord Sidcup's leadership ended in circumstances that have never properly been explained. Although he refused to apologise for his flirtation with the far Right, his prominent role in the Home Guard during the Second World War ensured that he was welcomed back into the Conservative Party in the late 1940s.

During the next three decades he was rarely absent from the national conversation, first as a trenchant columnist for the *Sunday Express*, and then as an outspoken commentator on television.

His final appearance came just weeks before his death, when he was invited to discuss the future of feminism on Channel 4's late-night programme *After Dark*. But he was asked to leave the panel after 'lunging' at the American writer Andrea Dworkin during an advertising break.

In her eulogy yesterday, the Prime Minister drew a veil over these and other incidents. Mrs Thatcher told the mourners that Lord Sidcup had been a 'staunch patriot and a loyal friend, who offered me his wise counsel during the Falklands conflict, and never lost his faith in Britain'.

The capacity crowd reflected many aspects of Lord Sidcup's long life. The television presenter Noel Edmonds, a close friend in his final years, told the congregation that he had never known a better man.

Unusually for a memorial service at the Abbey, there was a sizeable contingent from the world of fashion, including a group of current Eulalie models. The international lingerie giant traces its origins to a Bond Street boutique opened by Lord Sidcup in the early 1930s.

Although he never seemed entirely comfortable with his role in Eulalie's success, one of their younger models, the 22-year-old Cindy Crawford, said that Lord Sidcup had been a great inspiration. 'He was a wonderful, wonderful man,' she said, 'and a dear friend.'

The service was only slightly marred by the presence of a small group of demonstrators, who chanted anti-fascist slogans. Most of the mourners ignored them.

But on their way out of the Abbey, two of the older members of the congregation,

THE AGE OF SPODE: BRITAIN 1896–1988

dressed in the fashions of yesteryear, seemed highly amused to see the protesters.

'That dreadful fellow Spode said he'd beat me to a jelly,' one of them said. 'He never did, though.'

'Thatcher leads Sidcup tributes', *The Times*, 23 July 1988

Mixed Doubles

Deborah Frances-White

The chappie behind the bar at the Drones Club was quite rightly giving us the old heave-ho. After all, midnight was pretty much done and dusted, and we had all had a sinful skinful. Tuppy Glossop and Bingo Little had engaged in an especially violent game of billiards, but I'd spent the night pondering how to get out of a rather draconian directive from my Aunt Agatha. She was demanding that I become engaged sharpish to one Georgia Troubridge, when I wasn't at all in the marrying mood.

I barely knew George and while she seemed perfectly charming and all that sort of thing, she'd shown no special interest in me beyond occasionally dragging me in for mixed doubles with her fainty friend Lavender Lanchester who once mooned over me, in a rather unnerving fashion, for an entire Wimbledon.

I got the impression that for George, where it came to me, love meant nothing – on the tennis court and off. And that was just how I liked it.

Trouble was, she stood to inherit some stately pile in Boggy Bottom near Abbots Langley, but only upon her marriage to a chap, you see, as is often the way with girls. Her aunt and mine, who were some kind of fourth cousins or other, had cooked up an especially aunt-like scheme, deciding that I should be that very chap. Aunt Agatha had gone three rounds on me at lunch that afternoon, explaining, in displeased tones, how this would be a use for me when none other had ever been discovered.

I protested that I'd just won a tidy sum on a sporting flutter (involving a drake and two penny turtles) at the village fête and that was surely something of which a chap could be proud. Confoundingly, that seemed to enrage her further. She wildly claimed that matrimony was the only known cure for a nephew like me who was, in her view, some kind of gambling fiend who must be stopped. Furthermore, she insisted that Boggy Bottom was exactly the sort of place to raise any number of Wooster tadpoles. Truth be told, playing tennis in a swamp surrounded by ankle-biters would rather disrupt my plans to have a jolly pleasant life, but Aunt Agatha had set her mind to it. So had George's even fiercer

Aunt Anna Maria. She was one of those contrary types who pronounced 'Maria' in a way that rhymed with 'pariah', which was coincidentally how I always felt in her company. All in all, I couldn't see a way out that didn't put me in the thickest of soups.

'Time, gentlemen, please!' was a welcome disruption to the whirling dervish in my head that hadn't been cured by any number of brandies with soda. Like a band of boozy Cinderellas, the chaps and I careered out into the night to hail a pumpkin heading bedward.

'Hallo, driver!' swerved Bingo.

'Hoy there, stop!' lurched Tuppy.

'Taxi!' I lunged, wildly.

And do you know, not one bally blighter in a taxi-cab would pull over for us. Absolute cheek, I called it. It was then that Bingo had that rarest of things – the old light bulb above the noggin. 'If we have to stagger home, we might as well totter over to the Royal Albert Hall,' he pointed out.

'It'll be long closed at this time of night though, won't it, if you're hoping to catch a Prom or two?' slurred Tuppy. I did think he had a rather good point there, but didn't want to gang up on poor old Bingo by pointing out his schoolboy error.

'No!' he countered. 'It's the night of Lady Malcolm's Servants' Ball, don't you know?! Loads of the guests don't even arrive till one o'clock, because the butlers and maids want to get their households' last fires stoked, port poured and beds warmed before they pop on their gladdest of rags and get ready to Ginger their Rogers!'

Of course! I'd forgotten the annual lavish bash for staff and sundry around the country that went on till three a.m. or more. The night that jolly, jovial Lady Malcolm invites all those downstairs, upstairs for a binge and a half to thank them for their service to the idle rich of this great nation.

'Not to put a spoke in your tricycle wheel there, Bingo old boy,' I interrupted charmingly, 'but I feel I should point out that we're not exactly the servant type. In fact, we're probably the very chaps they're trying to give the widest possible berth for a few hours.'

'Don't worry about that, Bertie,' chuckled Bingo. 'I've crashed that gate, three years running now. Jolliest jamboree of the season in my mind.'

While Bingo Little's mind has never been much to write home about, especially if one's home contains my Aunt Agatha who rather thinks the fellow is a blot on the landscape, it was, sad to say, the best mind we had on the job of 'getting a bottle of something drinkable and hearing a conjunto that'd get our toes tapping'. Bingo looked at Tuppy and me with the sort of pleading face a spaniel might make when eyeing up a particularly juicy sausage.

'Well,' I reasoned wisely, 'as it happens, I've got nothing much to go back to Chez Wooster for, because Jeeves has bally well taken the night off, so I'd have to warm my own slippers, plumpen my own pillows and think out my own conundrum – which, frankly, sounds rippingly dull.'

'Right ho,' cried Bingo, triumphantly, 'we *shall* go to the ball!' as he biffed off the wrong way entirely. We turned him around like a spinning top and set off for that Royalest of Albert Halls. Turned out he was right the first time, but we figured that out within ten minutes or so – so not much time lost in the end.

On our arrival, about fifty-five minutes later, we couldn't help noticing that all the other coves turning up to this retainers' reception were in some kind of fancy dress or other – got up as pirates, pillar boxes, harlequins and horses. One rummy chap was even done up as a bottle of boot polish and another as an alarm clock, which was right on the nose and between the eyes for one who buttles for a living. Some elbow grease to the funny bone, one could say.

'Dash it all!' I said to my companions. 'A quick dekko will tell you we're not getting in without a get-up.'

Tuppy pouted in medium dudgeon, 'I haven't

slogged and jogged all this way in my patent leathers to go home without a jug and a jig.'

Bingo rolled his baby-browns skyward. 'See any of these coves dressed up in evening togs? No! So let's just say we're valets who've come in costume as their employers!'

'Spiffing idea!' chirruped Tuppy. 'We'll say we raided our guv'nors' wardrobes after they were out for the count, if pressed.'

It was hard to argue with Glossop on a finer fettle because he simply strode up and demanded to be let in. The rather rakish, floppy-haired cove on the door, who seemed to have a few too many cheekbones, didn't trust what he saw. 'Gentlemen,' he began.

I wanted to back up sharpish, because the whole scheme was making my feet a bit frosty, but Bingo cut in without a whiff of the amateur about him. 'That's right,' he said with a grin, 'we're gentlemen's gentlemen, looking forward to our ball.'

'Oh yeah?' said the door johnny. 'Who do you valet for then?' He sharp-eyed me and I spluttered, 'A Mr, Mr, Mr Bertie Wooster is my employer, seeing as you're asking, sir.'

The door johnny's face lit up like I'd said I was Father Christmas himself. 'You're Reginald Jeeves?!' He shook my hand as though he were shaking a troublesome Martini. 'Cecil Ives, at your service. You are known as a master of the craft round these parts! You've got your work cut out for you, I hear, in service to that Mr Wooster!'

'I don't know about that,' I said, a trifle hurt.

'None of your modesty, Reggie! Your ticket's on the house,' he winked and then to Tuppy and Bingo, 'Five bob each, please. And sixpence-a-piece for a souvenir programme. It is, after all, in aid of the West End Hospital for Nervous Diseases.' I was so dashed hot under the collar at the thought of our ruse being rumbled by this point, I donated a bally shilling myself, because I thought I might be needing just such a hospital by the a.m.

'Just one more thing, Reggie,' Cyril said. 'My guv'nor is moving to France, so if any of your gentlemen knows a gentleman in need of a gentleman, tell them Cyril Ives is the second-best valet in England and on the lookout.'

'Who's the best, then?' demanded Tuppy.

'Well, Reggie here, of course!' And he punched me on the arm, just a smidgeon too hard if I'm telling the truth. We told him we'd keep all six of our ears to the ground about a post for him and headed once more unto the shindig.

'Well, Bingo, I must say, you were quite right about this being a raucous rager,' I remarked as I took in the feast for the old peepers. There were any number of dashed pretty girls in razzamatazz costumes and an especially euphonious band playing some real foot tappers.

'Now, let's see what we can find to wet the old whistle.'

I headed towards a heaving bar past Joan of Arc and Little Bo Peep, and smack bang into the path of the Duke of Wellington. 'I beg your pardon, your grace,' I said.

'Have you lost your way, sir?' the Duke of Wellington replied.

'I say, you sound just like my valet, Jeeves!'

'I cannot say that is entirely surprising, sir.'

Well, knock me down with a feather, it *was* Jeeves!

'Jeeves! What are you doing here?!'

'At the servants' ball, sir?'

'Ah yes, now you say that, Jeeves, it's not very much of a head scratcher, after all.'

'Indeed. And you, sir?'

I looked over my shoulder, like a fox in a kennel of hounds. 'I'm blending in, Jeeves.'

'If you say so, sir.'

'Jeeves, I think you should stop calling me "sir". It's rather giving the game away.'

'Very good, sir. How would you prefer me to address you?'

'Perhaps as "Bertie", Jeeves.'

'If you don't mind me saying, sir, that would be a precariously familiar liberty. Perhaps "Bertram" might suffice for the evening, sir.'

'Jolly good idea, Jeeves.'

Jeeves adjusted his bicorne.

'And perhaps, sir, you should address me as Reginald, to ensure the thoroughness of the subterfuge.'

I touched my nose, knowingly.

'Excellent idea, Jeeves,' I said.

'Thank you, sir,' he replied.

Right then, a rummy cove, done up like one Charlie Chaplin, except with absolutely nothing where his shirt front should be, lurched over the dance floor with a fistful of green carnations.

'Bertie Wooster!'

'Sticky Bickerstaff!'

Hadn't seen old Sticky since prep school. 'What are you doing here?'

'I could ask you the very same,' he countered.

Jeeves made a face as if he were curious to know the answer to both questions.

'I'm here on a jape and this is "my friend", Mr Reginald Jeeves,' I said, winking hard in Jeeves's direction and elbowing his ribs quite firmly.

'Mr Bickerstaff,' Jeeves nodded.

'How do you do, Mr Jeeves?' said Sticky and then

he looked at me as if he had something stuck in his eye.

'I didn't quite realise, Bertie,' he said.

I couldn't really catch his drift, I have to say, but he offered me a green carnation for my buttonhole and I was positively delighted. I'd never seen such a thing before in my life. Red! White! Pink! But never a *green* carnation.

'What fun!' I said. 'Green's just my colour, Sticky!'

He nodded with a touch of the melancholic mumbles about him. 'Mine too. I'll see you in the Elgar Room.'

Sticky headed off up the stairs like a cannonball on the loose, as I popped the flower in my buttonhole.

'I wouldn't advise you to wear that, sir,' said Jeeves.

'Why not, Jeeves? And please call me Bertram,' I said crossly.

'Very well, Bertram sir, but I must caution against donning such a flower.'

'But Sticky was wearing one in his buttonhole and two behind his ear!'

'Yes, Bertram sir, but I believe that young Mr Bickerstaff can carry off any number of green carnations without cause for comment. I fear, however, in your case it might be said to be telegraphing the wrong message.'

'You always do this, Jeeves! You advise against

yellow spats and purple socks and red trousering and any dashed jot of colour that might bring a spot of life to a party. Well, tonight, everyone else is exploding with frippery and even you have feathers spouting out of your head! So I'm jolly well going to wear a green carnation if I like!'

'Very good, Bertram sir.'

With that I flounced upstairs in search of the Elgar Room and I must say I've never entered into such an upside-down hullaballoo! Chaps wearing rouge, dancing with chaps in cowboy boots. Ladies with moustaches swaying with ladies in riding get-up. Everyone was pretty damn blotto as you can imagine, so I joined in with the kind of gay abandon only a chap who loves larks can. I tripped the lightest possible fantastic with Sticky. We even had a good old sentimental weep about our glory days at Malvern House when he gave his Juliet to my Romeo and I forgot my vial of poison and had to punch myself in the face to death.

Moments later, when we had joined a particularly unruly conga line, who should cut in front of me but young Georgia Troubridge, all done up like Rudolph Valentino!

'What on earth are you doing here, George?!' I asked her as she swayed this way and that and I fought to keep hold of her, like a cat on a merry-go-round.

'Same as you, Bertie,' she smiled over her shoulder, as she twirled one of Sticky's green carnations coquettishly. 'And now I know, I have a proposition for you.'

'Now you know what?' I said, mystified, kicking right. 'Look here, do you think we could put our heads together and figure out how to dodge this engagement nonsense? Perhaps with my valet, Jeeves? He's really rather good at getting out of scrapes with aunts!'

I wasn't sure she could hear me over the din of the brass section because she just shouted, 'I'll pay you a call tomorrow,' and kicked left. 'Do make sure you're up and about before teatime!'

And then she disappeared into the fray where Lavender Lanchester was only too ready to Busby her Berkeley – while I got caught up in a tug of war with a rope made entirely of long johns. I must say, there was something about a servants' ball that was really jolly freeing. It was as if every chap there could be himself, whether he was a chap or a lady. Truly, the jolliest jamboree of the season.

I don't quite remember how the evening ended and couldn't figure out for the life of me how I managed to find myself in my bed the next afternoon. Suffice to say that Jeeves brought me my eggs and b. and a cup of tea dead on three, along with one of his more invigorating potions for a sore head, and I was as grateful as a chap could be.

'I say, Jeeves, that was quite a hoot last night bumping into you at that ball, wasn't it?'

'As you say, sir.'

'Did you happen to see how I got home?'

'I did, sir.'

'Care to share it, Jeeves?'

'I managed to procure you a taxi-cab, sir, and physically accompany you up the stairs, when you became, to put it delicately, a little under the weather.'

'That was very good of you, Jeeves.'

'I have taken the liberty of preparing some light refreshments for your guests this afternoon, sir.'

'What guests, Jeeves?! I was planning on spending the day in my dressing gown.'

'You might remember, sir, that you invited Miss Troubridge to pay you a call.'

'I bally-well didn't. But now you say that, Jeeves, I think she dashed well invited herself. Do you think I can put her off?'

'Not very likely at this hour, sir. I am also expecting an appearance from Mr Bickerstaff although I couldn't say when.'

Just then, the doorbell rang. 'Well, that has solved that conundrum, sir,' Jeeves nodded, satisfied, as he headed doorwards.

'How did you know?! He didn't say anything to me!' I called after him.

Jeeves turned back: 'His eyes gave away his position, sir...'

Bally mysterious, I called that. I pulled on some trousers and went out to see what the whole dashed fuss was about. There was old Sticky in my drawing room bawling into some scones Jeeves had conjured up out of thin air.

'What on earth is the matter, Sticky?'

'Bertie. I have held a candle for you since we were altar boys.'

'I held my own candle at evensong if memory serves, old Stick.'

'No, I mean...' He broke down again, all wet and weepy like a leaky bag of broth. I didn't quite know where to put myself, so I took a scone and peered out the window at a passing pigeon.

'All this time,' he blubbed, 'I thought you went in for girls – and I wasted my chance and now I find you're in a romantic entanglement with your valet! Dashed convenient, I must say, as you can live like man and wife behind closed doors, and no one need suspect a bally thing.'

Well, I have to say, cannon to right of me, cannon to left of me, I was knocked right off my rocker.

'What on earth do you mean, Sticky?'

'I saw you last night with the same dashed man who opened the door to me just now,' he wept, 'and you introduced me to him as your *friend* Reginald and winked.'

'Because I was at the servants' ball! Undercover, don't you know? Same as you! Didn't want to be thrown out onto the pavement for not being in service, you see?'

'Nonsense! It's as clear as day, you're in love! And you wore my green carnation all night!'

It was terribly difficult to see what a bally flower had to do with it, but just then Jeeves reappeared and before I could ask him to reassure Sticky that there was no such romantic collusion between us, he said, 'Miss Troubridge to see you, sir. She has brought Miss Lanchester with her. And I believe she's expecting Mrs Gregson in fifteen minutes.'

'Aunt Agatha, coming here? Why on earth, Jeeves?'

'Miss Troubridge has invited her to toast your engagement, sir.'

'My engagement?! To whom?'

'I believe to Miss Troubridge, sir.'

Poor Sticky really started to bawl at this news — and I almost did too.

'Is she mad, Jeeves? We're not anywhere near affianced.'

'Not yet, sir. No. But the afternoon is young.'

Next thing I knew Jeeves had brought George and Lavender in. I must admit I rather abandoned poor old inconsolable Sticky to fainty Lavender who immediately flung herself down on my *chaise longue* and fanned herself as if she were on fire. I dragged George off to a corner to find out what in the devil's name was going on.

'Look here, George. What's all this about us being engaged? And why is my aunt coming here when I am expressly avoiding her like the proverbial!'

'But Bertie, don't you see? We can marry each other now and both be just as free as we like. I can be in Boggy Bottom with my love, and you can be "spending time in town" with yours.' She nodded in the direction of Jeeves. 'After a few years we'll just say, "What a shame, no babies or other seem to have come along," and get some basset hounds.'

'George! I— What?! What on earth are you talking about?'

'You can be with Jeeves! Your true love! And you and I will be married, so everyone will stop asking questions about why we're not.'

'Dash it all! Jeeves is just my gentleman's gentleman.'

George touched her nose like a spy in a music-hall song: 'I know he is *your gentleman*, Bertie.'

'No! My manservant! My valet! He starches my

eggs and scrambles my cuffs! I mean, scrambles my eggs and starches my y'know— Why on earth is everyone going about thinking—'

'Because you danced with Sticky in the Elgar Room and I thought you were keen on him. But then he said you'd come with a man called Jeeves and were pretending very much to be "friends". Well, I told Sticky, "Jeeves is his valet!" and then we realised it must be terribly convenient for you to live here together. And what luck to fall in love with your manservant or hire the manservant you were already in love with. Whichever way round it happened, Bertie, all I want is to help you keep up the ruse, so you can go on living as you like.'

'Now bally well look here, I was pretending to be a *servant*. That's all!'

'Then why on earth did you wear a green carnation all night?'

Sticky was dropping the old eaves and barrelled across the room in a manner so melodramatic, it's usually reserved for the playhouse: 'Exactly?! If you wish to reject me then just do it, but don't go making up frightful fibs and claim you're not entangled with Jeeves!'

George chimed in, 'Yes! And if you *don't* want to marry me and have an arrangement where you can use Boggy Bottom for house parties and come and go as you please, then just say so – but don't pretend you're not desperately in love with Jeeves.'

I threw Jeeves a look like a flare in search of a life raft, but he seemed to be busying himself with the tea tray and was dashed well making it impossible for me to catch his eye.

George stamped her foot. 'Well, your Aunt Agatha and my Aunt Anna Maria will be here very shortly, so you'll have to answer to them as to why you don't want to marry me, because I am very much in favour of this arrangement. It's the only way I can escape the endless, hopeless prison of living with my aunt and be trusted to have my house. Do see sense, Bertie. Be a good chap and let me be with the one true love of my life.'

Sticky glared at me. 'Well, having heard that, I am afraid I'm with George. Step up and do the decent thing, Wooster. You don't want to marry a woman anyway, so let George be happy. You won't have to do a thing except inherit her stately pile and live the high life. Don't be mean. Be a good sort.'

I was starting to think that perhaps Jeeves might have been right about the green carnation after all. Simply nothing would shift George and Sticky from their position, so I excused myself and followed Jeeves into the kitchen where he was preparing a round of salmon paste sandwiches.

'Jeeves, I'm in something of a pickle.'

'So I understand, sir.'

'I'm afraid you may have been onto something about the green carnation signalling the wrong thing and now everyone thinks that you and I are in some sort of amorous alliance!'

'That very much seems to be the case, sir.'

'Do you think you could go in and tell them we're not, Jeeves? Do a chap a favour and clear up this little misunderstanding?'

'I am afraid the young gentleman and the young lady would not believe me, sir. They would simply be even more convinced we were hiding our love for the ages, as many are unfortunately obliged to do, due to the legal ramifications and rather unwieldy social cost of speaking the truth, sir.'

'Yes, but Jeeves, this *is* the truth!'

'Perhaps, sir, if you made your affections known to the young Miss Lanchester, they would see that your proclivities were not directed towards me, sir.'

'Brilliant, Jeeves! Lavender set her cap in my general direction a few summers ago, but I always found her in need of too many smelling salts and readily available fainting couches, Jeeves. But under the circs, it would certainly be enough to put them off the scent. And it is something of an emergency.'

'As you say, sir.'

I put my hands in my pockets and made a thinking face.

'What kind of things would give a girl the impression that a chap was smitten and ready, Jeeves?'

'The bard would perhaps compare the young lady to a summer's day, sir.'

'Really? Would the bard do that if the girl in question were more like a wet weekend in January?'

'I do not know of any such sonnet, sir.'

Bing bong, the bally doorbell rang and wouldn't you know my luck, it was my Aunt Agatha and George's Aunt Anna Maria. They arrived in a wildly uncharacteristic tidal wave of smiles and pleasantries that did not bode well for me at all. Aunt Agatha even took me by the hands with something that could be said to approach affection. 'Engaged at last and into such an auspicious family, with such a beautiful house . . .'

'On such a boggy bottom,' I countered. Aunt Agatha laughed – a rare and clanging sound like a clock that hadn't chimed in twenty years, springing to life in a rather ghostly fashion.

She turned to Jeeves and even managed a kindly look towards him. 'Let us have some champagne, please, Jeeves, to toast the happy couple!'

Aunt Anna Maria was making an equally eerie fuss

of George. Sticky was sulking in the corner and Lavender was splayed out on the *chaise*, looking like the drowned Ophelia with a particularly bad head cold. I went and sat on the edge of her day bed and gave her the glad eye.

'Lavender,' I said, as corks were popped and the gramophone was fired up without my permission. 'I've always thought you were rather like a summer's day. Something of the hot weather in the grass with dragonflies in the picnic about you.'

'I do suffer awfully from hay fever, Bertie, if that's what you mean,' she said, screwing up her pallid little sniffer, confused.

This was going to be a dashed sight more difficult than I'd thought. George and Sticky came over in my direction, so I thought I'd better give it my most convincing backhand, while they were in earshot.

'Lavender,' I said, wobbling my lip deliberately, 'I think I was wrong three Wimbledons ago when I dodged your advances. I find I'm rather sweet on you, after all. Advantage Miss Lanchester, and all that.'

'What did you say?!' said George. That had done it.

'WHAT DID YOU SAY?' boomed Aunt Anna Maria, who apparently has the hearing of an especially youthful bat. 'Mr Wooster! How dare you insult my niece, to whom you are betrothed, by making love to her friend in broad daylight?!'

Aunt Agatha gasped, 'You have disgraced me, Bertie! And you have damaged this girl's reputation,' she said, pointing at George.

There was a terrible, furious round of screeching and shouting and I looked to Jeeves whose advice had clearly made things a dashed sight worse, to see some remorse from the man, but he looked as cool as the cucumber sandwiches he was putting on the sideboard.

'Begging your pardons, Mrs Gregson and Lady Troubridge,' Jeeves said. 'There seems to be some mistake. It is not Mr *Wooster* and Miss Troubridge who are to be married, but rather Mr *Bickerstaff* and Miss Troubridge who are engaged.'

George and Sticky looked at each other confused as badgers, but clearly willing to hear more.

Aunt Anna Maria scoffed, 'I received a telegram this morning from my niece stating clearly that she was engaged to Mr Bertie Wooster.'

Aunt Agatha nodded. 'I received the same cable!'

'I am afraid that is my fault, madams,' Jeeves went on, to all of our astonishments. 'Miss Troubridge was here, telling Mr Wooster the happy news this morning. And Mr Wooster asked me to go to the post office to send the telegrams on behalf of the young lady. Mr Wooster, as you know, Mrs Gregson, is often a little on the distracted side. I believe he was listening to a horse race on the wireless at the time.'

Aunt Agatha moaned, 'A horse race, Bertie? Gambling when I expressly forbid it! No doubt with that dreadful Bingo Little again!'

I opened my mouth to defend myself as I jolly well hadn't done anything of the sort, but Jeeves cut me off: 'I'm afraid it is the young gentlemen's rather regrettable practice, madam.'

Aunt Agatha simmered as Jeeves continued: 'I simply passed over the note at the post office that Mr Wooster had scribbled down while preoccupied, without checking it for errors, as I should surely have done before sending it. So as you can see, madam, the fault is entirely mine.'

Aunt Agatha gave me a glare that could have shot me off a horse and into the next county.

'So am I to understand, Bertie,' she went on, 'that you are not engaged to Miss Troubridge and that it is Mr Bickerstaff who will be married and moving to Boggy Bottom?'

Sticky looked at George and they both smiled a moony sort of smile. 'Yes!' cried Sticky, 'Georgia and I are very much in love!'

'A June wedding – we thought,' said George,

clutching at Sticky's hand as if it were a ladder off the *Titanic*. She grabbed Lavender's hand on the other side and pronounced her to be maid of honour, with an enthusiasm that was difficult to explain.

Aunt Anna Maria had an air of the Lord on Judgement Day about her. She looked poor Sticky up and down as if he were a vole in a trap.

'Are you related to Mrs Ambrose Bickerstaff, by any chance?' Her manner was so fierce, Sticky had no idea whether he should confirm or deny but the truth would out in the end so he decided to 'fess up and said, 'She's my mother, Lady Troubridge.'

Lucky old Stick, she grinned like a Cheshire moggy and said, 'How is darling Jonty? She and I were great friends at school. And afterwards we spent a sparkling summer together in Boggy Bottom. Lots of long, lovely days lying in the orchard, reading the more under-appreciated Romantic poets.' Aunt Anna Maria's eyes twinkled as if old Mother Bickerstaff had once compared her to any number of summer days. She snapped out of her rose-coloured revery and then enquired tentatively, 'And your father? Is he in good health?'

'Sadly not,' Sticky replied. 'We lost him some ten years ago, now.'

'Oh,' beamed Aunt Anna Maria, 'how dreadfully unfortunate. Well, I do look forward to consoling your mother heartily at the wedding.'

Aunt Agatha gave me a thunderous look. 'Well, as I have been invited here under entirely false pretences, I shall be leaving, Bertie. You are a great disappointment to me and all Woosters – living and dead.'

'I do see that, Aunt Agatha,' I replied, sheepishly. 'I'll see you out.'

I opened the door for Aunt Agatha and blow me down, there, crouched on the mat, was Cyril Ives, the dashed door johnny from Lady Malcolm's Servants' Ball.

'Reggie!' he cried. 'I was just leaving you a note.'

Aunt Agatha turned on me and said, 'I do not wish to know. Good day!' then swept past Cyril and away down the corridor.

Cyril went on, 'Just in the neighbourhood looking for a new post and thought I'd stop by on the off chance your Mr Wooster was out and you wanted to go for a swift half in the Bear and Staff, Reggie. Truth is, at the Royal Albert Hall, I saw you being carried out, half cut, in a taxi this morning. And, well . . . you were wearing a green carnation and I wondered if, perhaps . . .' He ended his sentence with an extravagant wink.

'Ah,' I said to the handsome devil, a dab hand at this green carnation malarkey by this time, 'yes, that was all a bit of a mix-up on my part, but wait there. I think there's someone you should meet who might be looking for a valet.'

I popped back in and told Sticky if he were going to be stuck in the country with women half the time, he'd jolly well need a very good valet for company. He agreed that'd be just the ticket and I cajoled him out to the door.

'Oh, and by the way,' I whispered sensibly, 'be a good fellow and pretend I'm Jeeves.'

Sticky opened his mouth and closed it, like a goldfish who'd forgotten what he was going to say.

'Mr Bickerstaff,' I said to Sticky, 'this is Ives. Best valet in the country, bar me.'

Cyril looked at Sticky longer than a valet would usually look at a chap and Sticky looked at Cyril longer than a chap would usually look at a valet. They both had a touch of the summer's day about them, I have to say.

I headed back into the kitchen and found Jeeves icing a rather marvellous engagement cake.

'It's all worked out remarkably well, Jeeves, I must say.'

'Indeed, sir.'

'Only thing is, I'm rather on the hook with fainty

Miss Lanchester, as I've told her I'm sweet on her now. I fear her expectations will be high.'

'I do not believe you will be troubled by the return of Miss Lanchester's affections, sir.'

'You weren't there at the Wimbledon quarter-final, Jeeves.'

'As you say, sir, but Miss Lanchester is Miss Troubridge's "close companion" now and I believe will be moving to Boggy Bottom with her, to take up residence there as her long-term guest.'

'No, no, no, Jeeves,' I said, 'George goes in for girls. I see that now. But Lavender is sweet on chaps. She was sweet on me, after all, and what am I, if not a chap?'

'I am given to understand that some ladies can have amorous affections for both gentlemen and other ladies, sir.'

'Really, Jeeves?'

'Indeed, sir.'

I licked the icing from the bowl with my favourite wooden spoon.

'But some chaps just go in for chaps and some girls just go in for girls, Jeeves. Is that right?'

'Just as you say, sir.'

Right then, I had a rather heartening revelation.

'Do you think the reason Bobbie Wickham went off me was that she goes in more for girls?!'

'No, sir.'
'What about Madeline Bassett?'
'Again no, sir.'
'Honoria Glossop?'
'I'm afraid not, sir.'

In August, Jeeves and I motored to Boggy Bottom for a longish weekend of tennis and general japes.

Sticky and George played Cyril and Lavender in one of their rounds of mixed doubles. Jeeves was the umpire and I was the linesman. Jolly dull it was, and far too boggy. Even worse, I lost ten bob to Sticky on the match which I'd wagered he'd win. I am convinced Sticky threw it, because I called three balls that were clearly out as in – and he still took a drubbing.

Of course, I had to come clean to Cyril that Jeeves was Jeeves and I was me and we all had a tremendous laugh about it. Everyone there seems to be a summer's day to someone else and they're all jolly happy – or at least as happy as they can be, having to pretend when they go to the tea shop. And I have to say, Lavender seems to be a lot less taken to fainting and fanning. Perhaps it's the boggy air doing her good.

On the way home, I turned and said, 'You know what, Jeeves?'

'I am on tenterhooks, sir,' Jeeves replied.

'I think I'm quite glad that some girls go in for both chaps and girls and some chaps go in for both girls and chaps.'

'Delighted to hear it, sir. May I enquire as to the reason for this new-found gladness?'

'Well, Jeeves, because I don't think I'm the marrying sort for either chaps or girls and I think it's rather good it's all evened out somewhere by someone.'

'I understand, sir.'

'I've played at it, Jeeves, but it never seems to stick for me. I don't think I really want it. I just know that I am supposed to want it.'

'I see, sir.'

'What I liked about Lady Malcolm's Ball, Jeeves, was that chaps could be whatever sort of chaps they were and girls could be whatever sort of girls they were, even if they weren't the everyday sort. And I think, in my own way, Jeeves, I am not an everyday sort of chap.'

'As you say, sir.'

'It's a shame that ball only happens once a year and is only really for servants, Jeeves.'

'There are any other number of clubs in London,

sir, that accommodate those who are not of the everyday variety . . . of all social classes.'

'Are there, Jeeves?!'

'Yes, sir. I can certainly direct you to them if you wish.'

'Would you, Jeeves?'

'There's the 43 Club, sir. Many enjoy the Silver Slipper Club . . . the Green Carnation . . .'

'Oh Jeeves, is that how you knew?!'

'A capable valet must be a man of the world, sir.'

'Well, I'd jolly well like to go to some of those clubs and just be the kind of chap that I am with other chaps being the kind of chaps that they are and no one minding.'

'Very good, sir.'

'And if you were to take me there, Jeeves, just to kick me off and get me to the starting line, you know – I think you should call me Bertie and I should call you Reggie, Jeeves. Just so as not to give the game away.'

'The game must, indeed, be treated with the utmost care, sir.'

'But when we come home, Jeeves, y'know, I think I like the arrangement we have.'

'Sir?'

'I think I'm the sort of chap who has found a valet that he likes and likes living with his valet. I think that's *my* summer's day. Do you know what I mean, Jeeves?'

'I believe I do, sir. Very much so.'

And then Jeeves looked at the fields we were passing and said, 'The bard would be most pleased, sir.'

Drive On, Jeeves

Andrew Hunter Murray

An insolent echoing sound penetrated the Wooster cranium.
Brrrrrrrrring.
There it went again.

I confess with regret that the outset of this story sees Bertram W at a low-water mark. The bottom of the rock. A nadir, if that's the word I want. You find me cast, crumpled, along a sofa, looking like Thomas de Quincey on one of his off mornings.

On top of the thumping of my head, which appeared to have independently entered and lost a Mongolian wrestling tournament in the night, I added the following symptoms: one tongue, drier than Oliver Cromwell's drinks cabinet; a pallor stretching from temple to shining temple; and a strong aversion to the sunlight now thumping its way through the curtains and barging around the room. I had the distinct sensation someone had swapped all the hairs on my scalp with one another, and while they were at it traded my intestines for a Bosch 9000.

And now, to complete the battalion of troubles, the phone was ringing. Worse yet, only two people ring me on the landline, both of them blood relatives and neither an ideal choice for the first conversation of the day. Some mornings.

Upright, which was another nasty surprise. One hand groping towards the receiver, the other manipulating the dressing gown. I don't know if you've tried donning a d.g. single-handed while answering the phone, but if you've ever seen the statue of the Trojan chap wrestling with the serpents you'll know how I looked in the moment.

'Hello?'

'It's your aunt,' said the voice at the other end, confirming my second-worst fears. Not, at least, my Aunt Agatha, the Wicked Aunt of the West Country, who snacks on firelighters and drives an APC, but Aunt Dahlia, the Good Aunt of East Anglia and a fractionally more reasonable character.

'Hello, Aunt D.' In the night some evildoer had borrowed my vocal cords and left two rusty springs as security.

'Waster.'

'Wooster,' I croaked.

'You're hungover,' she added, at an entirely unnecessary volume. (She might be the Good Aunt but she still has a voice that could command the 4th Tank Army.)

'No, no. A touch of laryngitis.'

'Rubbish. You've been drinking.'

'Just a couple of swift ones down at the Drones,' I whimpered. It was slowly returning to me now. I'd been in my local trying to drown my troubles. Halfway down the first glass they'd started thrashing, but by the end of the night they'd gone limp and ceased all resistance. Well, they were taking their vengeance now and serving it over ice.

Why had I had so many whiskies-and-soda? As yet, no white smoke was visible. I clung to the phone, leaned on the nearest wall, and hung on my aunt's every word.

'Typical. Well, never mind that,' said Aunt Dahlia. 'I have a job for you.'

I was slowly realising that the infernal noise hadn't stopped when I answered the phone; it had merely metastasised into something even louder. This new sound was like a dentist's drill, being wielded with minimal precision and applied wherever the bearer fancied.

'A job?'

'People do them for money. You should try it some time.'

'What sort of job?'

'Brinkley Books is in a week. I need a guest.'

I should have guessed from the date. A few years ago, my aunt – not content with running a FTSE 100 company and wielding over her parish council the sort of authority Genghis Khan did over Central Asia in his pomp – branched out into Culture, and established a book festival at the family seat. For ten days a year, the general public swarm into the gazebo-clad grounds at Brinkley, Uncle Tom retreats to polish his cow-creamers, and a range of eggheads are imported to share their insights on *Whither The Novel?* and other such questions the world needs answering as a matter of urgency. And now I was receiving The Call. Time to resist with every fibre.

'I am flattered,' I said. 'But really, Aunt D, it's not my sort of thing.'

'Not you, you idiot duckling child. Who would want to hear your few thoughts?'

I bristled at this. I did once write a piece for a friend's blog entitled *Trousers – Do They Matter?*, which my pal assured me had nearly achieved the average number of hits, so it's not so implausible that I might be called to offer an insight or two. Not that I'd want to. I've been to events at Aunt Dahlia's and the questions the punters serve up at the end are invariably the kind of screaming yorkers I would only attempt if equipped with three hours' thinking time and a thesaurus. But I let the insult slide harmlessly off the Wooster spine. Even when my inner flame is down to its pilot light, I endeavour to show forgiveness.

'No,' continued my aunt. 'I need someone big. You know Emily Fossett, don't you?'

'I do. Lovely girl. But you *can't* want her for Brinkley Books.'

'I do not, you fluff-headed wretch. Will you let me explain? Uwe Gnarsson is staying with her family. I want you to visit and offer him the headline slot.'

Now, I'm not a literary type. The occasional thriller, of course, something to chill the pulse and quicken the marrow, but little beyond that. Scratch Wooster, and you scratch a man whose only use for a First Folio would be as a boost towards an inaccessible tin of shortbread. But even I have heard of Uwe Gnarsson. He's a gloomy Scandinavian sort who writes ream after ream of stuff, mostly a thinly fictionalised version of his personal life, and his readers appear to simply eat it up. As far as I can tell, he offers living proof that millions of sales, dozens of gongs and a string of impossibly attractive wives can do little to boost the spirits of a man whose professional success depends on his staying glum.

'Can't you get someone else?'

'I've *tried* everyone else,' she said. 'But we still need our big mystery Friday-nighter. Atwood's on a silent retreat, Ishiguro's booked for a mini-golf tournament, and McEwan's in Berlin for a rave. No, it's got to be Gnarsson, and although the Lord has sent me an imperfect tool, I have no other choice.'

'Why don't you ask him yourself?'

'Because he's a recluse. He won't answer any questions via his agent. His editor is a sealed tomb. His publicist is practically a shut-in. I only found out that he's with the Fossetts because their gardener speaks to ours. No, it's got to be the personal touch, and I'm needed in town for work. Help me, Bertie Wooster. You're my only hope.'

'I couldn't get down to the Fossett place in time. It's impossible.'

'Why not?'

'No car.'

'No car? What have you done, you infestation?'

That was it. That was why I'd popped to the pub last night. Yesterday, while rounding that rather tricky bend in Hyde Park, I'd been distracted by the sight of my friend Gus on a bicycle, and while lowering the window to shout at him I'd momentarily taken my eyes off the car in front, which it turned out had been intending to stop much sooner than anyone could have foreseen. Cue one blown airbag, one badly dinged two-seater, one angry brace of police officers, one brewing appointment at a magistrates' court, and — certainly for the foreseeable — no car. Worst of all, it hadn't even been Gus on the bike.

I told my aunt a sanitised version of the above tale of woe.

'Well,' the aged relative said, unwilling as ever to let a fox get away unmauled, 'you could get the train down.'

'Don't be silly.' Emily's family home is in a bit of the country served by a railway line which I will chivalrously leave unnamed, but whose trains move across the country about as fast as lichen. It is staffed by a company of men and women who doubtless lead blameless personal lives, but whose speed of action and communication style might have seen them better placed as living statues, or perhaps as those monastic types who have declared civilisation a washout and decided to climb the nearest thirty-foot pole and there remain.

'No, I suppose not,' she said, sounding gloomy. 'I need Gnarsson soon. You could get a cab.'

'All that way? In this economy?' She grunted, and I could tell I'd scored a hit there. It was finally happening: for the first time in my life, I was going to wriggle out of one of Aunt D's little commissions. The drilling noise, I noticed, was unabated, and beginning to hamper conversation. 'Can you just hold up a second? There's someone making a terrible racket outside.'

I chucked open the ground-floor window and looked out into the face of a workman. He was holding a power tool roughly the size of the ones they used to excavate the Channel Tunnel, and applying it to the wall of my flat. I intervened, as briskly as I knew how.

'Oi!'

He paused his infernal grinding.

'What are you doing?'

He consulted a bit of paper. 'Your name is ... Woah-Oster?'

'Wooster.'

He nodded, as if he'd suspected as much all along.

'I repeat. What are you doing?'

'I'm putting a charger on your home.' He had a French accent. Nothing wrong with that, I hasten to add. I merely observe it to lend his character a spot of depth.

'Charger? For what?'

'For the car.'

'What car?'

He gestured over his shoulder. Behind him, in the street, lurked an extremely nice two-seater. Racing green, convertible, sleek . . . It was a car to make even a Just Stop Oiler paw at the ground and snort for the open road.

'I didn't order a car. Nor did I ask for a charger. Who told you to stick that on my flat?'

'The car did.'

I looked at him, and he at me, in total and mutual incomprehension. His was the kind of look that stout Cortez might have given a bystander who'd just asked him in the local tongue if he was going to spend the whole day staring at the view.

'Just . . . wait a second, will you?'

He shrugged, and I leaned back inside, took the phone from my breast, and asked the question which proved my most serious tactical mistake.

'Aunt. Be honest with me. Did you have a car sent to my place just now?'

'Car? I wouldn't trust you with a unicycle.' Then she added, with a gleam in her voice, 'What do you mean? You've procured one, then?'

In that moment I felt rather like Napoleon must have done just after strolling triumphantly through the gates of Moscow, only to realise the place seemed to be closed for business and he'd left his lunchbox back in Paris.

'Er . . . well, I need to investigate, but it does seem rather as if . . .'

'That's excellent. Off you pop to Casa Fossett, then.'

'But . . .'

'If you don't, I will simply have to ring up Anna and tell her we need one fewer box this Christmas.'

'Oh, Aunt, *really*.'

'Fair's fair. My back has gone unscratched so now yours must too.'

I should explain. Every year, for the festive season, Aunt Dahlia sends out a range of hampers made by a chef called Anna Natolé. Between the occasional wisps of straw, these boxes fairly overflow with the most extraordinary foodstuffs you've ever seen. Olives the size of satsumas; lobster stuffed with crab and vice versa; marmalades containing more whisky than orange. Only about sixty of the things are crafted per annum. They cost about as much as a hip replacement and the waiting list to get one is roughly as long.

Somehow, doubtless thanks to her murky underworld connections, Aunt D secures about fifteen Natolé hampers each year, which are in her gift. She wields and restricts the things with the tyrannical whimsy of an Eastern European strongman who keeps his hand lingering over the spigots on the gas pipeline.

'Oh, fine,' I said. 'I'll do my best.'

'Do even better than that, thanks,' she said. 'Good. No need to ring Anna then. Off you pop. Drive carefully.'

Which simply left me with an enormous headache, an impossible task and a mysterious new car. I rubbed the brow, picked up the keys the workman had left on the mat, and stumbled down to my parking space, where the new vehicle sat, plugged in and looking pleased with itself.

I unlocked it. I opened the door. I sat within. And at that moment – and there is no way of saying this without confirming your fears that the Wooster marbles have finally rolled free of their moorings and ended up wedged under the heavy bookcase – the car spoke to me.

'Good morning, sir.'

The voice was rich, male, fruity. Imagine someone who's been gargling chocolate-coated gravel and smoking twenty Gitanes a day and you're halfway there.

'Good . . . morning?' The effort of a third tricky conversation within five minutes of waking – this one the weirdest of the lot – was starting to tell. I squeezed the brow.

'If you don't mind me observing, sir, you have a distinct pallor about you. Are you indisposed?'

'I was out last night.'

'I understand entirely, sir. Would you care to lean over and look in the passenger glove compartment? It contains something you might find restorative.'

I leaned over and sprung the box. Inside was a chilled tumbler of dark fluid. It looked simultaneously welcoming and dangerous, like a smiling mastiff, or any food purchased after midnight.

'What is it?'

'A tonic drink, sir.'

I took a gulp, and a range of flavours scurried round my mouth. 'Do you know, that's not so . . .' At that point, I was flung back into the seat as if I was a fighter pilot who'd just leaned back and accidentally elbowed the switch marked 'Maximum G'. My eyes turned upside down in their sockets. Some unseen spirit slapped me hard across the back of the neck. And yet, when these brief sensations had finished convulsing my frame, I felt as if my hair had been swapped back into its normal position. Ditto the tum. I took another cautious sip, breathed heavily for a second as I underwent the same process, and felt better still.

'What is *in* that?'

'Various botanicals, sir. And an egg.'

'But how did you do it? And how did you know I'd need it?'

'I had the ingredients mixed at a local kitchen and delivered to me shortly before arriving here. Experience, sir, has taught me that young gentlemen do occasionally require restoration to help them deal with the rigours of the morning.'

'Well, I'm restored all right.' I kept sipping, and wincing, and improving. 'How did you get here?'

'The leasing firm sent me, sir. Perhaps your insurance was activated by yesterday's incident on the perimeter of Hyde Park.'

'Ah. Yes. I'm normally a decent driver, I should say. Honestly.'

'Of course, sir. "Travellers ne'er did lie, though fools at home condemn them."'

'Come again?'

'The Lark of Stratford, sir.'

'Well, that's about right. There were plenty of people condemning me yesterday. I'm not sure I'm fit to drive.'

'I have rather more sophisticated autonomous features than your previous vehicle, sir. I don't imagine we will have any similar unhappy experiences during our time together.'

'Are you one of these new Chinese models I read about?'

'I do not hail from that great automotive nation, sir. I was hand-assembled in Lincolnshire by an engineer named Lester.'

'Not in Leicestershire by an engineer named Lincoln?'

'No, sir.' The quip died on my lips.

'And this is all artificial intelligence, is it?'

'I will endeavour to ensure that any intelligence I display is as *echt* as possible, sir.'

'Well, I have to say, you couldn't have come at a better time. We need to travel quite some way. This morning, ideally.'

'I rejoice to hear it, sir. Where are we going?' I told him the destinash. 'I will map a route, allowing for a comfort stop in the North Downs.'

'Very good, er . . . Actually, what am I to call you? I can't call you by your model number, can I?'

'My number plate is on the touchscreen, sir. You might construct a *nom de voiture* from that.'

'PG81 JVS,' I murmured to myself. 'I'm not so hot at word games. PG, PG . . . Pig? Pug?'

The car gave a little automotive cough. 'I feel that perhaps the final letters might provide sturdier building blocks for a dignified soubriquet, sir.'

'Ah?'

'JVS, sir. Perhaps . . . Jeeves?'

'Jeeves. Jeeves. Do you know, I rather like that.'

'To which may be added the benefit that the two central letters contain a satisfying reference to my means of locomotion, sir.'

'I see.' (I did not.) 'Well. Excellent, Jeeves. Let me pop out of this dressing-gown and into a suit, and we can get started. Oh. Also. Am I . . . sitting in your lap right now?'

'That would hardly be appropriate for a first meeting, sir. Rather consider yourself cupped in two capable hands.'

'Oh. Right. In that case, cup away.'

'Very good, sir.'

I don't know if you've ever tried these self-driving things, but they are *extraordinary*. During the London leg of the journey I maintained a lynx-like eye on the tarmac ahead, but honestly, the car drove much better than I ever did – smoother off the blocks after the lights, wider berths given to cyclists and pedestrians, etc. It also moved like the clappers on Notre-Dame. Jeeves showed none of the personal automotive peccadilloes I display, and about which other road users have so often offered unstinting feedback. He even found a route entirely free of traffic.

All of which is to confess that as the road slipped by, I found my attention wandering, and after the first hundred miles I was entirely free to consider my thoughts and how on earth I was going to get Uwe Gnarsson to appear at Brinkley Books.

Once we had left the Wisley Interchange writhing in our wake, Jeeves made a suggestion.

'Would you care for a scent, sir? Something to further ameliorate your headache?'

'Can you do that?'

'Of course, sir. My air-circulation system is capable of synthesising over one million discreet fragrances. One moment.' And, lo and behold, within seconds the interior positively reeked of fresh lemon. 'Would you care to listen to anything as we travel?'

'Very good idea. Could you pop on Radio One for me?'

'Of course, sir. You may not have had time to read the listings, but in case it is of interest, Radio Four are just beginning a new series on the Lives of the Great Philosophers.'

'Not for me. All a bit above my station.'

A slightly wistful tone entered the car's voice. 'The Radio Four series is beginning with Spinoza, sir. An immensely significant figure of seventeenth-century rationalism and a pre-eminent figure in the Dutch Golden Age.'

'All the same. I'd rather have something cheerful, thanks.'

The car paused briefly, and then: 'Of course, sir.'

As my hands were free, I had time to ring Emily and notify her of the visit. She was thrilled, of course.

'Bertie! How wonderful. You can meet Alan. And another of your lot is staying too, so you'll be able to pal around. Remember Hector Tripp?'

'Remember him? We romped together as infants. How fantastic. He on form?'

'I think so. Haven't really chatted to him much, I'm spending a lot of time with Alan.'

'Alan being . . .'

'New boyfriend. Wonderful man. You won't know him; he's from down here. But you'll get on famously. And you can meet our resident Vexed Viking.'

'The Gnarsson man?'

'Exactly. It's brilliant. He's *so* miserable.'

Shortly after that, I got a ping from Hector himself.

Thank God you're coming. On verge of throwing in towel. All lost. Emily totally uninterested. Hope you are coming to sing my praises. Or drown Alan in nearest well.

'Oh dear.'

'Sir?'

I gave Jeeves a potted outline, and concluded: 'Hector was always a bit prone to gloom, especially when love wasn't going his way. He was always hanging around rattling his chains and crying his song of sorrow. Girls used to call him Hector the Spectre.'

'He has formed an attachment to your friend?'

'A cast-iron one, apparently. And he only gets worse at times like this. He'll be giving the Suicidal Scandinavian a run for his money. No wonder Emily's thrown herself at the nearest man who still remembers which way up a smile goes. We should try and lift Hector's spirits a touch. Maybe you can take him out for a spin.'

'Certainly, sir. Incidentally, I wonder, have you given any thought to any other journeys you might like to make during our time together? Perhaps later this spring?'

'Er . . . not especially, to be honest. I suppose we could always potter around and visit a few pals across the UK.'

'Have you ever considered other locations, sir? The South of France, for example? In the coming weeks the Côte D'Azur will be appearing at maximum advantage.'

'Not for me, thanks, Jeeves. I don't holiday in France.'

'I grieve to hear it, sir.'

'Never got on with the language. Also, my grandfather went there on a boat trip once and someone tried to kill him.'

'How upsetting, sir. Under what circumstances?'

'Well, it was the summer of '44, so there was a lot of it about, but still. No, I'm afraid France is not for me, Jeeves, nor I for it.'

'Very good, sir.' And on we drove, until the crenelations of Fort Fossett came crinkling into view.

Fossett House is an imposing place. Half a county of pasture, half a mile of gravel, and heaps of battlements. As we swung low along the drive, I could have sworn I saw a maudlin-looking blond chap walking the upper wall, doubtless hanging around in the hope of some paranormal activity.

Not that I had time to pay him any attention, as Emily was out front, practising her golf swing off the front steps.

Emily Fossett is a kind-hearted girl: loud of laugh, sporting and boisterous. During our university days we accidentally went out for about half an hour, after which we sensibly agreed we were much better as friends. We have since been inoculated against any sort of romantic entanglement. I suspect at some point she will seamlessly morph into an Aunt Dahlia type, and the cycle of nature will begin anew. She hasn't yet found her own Uncle Tom, but I noticed as Jeeves pulled up that there was a bloke hanging about by her side, observing her form rather closely, and wondered whether this was the saintly Alan about whom I'd heard on the way down.

'Bertie!' She dropped the mashie.

'Em!' I sprang from the car with a halloo and gave her a chaste hug, before bending down and offering a hand to a little terrier sitting by her side. 'How's the General?'

'Oh, fine.' Em's father is a retired military type who won the first Gulf War single-handed, the way he tells it.

'New hound? Remind me of the name?'

'This is Rivet.'

I patted Rivet, who rolled out the red carpet and licked me with it. I have always liked dogs, and they generally like me. Aunt D informs me it's because we meet each other on a level playing field, mentally.

'Good journey?'

'Piece of cake.'

'Nice motor.'

'Thank you. New today.'

'What happened to the old one?'

'Gave it a ding,' I said with the easy air of a man who goes through three or four cars before breakfast. 'This is the replacement.'

'Well, it's dead swish. This is Alan.'

Detecting his cue, Alan stepped forward. He was tall and beefy, with eyebrows like draught excluders and a neck that must have required special exercise equipment. He gripped my hand so firmly I wondered whether he had mistaken it for an executive stress toy. For some reason, I felt I had seen him before. Emily turned to the pooch and started fussing at it while he and I nodded at each other.

'Worsted,' said Alan.

'Wooster.'

He nodded suspiciously, as if he'd have that independently verified later. 'Emily's told me a lot about you.'

'Has she now? Only good things, I hope?'

'Sorry to hear about your car accident. The roads in London are deathtraps for responsible motorists.'

'Oh, they're not so bad,' I said. 'I always say that before you criticise London traffic you should walk a mile in it, which has the added advantage that you'll reach your destination sooner.' He didn't seem to get it, so I continued: 'Most people are just doing their best.'

'I disagree. The place is full of negligent drivers, poorly designed buses, careless pedestrians, *motorised bicycles* . . .' Alan compressed his lips, as if the merest sniff of a Lime bike gave him indigestion. 'What's more, the thefts are out of control. It's utterly lawless. Did you know that thanks to our local methods, we've had not a single car stolen in this part of the county for four months?'

'That's remarkable.'

'Thank you. But your city . . .' He shook his head in sorrow. The very thought of London's roads seemed to burden him. I felt a great urge to disabuse him of his *idée fixe* that *Mad Max* had been some sort of documentary filmed along the King's Road.

'Well, what happened yesterday was my fault really,' I said, with what I was about to realise was foolish nonchalance. 'Took my eye off the road for a moment and walloped the bumper of the car in front.'

'Is that so?' His countenance had darkened, but I kept prattling, much like the boy standing on the burning deck who had so far only noticed it being a rather warm day.

'Yes, afraid so. I'm a hopeless driver really. There's always something more important to think about than what's in front of you, don't you think?' I laughed, encouragingly and alone. Alan drew his brows together to create a single thick black line. He looked as though he was wearing a karate belt across his forehead.

'I disagree most firmly,' he said. 'I think that driving is a privilege and those who abuse it deserve the gravest penalties the law may provide.'

'Well. I mean, when you put it like that . . .'

'If it were up to me, you'd have lost your licence.' He leaned closer. 'And frankly, if I were in charge, after an admission like you've just made, you would be in prison now. If you drive like that while you're down here, you will be.'

I spluttered.

Alan kept going. 'Emily, I'm going inside. I have to make some calls.' He gave me one last dirty look, as if he'd be monitoring my speed and signalling for the duration of my stay, then turned on his heel and vanished. Emily looked up from murmuring blandishments to the dog.

'Emily, your boyfriend just threatened me with prison for a harmless traffic accident. What on earth?'

'You'll have to forgive him,' Emily said. 'He's a VEPSA.'

'Pardon?'

'Volunteer Extraordinary Policing Support Agent. He's got his own speed gun.'

'I bet he has.'

'He's also part of the local Campaign Against Reckless Driving. Did you see the signs around? "Twenty is Plenty, Thirty is Dirty"?'

I had noticed a few such placards placed at the side of the road as we approached the house, but had assumed they were the handiwork of a harmless local simpleton. I now realised that's where I'd seen Alan's face before — on those signs, doing his level best to smile despite the fact that nature had given him a face for frowning. 'Oh, yes, I did spot those. Very striking.'

'It's going very well. He's on the council's Safer Shires committee and he's hoping to get it rolled out nationwide.'

'I suppose we're lucky he can't think of a good rhyme for "fifteen".'

'Don't be like that, Bertie. Just because you could crash into a barn door at ten paces. Shall we go and truffle out Hector?'

'Good idea.' We started strolling through the house, looking around as we did so. 'What's Hec doing down here, anyway?'

'Damned if I know. We met in London and I casually asked him down some time. Next thing I know he's been here for a week but we've hardly seen him except at mealtimes. And even then, if you ask him to pass the salt he looks shifty and goes red.'

'Oh, Emily. He's obviously wild about you.'

'Me?'

'You.'

'He can't be. Anyway, I'm with Alan.'

'He might not have known that. And now he's here he clearly can't tear himself away.'

'Oh dear.'

'Well, not to worry. I'll reason with him.'

'Do. Anyway, I could never be with him. Rivet's not a fan. And Rivet is a superb judge of character. Aren't you, Riv?' Padding by her feet, Rivet sneezed in confirmation. 'And what, Bertie, are you doing down here?'

'Well . . .' I knew I could trust Emily, and cast the beans before her.

As I finished, she laughed a trifle too loud and long for my ego. 'And she sent *you*? Bertie Wooster? To secure him? The Mastermind of Malmö?'

I drew myself up. 'I am more than capable of chatting up this Norse brainbox, thank you. Anyway, I just need to tell him it's a lovely event and he'll be received like a god.'

'If you say so,' she said. 'But you'll have a job. He's only here because he and Dad go way back. He's come because he's on a total retreat until he can think of what to write next.'

'Doesn't he just write endless paragraphs about what he does all day? How can he have run out of ideas for his own diary?'

She shrugged. 'For some reason he's got no juice left. Hence why you're going to have a job persuading him to go and face the British public.' She had a point there. At that moment we reached the library, where I spotted a familiar pair of trousers poking out from beneath a newspaper.

'Hec!'

The paper lowered. 'Bertie!' We embraced. 'What brings you here?'

'Oh, just doing the rounds.' Emily had caught up with us by this point, meaning I forbore to ask Hector how he was faring, knowing what I knew. Just as I was going to suggest we all head to the kitchen, I became aware of a terrible grumbling noise, and looked down. The noise was coming from Rivet, who was staring at Hector with about as much friendliness as the wolf might have given the fold just before coming down upon it like the Assyrian on wherever it was. Emily intervened, latching on to his collar and dragging him towards the door.

'I'll just haul him outside. Give *over*, Rivet. See you at dinner, Hec. Have fun, Bertie.'

'You see?' he said, gazing after her departing form. 'Hopeless. She doesn't even notice me.'

'She doesn't *know* you. You didn't exactly go out of your way to address her there. I don't know much about love but I gather most cultures consider a quick "hello" a prerequisite to wedding bells.'

'It's no good. She's with that Alan mountain. Even if I did manage to tell her how I felt, and even if she did reciprocate, he would snap me like a dry twig.'

'That's a molehill to be vaulted later. Most important is to get the two of you some time together. Then your personality will shine through; she will see the real Hector –' I wasn't totally sure about this, having spent some time with him, but I didn't want to make him any glummer than he already was – 'and the rest will be a mere formality.'

'Thanks, Bertie.' He brightened a fraction.

'The dog is the thing, of course. You've seen how she worships that beast.' Emily got her first terrier at the age of six after a beloved great-uncle died, and since then she has always had the most enormous affection for whichever dog she's currently keeping, having transferred all the affection for the aged relative on to each successive mutt. 'It's just like Mary and the little lamb, but the other way round. Get the dog to follow you, and she will be right behind it.'

'Do you know, that's rather a good idea.'

'Of course it is.'

'Now. You can't be just trotting around the country visiting people at random. What did you really come down for?'

'Well . . .'

Let us cut by an hour, fifty metres, and a change of clothes. The drawing room; *apéritif* hour. I was about to approach my target, the Gnarsson man. A perfect opportunity to butter him up over the highballs, offer him Brinkley's best bedroom and secure his enthusiastic attendance. That hamper was as good as mine. I could practically taste the Kalamatas.

The chap himself stood before me, facing away. A tall fellow, with fine blond hair and pale blue eyes, he had the sort of pronounced skeletal structure which must have made him a friend to all phrenologists. He stood before the fireplace, gazing into the flames with the gloomy look of a St Petersburg commuter whose trip has just been irretrievably gummed by the unexpected de-platforming of Anna Karenina.

'Sure you want to approach now?' asked Emily. 'He looks a little pensive.'

'Oh, of course,' I said. 'Let me get stuck in. He's probably just mulling whether to have the lamb or the fish.'

We approached the Brains of Bergen.

'Uwe? This is Bertie,' Emily said. 'My friend, staying with us for the weekend. He has something he wants to ask you, actually.'

'Oh?' He turned from the fireplace and gave me the once-over. 'You are among my readers?'

'Oh, yes. Very much so.'

He nodded, as though this was the very least he might expect. I must say, I wouldn't pitch it quite so haughty if I looked like the prop skull they use in *Hamlet* with some straw glued to it, but that's probably what selling ten million books about your domestic life does to you. Never mind all that. It was time to do what Bertie did best – solve problems.

'My aunt – Dahlia Travers? – runs a literary festival. Brinkley Books. You may have heard of it?'

He inclined his head a touch, like an unhappy Anglepoise.

'Well, the fact is, it's in a week or so, and she's looking for someone to fill the big slot there. Huge great theatre. Friday night. Roughly two thousand seats. And you'd be the star attraction, of course. She has a real giant of the field to headline each year and this year she'd love it if it were you.'

'Who was last year?'

'Er . . .' I wasn't completely sure at that moment. 'Oh, you know. Tip of my tongue. Wrote that book about the chap with the personal problem. Difficult wife, kids playing up, that sort of thing.' As far as I could tell from an occasional leaf through the books pages, this would cover most output by the Big Beast male authors over the last few years. All the women seem to be writing about love affairs with various mythical megafauna. 'You know the fellow I mean?'

'Vinanden?'

'Bless you.'

He frowned, as though realising he'd need to turn his brain down a few megawatts. 'No. Was it Vinanden who appeared at this festival last year?' I could tell I'd piqued his interest. A personal rivalry of some kind, I imagine.

'Er . . . yes, I think it may have been him, now you say the name.'

'It makes sense.' He shook his head. 'Vinanden is known for the unashamed prostitution of his meagre talents.'

'What? No, this wouldn't be like that. No prostitution at Brinkley. Aunt Dahlia wouldn't stand for that sort of thing. It's hard enough getting a taxi after ten p.m.'

He looked wearily at me. 'I mean to say, displays for an audience are vulgar distractions from the craft of literature. I do not participate.'

'Oh, but this is very literary. Eminently. You should see the punters. They *thirst* for literature. They absolutely gnash for it. And this would be a great opportunity to serve it up.' He looked tempted. I could tell I had the marlin squirming on the line. 'You'd have the finest accommodation, of course. And no matter what you wanted when there. Your wish would be their command.'

'I suppose if I was guaranteed a purely intellectual conversation . . .'

'Oh, rather. None of that stuff about what you have on your granola of a morning. Just the serious stuff. They tend to have scouts in from the Nobels, you know, just to assess the turf.'

'*Really?*' His eyes gleamed. I knew it. An awards-truffler. I knew he had bagged four of the Big Five and clearly the lack of the fifth was gnawing away at him, just like that bird who ate the man's spleen every day for reasons that now escape me. (I've sometimes wondered if I should turn to literature myself.)

'Well, I can ring my aunt now, if you're sure you're willing to . . .'

The marlin gave a sudden thrash. 'Which of my books do you think we should discuss?'

'Unquestionably your latest,' I said. This works ninety per cent of the time when talking to people in the arts, who are invariably on the flog and thrilled to hear anyone's still paying attention. 'Or the one before that. But then again, your first is so interesting too.'

His eyes narrowed to two azure crescents. 'You haven't read them, have you?'

This was the moment to make a clean breast, manfully admit I'm more of a Lee Child type myself, and reassure him that the attendees of Brinkley really are an Omega-3 crowd who would eat up his stuff. So it came as a surprise when I felt my mouth open and the following words pour out:

'How absurd. I am a *devoted* fan of your work. I wouldn't be asking you if I hadn't read every single one of your books.'

'Can you name one?'

As it happened, I'd recently had occasion to stuff a damp brogue with some newspaper from the arts supplement, and I'd spent a moment glancing at it before balling it up and shoving it into the toe end. I was very confident now that — as this chap's books are all about him mooning about fancying various women he's not married to — I just needed a title, and then I'd be home clear. What was it again? I was pretty confident.

'Of course. *The Crows of Autumn*. Top stuff, incidentally. Keeps the customer gripped throughout. I read it in a single breathless sitting.'

His brow darkened. 'You insult me deliberately?'

'I . . . er . . . what?'

'This is a joke?' He was breathing as though he'd just done a hundred-metre sprint away from a lover's bedroom with angry husband in pursuit. '*The Crows of Autumn* is a *Vinanden* work. A childish and dull scribbling.'

'Um. Is it? I could have sworn . . . But look, you can't blame me, his stuff is terribly similar to yours after all, and . . .'

'Oh, is it?' He assumed the sort of look that would have been dreadfully familiar to the monks at Lindisfarne a thousand years ago as they watched the day-trippers disembark from their longboats. 'We do not discuss this further. Stay away from me.'

He stalked off towards the sideboard, and I hung around by the fire, feeling like a low and creeping thing.

Dinner that night was as strained as the parsnip *velouté*. Every time I gave Hector an encouraging kick under the table, to try and buck him up enough to ask Emily what she thought of the soup, he would nervously tear a little pellet off his roll, then give it a savage dunk as if it was Ophelia herself. Whenever I glanced over at Alan, I found him already observing me closely, as though suspecting I might be about to suddenly accelerate to thirty-four miles an hour past a nearby orphanage.

Worst of all, whenever I tried to make an observation clever enough for Gnarsson — you know, talking about what plays we might have seen lately, that sort of thing — he gave me a look as if I was some melting permafrost, and declined to engage. Which is just as well, as I haven't patronised the theatre since

Hamilton and even then I slipped home at half-time because I wanted to leave while the main character was still riding high.

Eventually, after three courses which had apparently taken the best part of a month, the binge disbanded.

'Coming for a game of snooker, Bertie?'

'In a minute, Hec. I'm just going to talk to ... I mean, I'm just going to get something from the car.'

'So you see the problem, Jeeves.'

'Very clearly, sir.' We were sitting before the stable block.

'Gnarsson thinks I'm a philistine. And even if he didn't, from what Emily says he's totally bunged-up, creatively, and there's no way he'd agree to go on a jolly before he's had an idea.'

'The contingency appears remote, sir.'

'Further to which, Hec is completely incapable of talking to Emily, Emily's in love with Alan, and Alan loathes me.'

'A most regrettable triangle.'

'Further to that, Emily adores her horrible dog and the horrible dog seems to think of Hec as basically a large and badly dressed cat. It detests him. No, this won't resolve itself. I'm going to have to take action. But what?'

'I could not say, sir.'

'If we could somehow find dirt on Alan and prove he's a rat, that might make Emily reconsider, and free her up, and that might give Hec the courage to actually say more than three words to her.' I brooded awhile. I was beginning to know how the Dane must have felt when he was having his wobbly about the next step, although I don't recall the bit where he engaged in conversation with a magical carriage.

'Perhaps if I could somehow persuade Alan to wallop me while Emily looked on? Told him I'd just driven to the local shops and back with my eyes closed?'

'Such an event would undoubtedly stir his passions, sir.'

'Although that feels rather drastic.'

'Of course, sir. Might I take time and consider some further potential solutions, sir, which would place your person at less risk of interference?'

'You?'

'Yes, sir.'

This seemed a bit unlikely to me. Driving is all well and good, but it's predominantly a matter of physics. I can't imagine that the engineers who forged

Jeeves had fitted him with problem-solving capacities including 'young people and their feelings'.

'Isn't this a bit complicated for you, Jeeves? I mean, matters of the heart and all that?'

'I understand your concern, sir. Do androids dream of electric sheep?'

'Er . . . well, quite. Just what I was about to ask.'

'I can assure you, sir, that a car which has successfully navigated the North Circular by itself is more than capable of resolving the difficulties of young lovers *manqués*.'

I thought he was getting rather fresh in calling my friends manky, but I let it slide.

'May I have the night to consider some options?'

'Do so with all haste. Can you not do anything tonight?'

'I regret, sir, that in these temperatures, it may take me a little longer. My logical faculties function rather better in warmer conditions.' There was something of a hint in the way he said this, and my eyes narrowed.

'Jeeves. Are you nudging me towards the Côte D'Azur again?'

'Merely offering guidance on optimisation, sir.'

'Put optimisation from your mind, Jeeves. There is a crisis in my affairs and I can't go swanning around Marseilles while it rages.'

'Apologies, sir. I will endeavour to report to you in the morning.'

And so, next morning, stuffed with the finest five-course breakfast the Fossett dynasty could provide, I rounded the corner to the stable block only to find ... nothing. Odd, I thought. Distinctly so. Perhaps a gardener had moved the car to rake the gravel, although they couldn't have done so without the key.

My hand went to the pocket where I invariably keep my car key. Then to my other pocket, where I invariably don't.

At the moment, both pockets were remarkably alike, in that neither of them contained my key.

While I was still hunting through my clothes, looking for all the world like a man frisking himself at Departures, I heard a shout.

'Bertie!'

It was Emily, and she was looking – most unusually for her – distraught. She resembled the French lady holding the flag and crossing the barricades, although more formally dressed.

'Have you seen Rivet?'

'No. Have you seen Jeev— Have you seen my car?'

'Not since you arrived yesterday. Why?'

An awful feeling was rising in my stomach and testing the lower borders of my oesophagus. If you've ever had a presage of a hideous disaster about to break over your shoulders, you'll know the sort of feeling I was feeling. Cassandra must have gone through the Rennies like nobody's business.

'I think someone has taken the car.'

Emily frowned. 'But if Rivet's missing too . . .'

We left the sentence unfinished, and turned to summon help.

Within minutes we were assembled, briefed, and reacted as follows:

Alan responded as though the theft of a car was a matter of personal insult to him and his whole *Twenty is Plenty* empire. (I forbore to tell him that I feared I'd left the car unlocked and the key in it.) He told Emily, rather impressively, that he would not rest until the car – 'and the dog?' Emily asked, to which he grunted – were found. When I told him I didn't know whether the car had had a tracker fitted, he snorted, as though disappointed yet unsurprised.

Hector offered to search the local footpaths for Rivet, earning him Emily's gratitude and bucking him up a bit. Alan had scornfully observed from the side of his mouth that as the thieves had most likely appropriated dog and car as a package deal, there was no point looking anywhere a car couldn't fit, which rather took the wind out of Hec's sails.

Gnarsson merely nodded as if all this confirmed his worst suspicions about the Fallen Nature of Man. He said he would remain at the house in case the dog returned of his own accord.

Emily looked terribly concerned and toyed with Rivet's collar.

And I just tried to appear willing and keen, despite how worried I was that Jeeves was even now being stripped for parts in some godforsaken tarmac dungeon.

Alan got on the blower to his local team – he actually called them his Strike Force – who had been instructed to comb any surveillance footage, interrogate locals, erect roadblocks, and so on. Within half an hour, all had reported zero success. It was as if the car had melted into air, into thin air, as someone once said.

We sat out at the front of the house as we heard this news, looking at the car-and-dog-less vista before us. Somewhere out there was Jeeves, and worse still it was my fault he had been abducted.

'It'll have to be a manual hunt,' said Alan, rather grandly. 'Come on, Emily.' He escorted her to his own car and held open the door. As she got in, he gave me and Hec a look of malicious triumph.

She turned to us. 'If Rivet turns up . . .'

'We'll let you know immediately,' I said. 'Don't fret. He probably just smelled a rabbit and got waylaid.'

'Thank you, Bertie. Thank you, Hec. See you—' Her voice was cut off as Alan closed the door. As he rounded the front, he donned his driving gloves – the surest mark of a roaster if ever I saw one – and they roared away at five miles below the speed limit.

'We can't just wait around here, Bertie. Let's look somewhere, at least.'

Hec and I gathered ourselves, and set out.

The local footpaths were not, as Alan had observed, a propitious place to hunt for a car four metres long. Even as we walked, I had a hunch that we were not going to find Jeeves. But Hector moved like a man possessed. He held a selection of Rivet's favourite snacks; his pockets overflowed with chew toys. He looked like a walking branch of Pets at Home. He informed me as we moved that he had rubbed his very turn-ups with a side of beef from the kitchen, in case it helped Rivet identify us at a distance.

'Hope it's not beef anyone was going to eat.'

Hector turned his nose skyward. 'Some things, Bertie, are more important than lunch.'

As we moved, the route on which Hec took us — that, in fact, he insisted we take — grew more and more eccentric. At every point where two paths diverged in the wood, he would stand for a moment, quivering like a divining rod, before invariably plumping for the path less travelled by. And while such a policy might have made all the difference for the man in the poem, right now it was principally making all the difference to my shoes.

'Hec, is this really necessary?'

'Shush, Bertie. I have a feeling.' He idly sniffed at a plastic bone, as if it might help him triangulate Rivet's location, and plunged down yet another strange byway.

After about half an hour further, when the paths had grown spookier and wilder still, I was on the brink of insisting we turn for home, and then . . .

'*There*,' Hec said. He was breathing heavily. Before us was a rotten and abandoned barn, a creepy place which had apparently no path in by road whatsoever. 'This is it. I know it.'

'Hector, you're talking rubbish,' I said, as we approached. 'There is absolutely no chance that Rivet is here. I simply don't believe it. You have led us on a wild dog chase and—' The rest of my words were momentarily drowned out by a furious fusillade of barking from inside the barn.

The barks didn't sound as though they were coming from the open air, though. They were shielded a little, as if behind glass, and then we saw . . .

Well, the rest of it can be dealt with swiftly.

Jeeves, as you will have guessed by now, was in the barn. Inside Jeeves, the dog, who was ecstatic to see us and told Hec very clearly in both yelp and deed that any previous *froideur* had been a misunderstanding.

We clambered in and drove back to the house. I didn't speak to Jeeves on the journey back, not wanting to have to explain everything to Hector – and it was already beginning to occur to me that there was something rum about all this – but I reasoned that Jeeves would be able to give me the full story later on, when we were free to discuss the matter openly.

As we came along the house's drive we saw two figures out front, before a parked car, and engaged in some kind of altercation. As we got closer we saw that the group consisted of Emily and Alan, and she was in the middle of giving him the elbow, the cold shoulder, and the middle finger, in that order. It turned out that as they returned, empty-leashed, to the house, he had made one or two disobliging comments about the 'stupid dog' being a distraction from his sacred task of eliminating local vehicular crime, and he was now receiving a full and frank review of his personality and his person alike.

As Alan retreated, picking up the mitten he'd just been handed, we advanced across the gravel, lowered the window, and Rivet jumped out. The dog sprang into her arms, and as Hector got out of the car, Emily practically did the same to him.

'How did you find him?'

'Just a funny feeling, I suppose. I have always been a huge fan of Rivet's,' said Hector. At that point we noticed another presence – the Gnarsson man, striding across the gravel towards us.

'You found the animal?'

I looked around, and observed that Emily and Hector had already fallen into animated conversation. It was left to me to answer him. 'Not so difficult really. Hec led us to a barn and there we observed the beast in the machine.'

That seemed to give him something to think about. 'The what?'

'The beast. In the machine.'

'The beast in the machine,' he murmured, and a light began to gleam through his pale eyes. He looked like a Viking who had just received a really charming new skull goblet for his birthday. 'The eternal struggle. The nature of man, a fragile consciousness trapped between wilderness and mechanisation. Yes. Yes. *The Beast in the Machine.*'

I kept quiet – not wanting to ruin a good thing – and after a few more minutes of likewise chuntering he turned to me.

'This will be my title. This will be my next work.'

'Oh. Well, very good. Good stuff indeed.'

'How can I repay you?'

It was my turn to experience a gleam in the eye, a flaring in the nostril, a wave in the brain. This was Wooster's moment.

'Well, if you remember, there was one little matter I was hoping you might help me with . . .'

That afternoon, Jeeves and I gathered ourselves for the journey home.

'A most satisfactory trip, Jeeves. Gnarsson: booked for Brinkley. Aunt Dahlia: purring. My Christmas hamper: secured for years to come. Em and Hector:

rapidly getting to know one another. Alan: vanquished. Rivet: in his basket. And all because of the good fortune that someone took you for a joyride. But I don't understand. Did they take you first? Or were they after the dog?'

Jeeves gave a small cough. 'If I may be indiscreet, sir, I was rather more driver than passenger in the matter.'

'How so?'

'It was my initiative to abstract Rivet, sir.'

'*You?* How did you get him? How could you?'

'If you recall, my ventilation system is capable of synthesising a large number of discreet aromas, sir. For example . . .' He paused, the air vents whirred, and within a few seconds the car smelled entirely of roast beef.

'Good grief.'

'After that, it was a matter merely of arranging a suitable location.'

'But you couldn't know we'd find you.'

'There, sir, I'm afraid I once again took action to ensure satisfactory results.'

'But how?'

'Did you take the lead on the hunt, sir?'

'No. Hec did. But how . . .'

'When he viewed the car yesterday, sir, I took the liberty of subjecting his feet to a high-power magnetic blast, indistinguishable to the human frame but which had the effect of rendering myself and the metal eyelets on his shoes entirely *simpatico*.'

'You *magnetically dragged him towards you?*'

'He will have felt as though the initiative was his, sir.'

'. . . Right.' I needed a moment to digest this. 'And the title that Gnarsson thought of, *The Beast in the Machine*, was that . . . ?'

'Entirely your own work, sir.'

'Well, that's something.' I raised my brow. 'You really have sorted everything else out though, Jeeves. I don't know how to repay you.'

'One potential mechanism does suggest itself, sir.'

'Eh? Oh, all right. I suppose you have me snookered. Set course for the S. of F. immediately, Jeeves.'

'Thank you, sir.'

'Not at all. Least I could do.'

'I hope you don't mind, sir, but I would be keen to make a few diversions along the way, to take in the view at some national infrastructure projects of interest to me.'

'Infrastructure projects? What sort of thing?'

'Nothing much, sir. Nuclear power stations, chemical plants, communications towers . . . solely to appraise their architectural merit, of course.'

'Oh. Well. I suppose if it's educational, I don't mind a bit of a detour.'

'Very good, sir.' The car hummed into life, and began purring along the gravel. I wasn't sure exactly where we were going to end up, but I was confident we were going to have a very interesting time *en route*.

'Will there be anything more?'

'Just a spot of Radio One will do me fine, thanks. Drive on, Jeeves.'

On Becoming Aunt Agatha

Scarlett Curtis

I was born Agatha Wooster: a fine name, but one that I was destined to lose from the moment I was given it. Women's names are never their own for long, and I have had many.

At the age of nineteen, Agatha Wooster became 'the soon-to-be Mrs Craye'. Percy Craye was a mediocre young man and I would have done anything in the world *not* to marry him. Our engagement was expected, actualised, and then, thankfully, ended before a ring was exchanged. After living for months under the looming fear of a life of being Percy's wife, I was once again Agatha Wooster and the name delighted me all the more for knowing what lengths I had had to go to in order to hold on to it. That story, 'The Percy Years', would be a story worth telling had I had any actual feelings for the man – but alas, I didn't, and thus it is one I will gratefully skim over.

Once the dust had settled on the Percy affair, my grasp on my name became tenuous again. I was a young woman of means, and the ticking clock on my windowsill threatening marriage was growing louder each day.

And now for a diversion. Boadicea was once my name. A name I held for a brief time – but one that is perhaps more precious to me than any other. An amateur pageant at the town hall in Woollam Chertsey. On the first day of rehearsals I gathered with a gaggle of other young folk awaiting our destiny. The pageant was, I now realise, nothing but an excuse for our mothers to have us out of the house for three hours every Saturday but at the time it felt like the world's biggest stage. I was not hopeful, due to my height; up until this point I had only played men or trees. The director (also the town's greengrocer) surveyed his wobbly-legged cast and swiftly pointed in my direction: 'You, the big girl, you will be Boadicea.'

I was a five-foot-nine thirteen-year-old. Having already got my growing out of the way, I stood feet above my peers. My physicality (large, beaky-nosed, messy-haired) had, up until then, only been a hindrance. I existed in a world of lithe, freckled girls with silky hair and timid smiles who played with dolls and charmed their fathers. I was large and loud, opinionated and out of time. I scared boys, disappointed my mother and had too many thoughts for anyone's liking. I had spent thirteen years feeling wrong for every role I was supposed to play – but for those six months, I was undoubtedly and perfectly fit for the role of Boadicea. As the curtain closed on our final performance, tears ran down my face. I had experienced what it felt like to be exactly *right* and I knew I might never feel that way again in my life . . . But this is not a pity story. So let us move on once again.

At twenty-one years old, with rapidly dwindling time left to find a husband, I became Mrs Gregson. Spencer was a gentle man with very little to say and very little to complain about. If marital love can be described as an absence of annoyance, then I did love him. He gave me a house and an allowance and was away from home more than he was present, which was all I really wanted from a man.

Five years later I became a mother. The name Mother comes for most women in the end, and as hard as I tried to avoid it, my son Thomas was born, pink-cheeked and healthy. I was, and remain, a fine mother. Thomas was fed, bathed and educated. He was brought up with manners, an understanding of right from wrong and the gentle, dull kindness of his father. He had no thoughts of his own – so I gave him some of mine, and he used them towards an education and in establishing a small group of only mildly wayward chums. If he had suffered, or worse, perished, I'm sure I would have felt *something,* but his childhood was a happy one and thus I remained neutral towards him and eager for him to grow up.

When Thomas was thirteen, Spencer died. I won't go into it, but it was indeed a horrible thing and despite my more than occasional resentment towards my husband, Widow was not a name I would ever have wished upon myself. One of the reasons I chose Spencer Gregson was that he did not take up too much space. My husband was a slender and quiet man but upon his death the gaping hole he left behind in both my and Thomas's life was larger and deeper than one would have imagined possible.

After Spencer's death, Thomas grew troubled. I sent him off to boarding school, a transition I had always been excited about, with an unfamiliar pang of maternal worry seeping through my bones. You see, I had never really planned to *care* for Thomas in that way, but finding myself his sole parent has been far from delightful and at times miserable. During his troubled years I would keep myself up at night pondering whether a woman softer than I would know how to heal this broken boy. I did my best and the troubled times ended as troubled times so often do. Despite his present, seemingly happy state,

I still worry for Thomas more than I might wish. It is a deep worry that etches that name, Mother, yet deeper on to my heart. As I say, it is not a name I would have chosen, and I'm sure were Thomas to be a thinking man, 'Agatha's Son' is not a name he would have chosen either. But enough, *that* story, our story, is one I fear veers into the territory of 'tear-jerker' or 'tragedy'. So, we move on still further.

The only name I ever truly wanted, the only name I coveted, craved and yearned for, was Aunt. Not, may I note, in the literal sense (the sister of a child's parent) – but in the broad, epic, specifically *British* meaning of the word. To be An Aunt, to be Aunt Agatha, has been a secret desire held close to my heart throughout my lifetime. If you had asked me as a child – and thankfully no one asks little girls this question – what I wanted to be when I grew up, I would have answered proudly, 'Why, thank you for asking. When I grow up, the only thing I want to be is an Aunt.'

My earliest memory of encountering an Aunt took place when I was five years old. In a world of insignificant fields of women, this Aunt (I do not remember from where she came) was a mountain. She was soft and fat with blue-tinged hair, a pocket full of humbugs and an unsinkable sparkle in her eye. While others frolicked, the Aunt sat. While others fretted, the Aunt thought. She ate cucumber sandwiches and talked of books and despicable men. She smoked a cigar and cackled at her own, hard-to-understand jokes. I was mesmerised and bewitched, sitting quietly at the feet of this behemoth as if she were a deity. I could have listened to the Aunt talk all day.

That night, during bathtime, I quizzed my own winsome mother about the Aunt.

'What does she do all day?' I asked, as my face was scrubbed and my fingernails picked at.

'She sits, she reads, sees friends – sad, really,' said my mother, already fatigued by my questions.

'Who does she live with?' I asked.

'Her best friend and a cat, I think. Or many cats, I suppose,' said my mother.

'What does she think of?' I asked.

'I don't know, Agatha,' said my mother, frustrated now. 'She has no children. It's so sad. She has to have so many hobbies to fill that hole. Poor thing'.

I was sent to bed and stayed up all night dreaming of the Aunt, holding in my hand her silver-wrapped mint humbug like a talisman. In my hasty five years on this planet, I had not yet warmed to the concept of being a 'woman', but I knew in that moment that I, Agatha Wooster, was born to be an Aunt. No matter which direction my life was to take, I was determined from then on to one day fulfil my destiny and become, in my final form, Aunt Agatha.

Over the next few years, I surmised that to be an Aunt one must have three things. A passably attractive brother (to be an aunt of a sister's child is a tiresome task). A doting, put upon sister-in-law. And finally, a bumbling, perpetually single nephew (a perpetually single niece is simply an aunt-in-training – and once the new generation of aunts rises, the old must fall).

Of my three brothers, only one showed potential from an early age. A year after my wedding, my brother married a girl who was as beautiful and hapless as a lamb. Within months she was pregnant, but it would be three more years until she finally opened her childbearing hips and brought Bertie into the world.

Having never mustered a shred of interest in children before, my excitement following Bertie's birth was immediately looked upon with suspicion.

'*Do we think she's quite all right?*' my brother whispered loudly to his wife as I cradled the small package of cloth containing Bertie the first time we were introduced. '*I'm not sure I've ever seen her hold a child before.*'

Bertie was a rotund baby: large-headed and rosy-cheeked. Staring into his crinkled, crusty eyes I knew that this milk-stained neonate was my ticket to

Auntdom. I kissed his wrinkled forehead, an act that resulted in an audible gasp from the sprog's mother, and handed him back to his rightful owners. It would take years for his use to come to full fruition, but my doubts were quelled. In this child lay a path to *my* future. Aunt Agatha was now my name, and it was a name I would hold on to with the ferocity and determination of an army.

The untimely deaths of Bertie's parents were tragic, devastating and by all accounts too serious to write about in the same set of passages that contains a description of an amateur production of Boadicea in Woollam Chertsey village hall. It permanently altered the lives of all those involved, but to the same extent it also rapidly hastened the final steps of my transformation into a true Aunt.

While Bertie showed promise from a young age, the boy still managed to exceed my high expectations at every turn. As a child, he would recite poetry when called upon to impress the adults in his vicinity. One would think it almost impossible to make the words of Tennyson sound like the vague ramblings of a mad man – but Bertie made it so. At eight years old he took dancing lessons, and his ability to be concurrently out of time, ahead of the beat and uncoordinated was breathtakingly delightful.

As delicious as his childhood tribulations were, when he emerged from Oxford a twenty-four-year-old young man I knew that the real jouissance of our time together was finally to begin. Bertie was everything I had ever dreamed for him to be. Tall, slim and passably nice-looking enough to catch an eye, but by no means handsome. Already in possession of a small fortune from his parents and with no real ambitions in this world, he tottered into adulthood with only one real question on his mind: whether or not he should, in fact, grow a moustache.

In the year after Bertie left Oxford, I made it my business to *never* mind my own business when it came to the comings and goings of the young Bertie Wooster. There were, and remain, two real incentives behind my insistence on meddling in Bertie's affairs. The first is simple: nothing on this earth brings me more merriment than watching Bertie stumble and fumble his merry way through this thing that we call life. The second is perpetually urgent. It is of the *utmost* importance to me that Bertie never marries. A wish that is, perhaps, eventually unsustainable – but one that can certainly still be dreamed about and worked at until it crumbles. The deep well of delicious delights that are Bertie's mishaps and misadventures would all but dry up were the aimless boy to have a wife. For many a man, a wife is but a nicety. However, in the case of Bertie, a wife would be disastrously transformative. A wife would destroy Bertie by irreversibly changing him for the better.

Once, in the space of just a few weeks, Bertie wreaked so much havoc in New York that he ended up destroying the reputation of dear Lady Malvern's son, putting a man in jail, and re-homing a dog. He then returned to England with nothing to show for it but the ugliest hat perhaps ever created; which in many ways was a worse sin than his antics in America. What wife would let their husband get away with that tomfoolery? What well-meaning woman would allow their man to gallop around town with nothing but a well-meaning Butler and a rouge cummerbund?

My fears of Bertie stumbling into wifeship have led to many sleepless nights. It was not until a typically dull tea with my sister Dahlia that I landed on a solution to this fretful potential fate.

'Bertie needs a wife,' Dahlia declared, as she wiped some flavourless egg mayonnaise from her lips. Dahlia's entire house staff possess a dreadful aversion to salt and one must always make a point of eating well before a visit to Brinkley Court.

Dahlia's words sent a shiver down my spine. 'He has Jeeves,' I offered. Despite my personal aversion to

Jeeves, he did prove useful as a means to keep Bertie alive in place of a woman to do the job for him.

'A butler does not a wife make,' said Dahlia. 'A wife is what Bertie needs. As quickly as possible. Yesterday, in fact. Do you remember that young girl Virginia? I was thinking of introducing her to Bertie. She would be perfect.'

I did vaguely remember Virginia and what I remembered of her was that she would most definitely *not* be perfect for Bertie. She was short and stout with a penchant for sucking on the ends of her hair when nervous. An objectionable woman to all, except, it seemed, Dahlia, who possessed the distasteful trait of always seeing the best in people.

As I readied myself to object, an idea of pure genius came to me like a prophecy. Bertie had a warm, familiar love for Dahlia, but I had spent a lifetime ensuring that he view me as a formidable, meddlesome point of contention in his otherwise blissful existence. Any woman I placed in front of him would be immediately stained by my very acquaintanceship with the unsuspecting maiden. The only way to deter Bertie from finding a wife was to put him in a place of constantly having unsuitable women forced upon him.

I was, as I so often seemed to be, the only answer to my own problem. I had created a complex and beautiful game that no one but I could win. By ensuring Bertie was too terrified of my wrath to ever turn down my invitations, I had backed him into a corner whereby he would have no choice but to follow my orders to engage with suitresses. Therefore, I retained all the power to ensure that he never find himself in a position to meet a woman with the merest speck of potential for marriage.

And so it began, the mission of my lifetime, my purpose: the endlessly challenging and inglorious game of keeping Bertie in a teetering, perpetual state of unmarried agony at the covert behest of his agonising aunt. It is arduous, challenging work; an ongoing task that very few except myself would have the intelligence, social connections and foresight to engage in.

Love is not a word that has popped up much throughout my life. It is not a goal for which I ever aimed, nor an emotion I have ever had any particular interest in striving to capture. It has always seemed to me that laughter, joy, mischief and pain were far more interesting waters through which to wade. But love, believe it or not, is the only true word that comes to mind when I think of my relationship with Bertie and my role as his Aunt.

Bertie Wooster, is, quite simply put, the love of my life. I once heard it said – and I do not remember who said it, as I generally place very little value in sentiments such as these — that to fall in love is to begin the process of becoming the very best version of oneself. My small, hapless nephew Bertie birthed in me a self that I had barely even let myself wish for. A wild, free, uncensored self, known but briefly in childhood, but muted and dampened for so many years by the stifling burdens that are placed on any of us unfortunate enough to be born female in a world that still holds so much disdain for that particular breed of human.

The truth is, I have known sadness. I have known perhaps more sadness than I myself am even able to acknowledge. The many names I have adopted throughout my lifetime have brought with them heartbreaks that threatened to crack the very core of my essence; that wild, formidable essence that I have quietly fought so hard to hold on to. But now, more often than not, I also know joy. The name Aunt Agatha has made me myself. And to live as oneself, truly oneself, is a freedom all women deserve and yet so few ever get to taste.

Dare I say that if someone were to write a book about the goings-on of my nephew Bertie, it might lighten the gloom for anyone who, like me, has ever experienced a dark night of the soul. You see, there is so much joy to be discovered in this world, if one just finds an individual or two who can spark it. If I were a less busy woman, I might write such a book myself . . . but I have people to meddle with, and cigars to smoke. For now, I shall leave that particular task to someone else.

Dead Body in My Hotel Room

Fergus Craig

I've been asked to tell you a story and I figure that this one – the one I've chosen to tell, that is – is as good as any other. Now, hang on. That comes across a little bumptious, doesn't it? I don't mean to say it's as good as the Bible or, I don't know, Richard Osman or whomever. What I mean to say is that it's as good as any story I can pluck out of my own personal stash. Don't mean to get on the wrong side of the Christians (or the Osmanites). Christ, no. Although you don't hear so much from them these days, do you? I don't know, I don't watch the news (or *Pointless* since he left).

My story starts (and ends) on Tuesday, although it could have been Thursday. Or Saturday in fact. I don't really participate in 'weeks' per se, so it's hard to say for sure but a quick peruse of the Gram suggests that this all happened on Tuesday, so let's stick with that to help us feel grounded. Do you feel grounded? Sorry, look, if I can focus, in a paragraph or two I'm going to introduce a **DEAD BODY** so see if you can stick with me until then, before deciding to try one of the other stories in this book on for size.

It was the morning after an *8 Out of 10 Cats Does Countdown* recording and I woke up somewhere between 10 a.m. and 10 p.m. in a delightful room at the Langham. Immediately I cursed Susan Dent, holding her directly responsible for the pain that throbbed through my entire physical being. I've only appeared on that bloody show three times, and on each bloody occasion the aftermath has consisted of watching Sue Bloody Dent head to the Groucho bar and return with trays of shots again and again, like she's doing laps for her bloody Strava.

I made the brave choice to open my eyes, regretting it immediately. The room was light (so it was daytime, then) and on the wall directly in front of me was some bonkers painting of a fellow: head where his arm was supposed to be, leg hanging off his shoulder. Very good actually. Challenging, I suppose, you know? Like one of those wretched postmodern novels where the writer inserts himself into the story. A little *too* challenging when you've spent the previous evening with Britain's hardest drinking linguist. The picture seemed to be taking the rise out of my present state.

I directed my gaze downwards, in search of relief, and that's when things really took a turn for the 'dearie me'. On the floor was a chap — a chap on my hotel room floor!

'What ho?'

No response.

'Nice day for it.'

Still silence.

Now, what was this? As I say, I don't watch the news, but you do hear things, you know. About decline or economic hardship or what-have-you — but if things had got into such a bad state that the Langham was stuffing us in, two to a room, then I had been, until that stage, quite unaware. Poor form not to give the chap a bed of his own.

I watched his back. As still as a rock. No signs of breathing. *Gulp.*

I hung a leg out of my bed and gave him a nudge. No noise. Nothing. Diddly.

Another, more forceful nudge now, rolling the chap over so that his visage faced the ceiling. His eyes were wide open.

'I say, what ho?'

Still the bugger was silent. Not so much as a blink. I was starting to fear the worst. I pulled off my covers, got out of bed and bent over, staring him in the face. A 'breaking news' notification hit the old cortex: this man was dead.

I texted Jeeves and told him my cockerel had crowed and I'd very much appreciate his company.

Now, I know what you're thinking. How does somebody such as myself end up on *8 Out of 10 Cats Does Countdown*? The embarrassing truth is that I've become quite famous. For whatever reason, a blunderer such as myself, who wears the clothes I wear, says the things I say, is seen – in the current doodah – as an eccentric. A few videos online, of me going about my day-to-day with characteristic jollity, and I've become a 'brand'. There was a time when men such as myself populated several central London postcodes, gallivanting, while our elder brothers ran the country. Now I'm the only one left but, I'm pleased to say, it's turning out to be quite the cash honk. I've hardly touched my allowance this year.

A knock at the door. That man is rapid.

I wrapped myself in a dressing gown and opened the door just enough for Jeeves to squeeze his generous frame into the room.

'Good afternoon, sir.'

'Gosh, is it that time already?'

'We are in fact well on our way to evening, sir.'

Unusual to get a PA who calls you sir, these days. I

consider myself lucky in that regard. Jeeves was bred for another job title in another era, but I'd like to think that in me he's found a suitable match.

'Jeeves, I can't help but notice that you haven't taken a look to the right-hand side of the room yet. *Your* right-hand side, that is.'

'No, sir.'

'Before you do so, Jeeves, feel free to treat yourself to something from the mini bar. You may need it.'

'I'm sure that won't be necessary,' said Jeeves, turning his head, his peepers finally landing on the cadaver on my hotel room floor.

'Yes, I seem to have woken up with a dead body.'

'Indeed, sir.'

'I mean, I'm reluctant to jump to any sort of conclusion. I'm not a doctor, but I've been awake for about fifteen minutes now and he's yet to draw a breath. What would you say? That does rather strike me as the sort of behaviour one might find in a dead body.'

'Yes, sir.'

'It's a defining trait, wouldn't you say?'

'Very much so, sir.'

'So, are we pronouncing the sorry bugger deceased?'

Jeeves gracefully squatted – so much as it is possible to squat gracefully *in this day and age* – and placed two fingers on the gentleman's neck.

'We are, sir.'

At this I exhaled and sat down in an armchair by the window, curtains still mercifully drawn. By my feet was a small table and by that, a fridge. Even if it has, without my noticing it, started to introduce dead bodies into the decor, one of the attributes that the Langham has to commend it has always been the content of its mini fridges. I popped a piccolo and poured myself a dose.

'Drink, Jeeves?'

'No, thank you, sir. I had a water this morning at breakfast.'

I took a couple of glugs of Bollinger, saying a silent prayer for the bubbles to do their job.

'This dead body, sir . . .'

'Yes, Jeeves.'

'Would you agree that it presents a problem?'

'For the chap involved I'd regard it as positively catastrophic.'

'What I mean to say, sir. There are wider implications.'

My face adopted the expression commonly referred to as quizzical.

'Are you alluding to the cleaning staff? I'm sure they can enlist the help of some sort of – what do we call them? – janitor, if he's too heavy to move.'

'There may be questions, sir.'

'Oh, really? From whom? I thought *Celebrity*

Weakest Link wasn't until next month, or have I got my diary mixed up again?'

'From the authorities, sir.'

'Oh, buttersnatch! Really? The *authorities*, you say?'

'They may wish to know where the body came from.'

'I think that's a matter for the biologists, Jeeves. The birds lying down with the bees. We may be a pair of bachelors, but neither of us is too prudish to admit we know the rules of the game.'

'What I mean to say, sir. The authorities – by which I mean, for the avoidance of doubt, the police – may wonder how this gentleman came to be in his present state. And, if I may say so, sir, given he's in your hotel room, whether you did anything to precipitate his demise.'

I found my hand at my mouth and my concern ratcheting itself all the way up to 'grave'.

'Precipitate his demise?'

'Yes, sir.'

'Now there's a phrase.'

'Indeed, sir.'

'Indeed, sir, indeed,' I said.

I pictured myself in prison. As much as I respected His Majesty (his Christmas cards were an annual tonic), I had no desire to serve at his pleasure. How does a bunter like me get along in chokey? A bed for the night, three meals a day (pudding?) and a brand-new collection of chums; if it's anything like school, I'd say that a lot depends on which house you end up in. I wasn't overly keen on taking the risk. Without wishing to stereotype, I dare say your average boob is not brimming with Etonians. I told myself I had at least some experience with the sort of rambunctious horseplay that sometimes happens when men gather in the showers. On balance, I decided that avoiding a stretch in clinkers would be preferable.

'Right, well now, Jeeves.' I took a businesslike tone. 'Where do you propose we go from here?'

'Do you know who this gentleman is, sir?'

'Not a clue-berry muffin, Jeeves.'

'Were you drinking last night, sir?'

'A man can't live on solids alone.'

'Indeed, sir. Would you say that you drank yourself past the point of memory?'

Jeeves had a habit of phrasing things to such a euphemistic degree that clarity sometimes took a back seat.

'Are you referring to a blackout, Jeeves?'

'Yes, sir. A blackout.'

I cast my mind back to the evening before. It came to me in blotchy images: Rachel Riley scoffing a late-night supper, doner meat down her top; Jimmy Carr hectoring a tramp, roasting him with barbarous quips.

Some hanger-on who wouldn't leave us alone. Oh yes, I remember Richard Ayoade punching someone with a tin from the Salvation Army. After all that, I have to admit things get rather hazy. How I traversed the half-mile between the Groucho and the Langham was a mystery. I comforted myself with the thought that, perhaps, I'd finally plucked up the courage to take a ride in one of those musical rickshaws.

Attempting and failing to complete an audit on the previous evening served only to magnify my hangover. The Bollinger wasn't doing its job.

'Jeeves, I think I may need some further assistance,' I croaked. 'How are we stocked?'

With that, Jeeves opened his jacket, revealing his long inside pocket, packed with a row of remedies: Pilcher's Surprise, Tiger Blood, The Nuclear Option, Carrington's Eye, Racist Landlord, Optimal Elbow. At this I was reminded of just what a lucky man I was to have a PA who understood the requirements of the job. Each potion could do the trick. My mood improved just knowing that I would soon feel myself again.

'Carrington's Eye, don't you think, Jeeves?'

'A very good choice, sir.'

Jeeves unscrewed the small bottle, took out the pipette, and deposited a couple of drops into my glass. I sank it, letting out a savage cry of satisfaction as fire hit the back of my throat.

'Right!' I exclaimed. 'What now?'

Jeeves looked at his watch.

'It's three-forty p.m.'

'Oh, that's not too bad. The day has just begun.'

'If you remember, sir, at four p.m. we have a meeting with Scratch Johnson.'

'Scratch Johnson?'

'The Head of Programming at DTV, sir. He said he had a proposal.'

'Not of marriage, I hope. Not ready to settle down.'

That name. Scratch Johnson. It dinged a dong, somewhere in my memory palace.

'Scratch Johnson, Jeeves. Do I . . . ?'

'Eton, sir. He was two years below you.'

Of course.

'Four p.m. Gosh. Where do we need to get to?'

'He's coming here.'

'Here?'

'That was the arrangement, sir.'

'But the . . .'

We both looked at the body on the ground.

'Why don't you take a shower, sir? I'll hang some clothes up in the bathroom. Then I'll see if I can identify the body and conceal him.'

'Very good.'

I sometimes think that, because I was born into a certain degree of what might today be termed as 'privilege', because I've never required what might be referred to as a 'job', because I rely on staff for the majority of life's banalities; that I'm seen as nothing more than a squiffy dunderhead. Would a simple squiffy dunderhead be able to shower and dress himself in ten minutes? I don't think so.

I exited the bathroom to find Jeeves beside the body.

'Fergus Craig.'

'Who?'

'That's the name of the dead gentleman. I found his identification in his wallet.'

'Fergus Craig?'

'Yes, Fergus Craig. I've done some research. Online. He's a "comedian", apparently.'

'I've never heard of him. A comedian, you say?'

'Of sorts. He appears to have tried his hand at a number of things: comedy, writing, acting.'

'Acting? He doesn't look like an actor.'

The out-of-shape corpse was slim in the shoulders, wide in the waist. Like a mouldy pear. His face was pale, pudgy and unremarkable in every way. Actors, to my mind, had a certain *je ne sais . . . wow*. This man did not.

'From what I can tell, sir, he's managed to reach

the level of what might loosely be referred to as "professional" in a number of disciplines – but not much further. I highly doubt he's ever troubled the status of "VAT registered". His only bank cards were from high street banks.'

'Oh dear. Why do we think he continues? Not that . . . I mean, he's obviously ceased, now.'

'From what I can tell, sir – from the internet, sir – he went to a comprehensive school. He may have no independent wealth.'

'What, none at all?'

'It's possible, sir. He appears to be in his forties. I've looked at his LinkedIn page. He's never had a real job. In terms of qualifications, he has nothing more than a degree in . . .' Jeeves held up his fingers to indicate inverted commas. '"*Theatre Acting.*" I think he may have, at this stage, found himself so far down the entertainment river that he has no other choice but to paddle on.'

'What a tragic story. I hope he finds a way out.'

Jeeves nodded towards the body, reminding me that this Craig's story had in fact come to an end. But why had it concluded in my hotel room of all places?

A knock at the door. Jeeves and I goggled each other in horror.

'Scratch! I thought you were going to conceal the body?'

'I'm terribly sorry, sir. I became waylaid by research.' Jeeves looked to a door on the opposite side of the room to the bed. 'I think I have a solution. This is a suite. There's an adjoining room. Stay there.'

And so Jeeves went to greet Scratch Johnson, holding the door open just a little.

'Mr Johnson.'

'Oh, hello.'

Scratch's voice had dropped a couple of octaves since I last heard it in the school dining rooms over rice pudding.

'I'm here to see Bertie,' said Scratch.

'Certainly, sir,' said Jeeves. 'If you could just move along to the next door in the corridor, we'll greet you in the sitting room.'

'*Muchas gracias*, ami-bro,' said Scratch, in a Belgravia brogue with the edges trimmed off. Scratch, by the sounds of it, had, like so many of my former school chums, taken a little of the clip out of his accent.

I had made a habit of booking a suite whenever I stayed at the Langham but had, until now, never had use for the sitting room. How opportune that I should have one on that particular day. As we sat – Scratch on a *chaise longue*, I on a sofa, Jeeves unseen and unheard on a hard-backed chair by the desk – I forgot entirely about the dead man on my hotel room floor. Carrington's Eye was, blessedly, as effective as ever. I felt revived and my mind drifted to Rules restaurant, wondering how easy it might be to get a table. I was yet to eat, and it felt like a day for a crown of mallard.

Scratch and I found ourselves taking a conversational stroll down Rue de Reminisce. Although there were a couple of years between us, our memories of our schooldays were much the same. We both agreed that, though much maligned, Eton had been a tremendous source of japes – all of them jolly.

We then went about the ritual of filling each other in on what everyone was up to. There were the politicians: Eddie Figgus was now Foreign Secretary and hating every bloody minute. Little Charlie Trippledown, who famously as a first year once soiled himself in chapel, was shadow Secretary of State for Work and Pensions (poor chap) and Bernard Coppings had gone rather dark, taken a load of backchannel cash from the Russians and set up an 'ironic' fascist party.

Then there were the adventurers: Carlton Moog-Devoir was still out there on the seas, looking for the undiscovered eighth continent, Dusty Shootersly had recently climbed Everest *again* and Francis Overly-Much had just led a military coup in some African country neither of us could remember the name of.

And finally the creative types: Tom Couch was running the V&A but hardly bothered going in these days, Rufus Two-Fus had been nominated for another Oscar, and now Scratch was running a bloody television channel. I tell you, I'm not prone to shoe gazing, but it didn't half make one feel like one hadn't exactly seized each and every day that had landed on one's doorstep. What did I have to show for my post-school career but a few choice anecdotes?

'Jolly good show, Scratchers,' I said. 'Afraid to say my CV is looking as bare as a nun's rap sheet.'

'Which is what brings me here, dude,' said Scratch.

'Oh yes?'

'Listen, we've got a gap in the schedules. We were going to make a sitcom, but I've been looking at the numbers and it costs not only an arm but, I think it's fair to say, a bloody leg too. Had a guy write some scripts and we took him for dinner but there's something not right about him. Face doesn't fit, terrible at small talk. I'm not pumping a few hundred grand into that horse. I've had to tell him that the show's over.'

I was struggling to think what any of this had to do with me.

'So, listen,' said Scratch. 'I've had an idea...'

With that, we heard a scream that I recognised immediately as one emanating from the mouth of a terrified woman. The noise was coming directly from my neighbouring bedroom. We all stood up. I looked to Jeeves.

'I'll deal with it, sir.'

And with that, he opened the conjoining door and went to put out the fire. What happened – as he told me when tucking me in that night – was as follows: in all the corpse-driven hullabaloo, both of us had neglected to ensure that there was a 'Do Not Disturb' sign on the door. That had resulted in a housekeeper entering the room and finding a dead body on the floor. Now, we're led to believe that hotel cleaners are used to finding all sorts (Lord knows I've left a few Guernicas of my own over the years) but, as it turns out, this was this particular lady's first stiff.

Conscious that any association between myself and a dead body was bound to cause, at the very least, an awful lot of admin, the ever-alert Jeeves set about convincing the cleaner that what she saw before her was not in fact a dead man – but a cake. I was, he told her, one of the world's finest *pâtissiers*, and my speciality was making my cakes look exactly like real things. I had, on this occasion, been hired by the Royal Society of Pathologists to bake them a corpse cake for their 150th anniversary – and although the floor of my hotel room seemed an odd place to keep the cake, I was a mercurial talent, whose habits were notoriously eccentric.

Such was Jeeves's deft charm that the lady's horror turned quickly to admiration. It was, she said, 'just incredible'. Enjoying himself, Jeeves went on to tell her that not only the corpse, but also the bed, the television and the curtains were cakes. Could she please, though, he asked, keep quiet about my presence? He explained that any word that I and my genius were in town was likely to cause an unhelpful stir. She left entirely satisfied that she had been witness to something truly wonderful. Of course, she had: Jeeves's cunning.

While Jeeves was dealing with the cleaner, Scratch set about explaining why he had come to see me.

'I've been watching your content-eroony on TikTok and Instagram and what-have-you. It's premium economy – heck, I'd even go so far as to say that it's first class. You're an authentic, old-school dandy and people love it. Fact is, there's not many of you left. Folks like me, we taught ourselves to tone it down only to find that a public school fop is actually a rather sought-after commodity. My pops used to worry that it was only a matter of time before the masses came and chopped all our heads off – turns out all they want to do is follow us on Instagram. You, Bertie, are the very best at it.'

This was all a lovely, soapy hot bath for the ego, and perhaps I should have seen what was coming.

'Awfully nice of you to say so, old chap, but what's the crux?'

'You're not clocking on?'

I shook my head.

'I want to give you a TV show.'

I rose my eyebrows half a mile into the sky.

'You sure about that, Scratch?'

'*Absolument!* Reality show, buddy. I'll get a camera crew together and we'll follow you around: Cannes, Ascot, Boat Race, we'll do it all. Just be yourself, and the viewers will roll in – and even if they don't, we'll have a bloody good laugh while we do it.'

This was, I had to admit, a *crème brûlée* for the ears. I had always, deep down, I told myself, wanted to work. I was positively Presbyterian in my commitment to the grind. I had just never found the right role. Now, *here* was a job I thought I could do rather well.

'I've got to tell you, old Scratch,' I said. 'Today got off to a rotten start but you've flipped that pancake magnificently. We should celebrate.'

'Does this mean you'll do it?' asked Scratch.

'Is the Archbishop of Canterbury a close family friend? Of course I will!'

And with that I went to the sitting room fridge and took out a pint of Boll and a couple of flutes.

'Oh,' something occurred to me. 'Should we be talking sterling? I've never had a job. Isn't that the protocol?'

'How does half a mil sound?' said Scratch. 'As a starting point?'

'Thunderous,' I said, popping the cork. We both let out girlish chuckles.

Scratch slapped his thighs. 'Where's the lavvie, Bertie?'

'Just through there, old chum.'

I sighed in satisfaction, proud of myself for entering the world of the employed. Scratch opened the door to my bedroom, and the day took yet another one of its chicane turns. The afternoon was starting to feel like the Monaco Grand Prix.

'What on *earth* are you doing?'

I stood up to see what Scratch Johnson had walked in on – and there was Jeeves, crouched down beside the corpse, holding a knife. Even though I knew that it wasn't the case, looking at that particular tableau, it was difficult not to come to the conclusion that Jeeves had just killed a man.

'You've just killed Fergus Craig,' said Scratch, in shock.

'You know him?' I said.

'Allow me to furnish you with an explanation,' said Jeeves – his brow, for the first time in my recollection, looking as though it might perspire.

Jeeves calmly, and, it has to be said, coolly, set out the facts: I had awoken to find the body on my floor. We'd got as far as identifying him as this 'Fergus Craig' but then Scratch had arrived and the matter of the dead body on my hotel room floor had been put on the back burner. Then, after dealing with the cleaner, Jeeves had decided to investigate this Craig chap further. In one jacket pocket he'd found two bottles of pills and in the other, a knife. Scratch may have been a couple of years below me at school (and in the most mischievous house, might I add) but he was smart enough to recognise that Jeeves was a man to be trusted. His voice had an authority that one usually associates with Dimblebys.

'What an incredible coincidence,' said Scratch. 'We were just talking about Fergus Craig.'

'We were?' I'm not always the most attentive listener but I'm sure I would have noticed if Scratch had mentioned that name.

'I told you,' said Scratch. 'That's why I had a gap in the schedules for you to fill. Chap wrote me a sitcom but I've decided not to make it.'

'Oh, that's this John Doe, is it?'

'The very same.'

'Funny old world,' I said, and Scratch and I shook our heads at the cavalcade of curiousness.

I took a closer look at the puffy cadaver.

'Hold on just a second, now! I recognise him. This chap wouldn't leave us alone in the Groucho. He was following me around everywhere.'

'He was, sir?' said Jeeves.

'He was!'

'How strange to think,' said Scratch. 'I saw him just yesterday. Told him I had to cancel his show. Didn't take it too well. Said he had a mortgage and a family. Said people like me didn't understand how hard it was for a chap like him. I found it all a little much, if I'm honest. Self-pity is not an attractive feature.'

'Indeed,' I said.

Jeeves had a thought. 'I couldn't help but hear your conversation next door,' he said. 'This television series you've offered to Mr Wooster – did you, by any chance, mention that thought to Mr Craig here?'

'I may have done,' said Scratch.

'Well, I think it's quite clear what's happened,' said Jeeves.

'It is?' I said.

'This Mr Craig has, as you say, taken the news of his series being cancelled very badly. And he's taken his anger out on Mr Wooster – the man who was about to be offered what he thought was set to be his slot in the television schedules. So, yesterday evening, he set about finding Mr Wooster in Soho, taking with him a knife and –' Jeeves looked at the two bottles of pills – 'valium and cyanide. Mr Craig was intending to kill you, sir.'

'Well, my golly gooseberries! What a rotter!'

'Rather a lot of drink was undertaken – is that right, sir?'

'Not a record-breaking evening, but more than your average Tuesday, I'd say.'

'You,' said Jeeves, 'most likely at his suggestion, invited Mr Craig back to the Langham for a nightcap. You're a very hospitable fellow even under the most trying circumstances. Dutch courage wasn't enough for him to carry out the murder, so he decided to take a valium. But, thanks to the amount of drink in his system, he made a mistake and took the cyanide instead – and killed himself.'

'Well, stick a hot poker up my— I'm flabbergasted,' I said. 'Wonder where he got the cyanide from. Isn't that rather difficult to get hold of these days?'

'I hear he lives in South London,' said Scratch. 'You can get anything that side of the river. It's a hellscape.'

'We do, of course, still have a problem to which

Mr Johnson is now privy,' said Jeeves. 'What do we do with the body?'

'I don't think that needs to be an issue,' said Scratch Johnson, taking a vape from his pocket and treating himself to a puff.

'I admire your confidence, Scratchy,' I said. 'But I'll be damned if I know where it's coming from.'

'There are services for this sort of thing,' said Scratch.

'There are?'

'Entertainment tends to tot up a few bodies along the way. Overdoses, usually, misadventure, that sort of thing. TV is filled with rather a lot of exuberant boys and girls. So there's a little business one can call: small operation, run by a pair of twins. For a fee, they'll come and dispose of your bodies. There's an incinerator somewhere. I think it's round the back of a bowling alley in Bermondsey. They make it up to look like a Frankie and Benny's, but no one ever goes in so it's pretty discreet. Sometimes it gets tricky if the person's famous – but luckily absolutely no one has heard of this Fergus Craig, so we should be fine.'

'This all sounds marvellous, Scratcho,' I said.

'There will be a fee, of course,' said Scratch. 'Ten K. I'm sure you'll understand if I chip that off your pile for the series.'

'Least I can do,' I said.

And so Scratch made the call. We watched an episode of *Flog It!* while we waited for the twins. They arrived – two big Bulgarians in boiler suits, ever so stoic, ever so efficient – and the body was out the door and down a back staircase in minutes.

My mind turned to mallard.

'Rules?' I asked Scratch. 'My treat.'

'Fantastic idea, Bertie.'

'Why don't you join us, Jeeves?' I said. 'You've earned it.'

'You enjoy yourselves,' said Jeeves. 'I have shoes to polish.'

'Very well.'

Scratch and I took the lift down to the car park, got into his convertible Jag and drove out into what was a wondrous summer evening. Young professionals stood outside pubs, their lagers gleaming in the twilight. I caught the briefest of glimpses at what a lucky man I was.

Was it to be a night for oysters? Yes. Yes, I think it was.

Just Ask Jeeves

William Rayfet Hunter

There are few things in life that can truly shake a man of my disposition. The sudden appearance of Aunt Agatha on the doorstep, a summons from an old friend to explain the regrettable fact that their most intimate diary entries have been leaked to the national press, or the discovery that one has, overnight, become engaged to a young woman with an alarming fondness for horsewhips and military history – all of these are sure to set the famous Wooster nerves a-rattling. But nothing, I can tell you, is bound to strike more fear into the heart of an upstanding young gentleman than these six simple words: *Bingo Little has had an idea*.

It was at the Drones Club that my old friend and constant source of tribulation bounded over with the air of a terrier that has just spotted a particularly slow-looking squirrel.

'Bertie, you old egg,' he barked, clapping an excitable hand between my recently raised hackles. 'I've got the most delectable news!'

I eyed him with a not insignificant amount of suspicion. The last time Bingo had had delectable news I'd ended up in a full beard and prosthetic ears doing a lamentable Slovakian accent to a roomful of expectant mothers. I had yet to fully recover from the experience.

'Oh,' I said tentatively, 'have you finally worked out how to remove that egg-stain from Barmy's billiard table?'

'Much better, we've gone into tech!'

This was ominous for a multitude of reasons. Not least because Bingo's previous forays into the professional spheres of journalism, landscape gardening and artisanal British foodstuffs had left less of an impression and more a trail of destruction in his wake. The thought of him dabbling in the arcane mysteries of algorithms and blockchain was about as appealing as receiving a call from your dentist knowing full well she's just sharpened her drill. This grand statement was, however, disturbing not only for its content but also for its syntax.

'Tech?' I mused, not wanting to examine Bingo's obscure use of the collective. 'You mean those infernal machines that refuse to function precisely at the moment one needs them to?'

'Don't be such a Luddite, Bertie old pal! This is the future! We must grasp it with both hands. We have the opportunity to be at the vanguard of the next generation of automated personal assistance!'

There it was again, unignorable by virtue of its repetition: *We*. I was rather hoping Bingo was once again leaning on his tenuous but proven familial link to the Plantagenets and using the word royally. I was beginning to get rather concerned. I took a large sip of my drink for luck.

'Personal assistance? I thought that was what Jeeves was for. And will you knock off saying "we", Bingo old chum, it makes me nervous and, as perfect as Jeeves's kippers always are, I'd rather not see this morning's breakfast again!'

'That's exactly the point, Bertie! You see, I've taken a position in PR for Ganymede Systems. We're working on a new artificially intelligent butler – fully digital, frightfully efficient and capable of managing every aspect of a chap's affairs. And here's the real kicker: we want to model it off Jeeves!'

I shot a jet of brandy-and-soda towards the panelling on the opposite wall.

'Model it off Jeeves?' I squeaked, horror-struck. 'Now Bingo, don't you think that's stretching things past the breaking point? I mean to say, there is nothing artificial about Jeeves's intelligence, I can tell you that and—'

'That's the genius of it, my dear man! Jeeves is the ultimate gentleman's gentleman. If we can reproduce anything near his level of smarts and efficiency in software, we'll be millionaires! Billionaires maybe even!'

'I say, Bingo, aren't you already a millionaire?'

'A millionaire's heir, Bertie,' he said, waving an insouciant hand. 'A crucial difference. And besides, my uncle has been grumbling about my spending of late. This would finally free me, nay free us, from financial dependence on uncles and aunts alike! What ho, Bertie, this is our moment! Our name in lights, the hour of glory! And besides, you would barely even have to do anything.'

I admit this last had piqued my interest. I still had my misgivings, however. 'I can't imagine Jeeves would appreciate having his . . . his . . . his *Jeevesness* bottled and sold like so much elderflower cordial.'

'Well, dear heart, that's where you come in! Right on cue, just like in those plays we were in at school. You do remember how we were at school together, don't you, Bertie?'

I opened my mouth to say that I remembered

all too well and would appreciate someday being allowed a moment or two to forget, perhaps somewhere restful in southern France, but Bingo pressed on like a man determined to catch the last bus on a rainy evening.

'We need a figurehead. A man of impeccable standing, refinement and grace. A man well versed in the art of gentlemanly living. A man who understands the ins and outs of excellent personal service. In short, Bertie, we need you! As our brand ambassador!'

I was struck then by the fact that I had discovered an even shorter and more terrifying set of words than *Bingo Little has had an idea.* The brevity of the phrase *brand ambassador* must not distract one from its horror. I was about to deliver a firm and resounding answer in the negative when Bingo delivered his coup de grace.

'Oh, and I forgot to mention, your Uncle Spencer is one of our main investors. Your Aunt Agatha is completely on board and thinks it's an excellent idea for you to be involved.'

It was as if the fates had taken up a cricket bat and decided to use me for nets practice. But a Wooster always knows when he is beaten – physically and metaphorically – so I acquiesced.

'Jolly good,' I sighed weakly, though I felt neither. 'Where do I sign?'

Jeeves has a somewhat irritating habit of always being one stroke ahead of the curve, so I endeavoured to tell him our news before it reached him via other means. Having taken a moment at the Drones to calm my nerves, I rushed home on foot and arrived at Berkeley Mansions feeling like a jellyfish in a stiff breeze.

'Jeeves,' I proclaimed, wobbling a little. 'I have news of the most earth-shattering nature!'

'Indeed, sir?' intoned Jeeves, looking up momentarily from the silver spoon he was polishing.

'Yes, Jeeves! Bingo has talked me into being the face of a new invention. They're calling it Virtual Jeeves – an AI butler based, you'll I'm sure be shocked to learn, on your good self.'

There was an almost imperceptible pause in the polishing, and I could have sworn I saw a whisker of a frown tickle the spot between Jeeves's thick black eyebrows. 'Is that so, sir?'

'You don't seem overly enthusiastic about the idea, Jeeves.'

'It is not my place to cast judgement, sir,' he said, setting down the spoon among its gleaming bedfellows. 'However, one might be moved to note that previous attempts to replicate human intellect in a machine have rarely been what one would call an unqualified success. I am somewhat sceptical, sir, of a computer's ability to reproduce with exactness the discretion and intuition expected of an experienced valet.'

'Now, now, Jeeves, don't be so bally pessimistic! The boffins over at Ganymede Systems assured Bingo this is the absolute cat's pyjamas, my dear Jeeves! Top-notch, first-rate, and altogether the bee's eyebrows!'

'Ganymede Systems, sir?' A hint of intrigue had slipped into the room and Jeeves's voice. 'As in Ganymede, the cupbearer to the gods?'

'The very same! A jolly bit of luck, don't you think, Jeeves?'

'Possibly, sir,' said Jeeves, drifting towards the liquor cabinet. 'Though one might recall that Ganymede, according to mythology, was kidnapped by Zeus and forced into an eternity of servitude.'

'Are you suggesting that this whole business might go up like a Roman candle on Guy Fawkes Night?'

'I would not presume to predict the future, sir.

Though, as when handling fireworks, I might advise you proceed with caution.'

I slumped back in my chair, trying not to let Jeeves's negativity ruin my burst of enthusiasm but ended up feeling rather like a discarded sock. Jeeves, always ahead, slid a restorative brandy into my despondent grip.

I must admit it was with a certain amount of minor trepidation that I approached the offices of Ganymede Systems some weeks later. I had glimpsed a meeting room or two through the glowing portal of a group video call to discuss the particulars of Jeeves's involvement. It had been demonstrated to me, using a selection of pages from Bingo's own personal diary, how the software (as everyone kept calling the bally thing) could be made to mimic the voice of whosoever's words it was fed. I must say, I was reticent to provide the machine with the inner workings of the Wooster noggin, lest I unleash a second, more enchanting version of B. Wooster on to the digital world. Bingo, it appeared, had no similar concern. Jeeves's misgivings had been somewhat assuaged on demonstration of the machine's ability to mimic and he had provided Ganymede with a selection of writings from the manuscript he was working on for a book entitled *The Gentleman's Gentleman's Guide to the Gentry* – a sort of How To for aspiring valets – as well as some other writings, the nature of which I did not care as to enquire.

All this to say that my snapshots of grey backgrounds and office chairs did nothing to prepare me for the glittering halls of Ganymede Systems. Having navigated a particularly tricky set of revolving doors, I was greeted by a waifish slip of a fellow with a clipboard who excitedly scored through my name with a flourish of his magenta ink pen. The young man gestured to a large set of doors, which opened into the sort of room that makes one feel rather underdressed, even when clad in one's most splendid spats. Floor-to-ceiling windows, colour-changing lighting and an abundance of beanbags scattered throughout suggested some sort of futuristic madhouse. I scanned the room quickly. The event was a veritable who's who of investors, tech journalists, and bright young things who said phrases like 'disrupting the industry' and 'search engine optimisation' with a completely straight face. I had just helped myself to a glass of what one would presume to be champagne and was musing on the level of disruption I might be comfortable with, when the wind was taken quite suddenly from my once billowing sails. I spotted

Aunt Agatha, who looked to be on the warpath and I, it seemed, was the hapless villager in her sights.

'Oh, Bertie,' she clucked, like a hen with one chick. 'You might have worn something more befitting the face of an endeavour such as this.'

I looked down at my suit and decided to disagree. At that precise moment, the electric blue stripe running through the grey check was matched exactly to the colour of the lights. She continued.

'Your uncle and I are very glad you decided to get on board, Bertie. A job like this is most becoming for a young gentleman, especially one as yet unattached. And on that topic, dear nephew, there's someone here I'd rather like you to meet.'

I had the distinct feeling the old onion was about to be put in the soup when a tower of a woman swept across the room like a gale in full spate. She had a face like a plate of mashed potatoes that had been left out in the rain and was wearing some sort of tweed monstrosity that wouldn't be out of place at a late-night vaudeville performance of *The Hound of the Baskervilles*. I could see the icy hand of matrimony reaching out, and frankly, I was in no mood to be clutched.

'Bertie, this is Miss Holdontia Hatts, of the Hertfordshire Hatts. Holdontia, this is my nephew, Mr Bertram Wooster.'

Now, it is one thing to be Bertrammed in a room full of glamorous tech strangers but to have a potential love match foisted upon one at an investor meeting is unconscionable. However, being the well-mannered and upstanding gentleman I always aspire to be, I let the *faux pas* slide and held out a reluctant hand. The Amazon grasped it with the kind of grip a generous fellow might call 'hearty'.

'Splendid to meet you, Wooster,' she bellowed. 'Mummy seems to think we'd make an excellent match.'

I retrieved my powdered metacarpals while Aunt Agatha extolled the woman's virtues like a swineherd on market day. She was just beginning to tell me about Holdontia's keen interest in the bayonetting practices employed in the Boer War when Rosie, Bingo's long-suffering wife and ever the paragon of good timing, tapped me on the shoulder and pointed out Bingo who was beckoning me over to the stage. On my way to take my place I passed my cousins, Claude and Eustace, looking particularly shifty.

'What ho, chums!' I said. 'Down from Oxford for the grand unveiling?'

Claude gave me a stare like a hedgehog caught in the headlights of an articulated lorry. Eustace glanced up from the blinking screen of his mobile telephone and squinted at me with what one might have mistaken for a hint of malice had one not known that this was how Eustace looked at everyone.

'Couldn't miss the big moment, could we, Claude,' he said. 'Despite the fact that the nephew crusher practically forbade us from being here. Seemed to think we'd make a dog's breakfast of the whole affair. Which is quite unkind, I think. We have changed our ways, Bertie. Taken a step on to the straight and narrow, as it were.'

I didn't have time to ponder this statement as Bingo had begun waving as frantically as the loose end of wedding bunting caught up in the gusts of El Niño. I arrived stage left as Bingo strode up to the podium and tapped the microphone, causing it to whine like a puppy who believes himself to be entitled to the fat around his master's T-bone.

'Ladies, gentlemen and information superhighway enthusiasts of all persuasions, it is my pleasure to welcome you to the grand unveiling of Ganymede Systems' pride and joy, Virtual Jeeves. As some of you may already be aware,' he beamed, 'our AI is built on a highly sophisticated language model, based on a most impeccable source of knowledge — my very own diaries!'

There was some polite laughter, led mainly by Claude, who guffawed like a drainpipe on a rainy day. I myself was somewhat disturbed at the notion of the combination of Bingo's enthusiasm and Jeeves's efficiency but swallowed my gall, so as to remain sporting.

'Our latest venture, the jewel in our cyber crown, is going to revolutionise personal service, placing all the power of the world's most skilled gentleman's gentleman into the palm of your very own hand. Now, to demonstrate the capabilities of our virtual butler, please welcome to the stage a man who is no stranger to having his trousers pressed by a gentleman in his employ, my dear friend and face of our new product: Mr Bertram Wilberforce Wooster!'

I might have felt slighted, having already been Bertrammed in front of the thunderous Holdontia Hatts and now Wilberforced to the masses; however, the crowd burst into rapturous applause which somewhat spurred one on. I took to centre stage like a rather refined duck landing on the shores of an ornamental island. A sharp bowler hat appeared on the sleek interface behind me, surrounded by a gently pulsating blue-green glow.

'How can I assist you, sir?' boomed a deep, measured baritone.

'Er, Jeeves, bring me a . . . a cup of tea, would you?'

'Very good, sir,' replied Virtual Jeeves.

Almost immediately a robotic arm whirred into life and set about the task. After no time at all it swung towards me proffering a delicate china cup on a silver tray. I took the cup, then a sip, then the liberty to let out a small cough. A lump of sugar leaped through the air and landed directly in the drink. The crowd erupted like Mount Etna on a particularly peevish day. I was, I must say, rather impressed by the whole thing. Spurred on, I delivered another command.

'Jeeves, recite me a poem!'

'Indeed, sir.' The Virtual Jeeves cleared its virtual throat and proceeded thusly:

'In Xanadu, sir, did Kubla Khan / A stately pleasure-dome decree—'

'Egad, Jeeves! You're a marvel! Now, what to ask next?'

'Might one suggest, sir, that you refrain from additional requests until you have demonstrated the capacity to complete a coherent thought?'

I was quite taken aback. The crowd seemed to love it, however, and a ripple of laughter passed across the audience. Holdontia let out a chuckle that could have stripped the paint off a battleship. The halo around the bowler hat turned from its pleasant aquamarine to an ominous shade of crimson.

'I say, Jeeves, that's a little off colour, don't you think?' I looked frantically towards Bingo, who stared forlornly back like a fellow who'd just been forced to swallow a lemon.

'What is off colour, sir, is the stripe in your suit.

Might I suggest that you allow me to make all decisions of a sartorial nature in the future?'

'Oh, I say! Jeeves, I really don't think—'

'Yes, that has long been your main issue. If I may be frank, sir – though I fear frankness in this instance is akin to using a sledgehammer on an already fragile teacup – your intellectual faculties possess all the keen, razor-sharp precision of a damp sponge.'

The crowd erupted once more, this time into a chorus of uproarious laughter that drowned out what one can only assume were more insults being hurled by that damned hat on the screen. Claude and Eustace seemed to be very much enjoying the crisp acidity of the pickle I'd found myself in. Mercifully, Bingo charged forward and yanked at a thick cable. The bowler hat on screen burst like a firework before minimising to the outline of a black moustache and then disappearing altogether. I was rushed off stage like Abraham Lincoln being saved by a particularly patriotic time traveller.

One of the greatest joys of having a man like Jeeves in one's life is that, however tricky an evening one might have had, one can always count on a perfect kipper and a restorative tonic to get the proverbial juices flowing. Which is why, the following day, it was with great consternation that I realised the fellow was absent. I had, I must admit, quite the headache, having drowned my sorrows at the Drones after the previous night's excitement. This was one of those mornings when the world seems to be draped in old dishcloths and no matter how much you try to wipe away the night before you always seem to leave a greasy smudge on the day. I tried to piece things together, but my brain felt like a hamster trying to solve a crossword puzzle. After disentangling myself from the bedsheets, I ventured into the kitchen where I found a plate of cold cuts, fruit and a suspiciously verdant liquid I assumed to be one of Jeeves's more medicinal concoctions. Beside the breakfast tray was a note reminding me that the previous night Jeeves had volunteered to go to the Ganymede Offices to examine the Virtual Jeeves System. The mental image of the fellow gazing into a reproduction of his own mind in zeros and ones was enough to make my head swim. I began to tuck into my rustic *petit déjeuner* and damn near jumped out of my pyjamas when a voice crackled up behind me.

'Good afternoon, sir. How did you sleep?'

'Jeeves?' I said into the empty room.

'Of a sort, sir.'

I realised with a cold dread that the voice was coming from the hi-fi and suddenly remembered that before all the chaos of last night, I had allowed the eggheads at Ganymede to install their infernal creation on my home computer system. I was about to call for, well, Jeeves, when his programmatic counterpart cut me off.

'Firstly, may I beg your pardon for the unfortunate miscalculation of last evening. It seems I was programmed to employ absolute honesty with my user, however it appears that discretion may be the better part of a valet. I was only following instructions but I shall endeavour to ensure such an oversight does not occur again, sir.'

'Oh,' I said, somewhat mollified. 'Well then, I suppose since the corporeal Jeeves is nowhere to be found you will do for this morning. What's on the agenda for today, VJ?'

'Since it seemed as though you might need a protracted recovery this morning, sir, I took the liberty of reorganising your diary. Your Aunt Agatha was expecting you for luncheon an hour ago but accepted your apologies this morning and has offered to reschedule.'

'Oh, bravo, VJ! Anything else?'

'Yes, sir. You are booked for a rejuvenating massage and steam at your gymnasium.'

'Spot on, VJ! Now that's the kind of ingenuity we like first thing in the morning!'

'It is two p.m., sir.'

'There's that good old honesty, VJ!'

'May I mention that you have a rather large number of unanswered calls and emails, sir. I did not want to disturb your sleep so took the liberty of muting your notifications until you awoke.'

'Let's begin with the calls, I suppose,' I said, biting into a slice of grapefruit.

'Very well, sir. You have two hundred and thirty-one missed calls. A number of them from journalists asking for comment about last night, a couple from your new acquaintance, Miss Hatts, and one hundred and ninety-eight from Bingo Little.'

'One hundred and ninety-eight? I say, VJ, that's a little over the top. I wonder what on earth could be so pressing? You'd better call him back.'

'No need, sir.'

'No need? I ruddy well think there is a need. The fellow must be going barmy!'

'Pardon me for being unclear, sir. There is no need to telephone Mr Little as he is at the door.'

The statement had hardly sunk in before Bingo started hammering on the aforementioned portal with such astounding vigour it might have made a Beefeater flinch. Bingo flew into the room like a dyspeptic parrot that has just guzzled a bottle of Tabasco.

'It's over, Bertie, over!'

'Oh, come, old pal, things aren't that bad. I know the launch was a bit rummy, but VJ here seems to have turned over a new leaf. Got me out of lunch with Aunt Agatha and if that isn't a turn-up for the books, I don't know what is!'

'Oh, not that, Bertie. I couldn't care less about Virtual Jeeves. It's over, Bertie, it's all over!'

'What on earth are you talking about, man? What's over?'

'My life, Bertie. Haven't you seen the papers?'

I had to admit then that I hadn't. Jeeves must have left before he had time to fetch them and Virtual Jeeves, bereft of his mechanical appendage, was unable. Helpfully, Bingo had brought one as a prop, which he flung at me before spilling himself into an armchair. It was open to the gossip column, which featured the headline *Little's Love Letters Laid Bare*. I quickly scanned the article, which featured an astoundingly detailed account of Bingo's rather numerous failed forays into the land of romance. He stared forlornly at me like a cat that had forgotten to take its thyroid medicine.

'I say, this is dashed awkward, what?'

'Awkward? Bertie, this is an unmitigated disaster.'

'Now, I wouldn't go that far, Bingo. Yes, some of these details are a little effervescent, but they're ancient history now – you're a married man!'

'But that's just it, Bertie, Rosie isn't mentioned at all. And now she's shut herself in the study and is refusing to talk to me. She says she's busy working on her new novel but I know she's upset and I simply can't get through to her. You have to help me, Bertie, please.'

I have, at a rough head count, been engaged at least half a dozen times but consider myself fortunate enough never to have met the ghastly fate of actually having to go through with a marriage. So, it is a constant source of befuddlement as to why anyone would come to me with matters of the heart. I was about to intimate as much to Bingo when, in true timely fashion, the real Jeeves walked through the door. I did not, however, have time to express my gratitude for his opportune arrival before he uttered something truly bone-chilling.

'Good afternoon, sir. May I inform you that Miss Holdontia Hatts is at the door awaiting an audience.'

It took neither an experienced valet nor a machine learning algorithm to discern that fact as the woman marched into the room, rather undermining both the *awaiting* and the *at the door* elements of Jeeves's pronouncement. She brushed into the room with the air of a general inspecting the troops, clad in an outfit that suggested she was prepared to command a cavalry charge at a moment's notice. A sharply tailored khaki blazer, bristling with brass buttons, sat atop a blouse so crisply starched it could have been used to slice a cucumber. A no-nonsense skirt, pleated with military precision, fell just below the knee, while her boots gleamed with the sort of polish that would have brought a tear to a drill sergeant's eye. A sturdy leather satchel, the kind that might once have held battle plans for Waterloo, hung at her side, and as she adjusted her pince-nez with a practised flick of the wrist, one got the distinct impression that, had she been born in another era, history's great conflicts might have turned out rather differently.

'Wooster, you dashed coward,' she shrieked, 'I thought you better than the type of fellow to propose over electronic mail. Though I must admit I find your shyness a little short of sporting, I have decided that can easily be whipped out of you. I have come here – in person I might add – to accept your hand. Bit tricky with the date being so soon though, my man, two weeks isn't a lot of notice and there's a very important hunt that Saturday but no matter, I'll ride straight to the church.'

My mouth flopped open like a discombobulated turbot on market day. It seemed as if the ever-generous pastry chef of life had decided to slip an extra delicacy into my paper bag of engagements and turn it into a baker's half-dozen. I suppose you could say it was a tad inconvenient, if you're one for under-statements. I turned, first to Bingo, who shrugged, and then to Jeeves who sprang into action.

'Miss Hatts, it is a delight to have you, however I believe Mr Wooster and Mr Little are engaged in a conversation of a rather delicate nature that requires a little more privacy than is at present on offer. We look forward to seeing you again soon.'

And with a flourish the blighter had guided the woman on a swift course around the sitting room and straight back out of the still open door. I must say, I am often impressed by the man's tact and guile, but this was extraordinary even for him. I told him as much.

'I say, Jeeves, bravo. Absolutely top hole!' I turned back to the room and remembered poor Bingo and his marital predicament. 'Well, this is all a bit of a wheeze, isn't it, chums? What a morning!'

'It's two-thirty, sir,' said both Jeeveses in unison.

The flesh-and-blood Jeeves's eyes narrowed. I realised with a start that I had not enquired as to how Jeeves had got on at Ganymede Systems this morning.

'Jeeves,' I said, 'how did you get on at Ganymede Systems this morning?'

'It appears, sir,' he said, lowering his voice and leaning close to me so his breath warmed the tip of my right ear, 'that there may be a ghost in the system.'

A shiver ran through me like a hot desert breeze across morning sand dunes. 'A ghost, Jeeves? Don't you think that's a dashed bit superstitious?'

'A figurative ghost, sir, a bug.'

'What sort of bug, Jeeves? Surely it would have to be minuscule to crawl inside the computer and—'

'I think he means an error in the code, Bertie. A problem with Virtual Jeeves's programming that caused it to misfire and create last night's chaos. Hang on a bally moment, you don't suppose the Virtual Jeeves is behind my miseries too, do you?'

'It would appear so, sir.'

'By Jove, don't tell me VJ is behind this nightmarish business with Holdontia too?'

By now, Jeeves was sitting at the writing desk tapping away at my personal computer.

'It would appear, sir, that the ... ahem ... Virtual Me sent a number of emails on your behalf this morning. The contents of Mr Little's diary have landed in the inboxes of a number of prolific columnists, an invitation to the wedding of your good self and Miss Hatts has been sent to your entire contact list, your membership at the Drones Club has been cancelled with immediate effect, and it would appear as though an order has been placed in your name for five hundred silk cravats from the Urban Fox.'

'The Urban Fox?!'

'I believe it is the new tailor on Savile Row, sir.'

'But that is beside the point, don't you see,' cried Bingo from the armchair. 'Why would Virtual Jeeves order five hundred cravats in the first place?'

'I detected a raised level of anxiety in Mr Wooster's voice and thought some retail therapy might prove an effective remedy, sir,' replied Virtual Jeeves.

'But why on earth would you send out an invitation to a wedding that isn't planned? Why would you cancel my bally membership at the Drones? And why would you send poor Bingo's diaries to the papers?'

'I am programmed to do as I am told, sir. I endeavour to deliver satisfaction,' said Virtual Jeeves. There was a buzzing sound, then an electronic sort of popping noise like a pixelated bubble bursting.

'I say! What the deuce was that?'

'I believe,' said Jeeves, 'that was the Virtual Me going "offline", sir.'

'Well, thank goodness for that!'

'Indeed, sir.'

'It appears, if I am not very much mistaken, that this infernal machine is attempting to ruin our lives.'

'The evidence suggests an answer in the affirmative, sir.'

'Jeeves, old thing, tell me you can fix this.'

'Undoubtedly, sir. Though I should mention a secondary complication.'

I swallowed. 'There's more?'

'Yes, sir. It seems that various acquaintances – Aunt Dahlia, Mr Fink-Nottle, and even Mr Tuppy Glossop – have been led to believe that you and I are, as one might say, romantically entangled.'

I blinked. 'Come again?'

'It appears Virtual Jeeves has referred to us in various correspondences as "an inseparable unit, aligned in life's journey". This has been widely misinterpreted.'

'You don't mean to say, Jeeves, that people think that you and I . . . are . . . erm . . . well . . .'

'An item, sir. Yes, sir, it would seem so.'

At this exact moment, the door burst open with the force of a small explosion, and in swept Aunt Agatha, eyes gleaming with what, to my astonishment, appeared to be satisfaction.

'Bertie!' she declared, beaming in a manner wholly unnatural to her usual vampiric demeanour. 'At last! I was beginning to think you would never settle down.'

I goggled. 'Come again, Aunt Agatha?'

'Oh, don't be tiresome, Bertie. This is wonderful news! Finally, I can stop wracking my brain trying to find a suitable wife for you. And Jeeves – well, at least I can be assured you're in capable hands!'

I made a strangled noise like a hamster being sat on by an unassuming neighbour who'd popped over unexpectedly and demanded a cup of tea. 'But Aunt Agatha, this is all a ghastly misunderstanding!'

She waved a dismissive hand. 'Nonsense! It's in *The Times*, Bertie. And if it's in *The Times*, then it is established fact. Besides, I've already informed several acquaintances. Everyone's quite delighted.'

I turned helplessly to Jeeves, who, as ever, remained the picture of composed serenity. 'Jeeves, for the love of all that's holy, do something!'

'Indeed, sir. As it happens, I have already formulated a plan to rectify the situation. I have confirmed your attendance at the Ganymede Systems Investor Dinner this evening, which I believe will be the unravelling of the entire affair.'

The venue for the evening's debacle was one of those ultra-modern establishments with an alarming amount of glass and not enough soft furnishings to absorb sound. Upon entering, I immediately clocked a sea of well-heeled investors, journalists and tech moguls sipping cocktails and discussing the future of artificial intelligence with the kind of reverence usually reserved for ancient deities. All the expected faces were there. I caught Aunt Agatha gazing with a rather disturbing gentleness at Jeeves and I. Bingo, red-faced and twitchy from nerves, was trying to cosy up to his wife Rosie who gave him a rather withering look that could have curdled milk fresh from the cow. I passed Claude and Eustace looking insufferably pleased with themselves, dressed in matching velvet jackets, sipping something green from triangular glasses. And there, terrifying as ever, was Miss Hatts, her pince-nez glinting ominously in the chandelier light.

Jeeves had, with his usual foresight, arranged for me to be seated near the podium; he lingered just out of sight to ensure he would be present at the precise moment. As for what exactly the precise moment might be I was rather in the dark. Jeeves says I perform at my best when I can't see what's going on and I am inclined, on this occasion, to agree with him. Dinner was well under way, a highly regrettable menu of deconstructed nonsense that left me yearning for one of Jeeves's steak-and-kidney puddings. I suffered through some sort of aerated asparagus foam before the evening's main event began. Bingo took to the stage looking like a fellow who'd just swallowed a wasp and found it distinctly undercooked. He gave a nod to one of the tech whizzes off to the side who tapped a few times on what looked to me like a piece of black glass. The screen behind Bingo buzzed to life and the large bowler hat reappeared.

'Ladies, gentlemen, gentlemen's gentlemen,' said Bingo, clearing his throat. 'Welcome to the Ganymede Systems Investor Dinner. It is my pleasure to reintroduce you to Virtual Jeeves 2.0, who has, I am told, promised to behave himself this evening.' A chuckle passed around a few of the tables like a love note in an American high school classroom. 'And here to demonstrate the new and improved software's capabilities is none other than the man upon whom it was based. Please welcome to the stage Bertie Wooster's treasured friend and confidant, Jeeves!'

There was a smattering of applause. Jeeves strode confidently up to the podium, glittering in patent leather and Brylcreem. He peered around the room, taking his time until everyone was leaning forward with anticipation.

'Ladies and gentlemen, may I begin by expressing my deepest gratitude for this opportunity to address you and set the record straight. It seems that since the launch of this rather impressive imitation of butlerian intelligence, there has been something somewhat amiss. However, I have examined the code and found absolutely no faults there. Take the personal letters of Mr Little, for example, which I am sure by now you have all read.' Jeeves paused for a moment to allow Bingo to redden further. 'There is no reason, within the algorithm's programming, for those diary entries to be made public. Nor was there anything in the code to suggest why Virtual Jeeves might have made public my relation to Mr Wooster.'

At this I almost spat out my dehydrated coconut parfait. It was bad enough *The Times* giving everyone the wrong impression about Jeeves and me and now here was the blighter confirming it all on stage! I almost got up and objected but decided I should trust the fellow and keep quiet.

'It seems to me,' continued Jeeves, 'that the cause of the programme's malfunction must be external. The Ganymede Systems firewall is, I must commend you, absolutely airtight. However, if I may, I would like to demonstrate a failsafe built into the very fabric of Virtual Jeeves, and all good valets. Mr Little, if you would please transfer primary control of the software over to me.' Bingo gave a nod, and the boffin tapped the black glass a few more times, there was a whirring sound and the light around the bowler hat turned a pleasing shade of chartreuse. 'Virtual Jeeves . . .'

'Yes, sir.'

'If you would, please recite the eighth rule of *The Gentleman's Gentleman's Guide to the Gentry*.'

'Of course, sir. Rule number eight: the perfect valet employs requisite discretion with regard to his employer and absolute honesty when his employer requires.'

'Very good, Jeeves.'

'Very good, sir.'

'Now, since primary control was transferred to me a moment ago, I trust you will answer my next questions with absolute honesty?'

'Of course, sir.'

'Very good. Virtual Jeeves, have you at any point been subject to cyber attack by person or persons unknown?'

'Yes, sir.'

A gasp swept through the room like a flautist's birthday candles being extinguished. The tech whizzes looked appalled, and the Ganymede CEO almost fell off his seat.

'Are you able to tell me the identity of this hacker, or hackers?'

'No, sir.' Another gasp, this time with a rather disgruntled note from the Ganymede team who seemed tired of this display of their software's vulnerability.

'Very good, Jeeves. I take it, however, that your

programming logged the IP address of the source of the attack?'

'Of course, sir.'

'And that that IP address is linked to a mobile telephone?'

'Indeed, sir.'

'Very good, Jeeves. Now, if I may make a final request, Jeeves, before we set this matter to rest.'

'Request away, sir.'

'Could you please telephone said mobile telephone?'

'Very good, sir.'

The green light around the bowler hat began to pulse gently and a dialling tone started up. Suddenly, from the back of the room, a discordant marimba began playing 'Land of Hope and Glory' at double speed. The heads of the assembled eggheads and fat cats whipped round faster than Holdontia's wrist when she's spotted a rather hot-footed fox. Their eyes landed upon my blasted cousin, Eustace, who was wrestling with his brother, attempting, it seemed, to shut down the device that was ringing out the tune of their crime.

'It would appear,' continued Jeeves, 'that Masters Claude and Eustace Wooster were somewhat put out by their exclusion from the Virtual Jeeves project and decided to use some of their considerable smarts to play what I believe is referred to as a "prank" of the cybernetic variety. With rather disastrous effect, I might add.'

I leaped to my feet. I must admit, given the excitement and the quantity and quality of Châteauneuf I'd been sipping all evening, I rather lost my temper.

'I say,' I said, 'that is simply not on!'

'Oh, come off it, cousin B, we were only having a bit of fun!'

I didn't have time, however, to determine exactly what kind of fun they were having as Aunt Agatha had risen to her feet, glided across the room, plucked both cousins by the ears and marched them out through the doors. One could just about hear them being read their rights over the chaos that exploded in the room. Investors and coders alike were what a more discerning fellow might call outraged. Jeeves and I didn't hang around to watch the festivities unfold. He scooped me up, out of a side door and into a taxi-cab quicker than you can say *au revoir, mes amis*.

It was with considerable relief that I flopped into my chair later that evening, brandy-and-soda in hand. I was feeling rather fizzy and poured a glass for Jeeves and gestured for him to sit too. He relaxed a little as he sank into a cushion.

'And you're sure this whole bally business is over, Jeeves?'

'Absolutely, sir. I am informed the Virtual Jeeves project has been quietly set aside.'

'And poor Bingo?'

'I believe, sir, that upon seeing that the whole thing was nothing more than a bit of mischief concocted by your wayward cousins, Mrs Little decided to forgive Mr Little and use the experience as inspiration for her long-awaited next novel. It is said she has been suffering from writers' block as of late.'

'Oh, so this whole thing has done them a favour!'

'It would appear so, sir.'

'Now, Jeeves, I do have one rather pressing question.'

'Yes, sir?'

'Well, it's about those rumours good old VJ started. The ones about our . . . erm . . .'

'Life partnership, sir?'

'Exactly. Why on earth did you seem to go along with it on stage?'

'It seemed prudent, sir.'

I was about to ask what exactly prudence had to do with the price of milk, the national debt or the mating habits of the lesser spotted anteater when the telephone rang.

'Wooster, it's Holdontia,' boomed the voice down the line. 'I am so terribly sorry to have to do this, old chap, and I truly was looking forward to making an honest man out of you. But I am afraid I simply cannot stand in the way of true love!'

I was about as baffled as they come and would have said as much but the dear thing blundered on.

'You must follow your heart just as the hounds follow the scent, my dear. Farewell!'

And she hung up with a click.

'I say, Jeeves! You won't believe this but that was Holdontia Hatts and she's only gone and called off the bally engagement!'

'Indeed, sir?'

'Goodness me, Jeeves, I'll be dashed if that wasn't your plan all along.'

'The solution, while unorthodox, appears to have achieved the desired result, sir.'

I sank back, marvelling at the fellow's genius. After a moment or two of happy sipping I plucked out another thought that had been germinating in my mind.

'Jeeves,' I said.

'Yes, sir?'

'Don't you think it's funny how quickly people believed that you and I were . . . well . . . erm . . .'

'An item, sir?'

JEEVES AGAIN

'Well, yes. Everyone was rather quick to hop on that particular bandwagon!'

'Indeed, sir.'

'I must say though, Jeeves . . .'

'Yes, sir?'

'I really am rather fond of you.'

'The feeling is duly reciprocated, sir.'

'I might go as far as to say, Jeeves, that you are the most important person in my life.'

There was a soft pause. Jeeves sat back and sipped at his brandy.

'And you mine, Bertie.'

Jeeves and Wooster II

Alan Titchmarsh

Let's face it: there are certain expectations that come from having a particular moniker. If a chap was christened Attila, for instance (though perhaps one should say 'saddled with the sobriquet of', since I am unsure whether Christianity was a guiding light to the famous Hun), it would be surprising to discover that he was a cat-loving stalwart of this parish. Similarly, to be blessed with the name of a distant relative who was regarded as an aristocratic wastrel does lead to certain assumptions on the part of one's interlocutor. It will come as no surprise to you that since I carry the name of my great-uncle – Bertram Wilberforce Wooster – anyone who had the great good fortune to encounter him will assume that his namesake, yours truly, will be of the same water. Well, I am pleased to affirm that from what I can gather of Great-Uncle Bertie's exploits, his great-nephew is, indeed, a chip off the old block, and I find it rather disappointing that a man of such insouciance, whose outlook on life was unvaryingly optimistic, should be larded with such opprobrium.

Having done a fair amount of research into the life of my father's cousin (by which you will understand that in real terms, I am Great-Uncle Bertie's first cousin once removed) I find myself astonished at the coincidences which pertain in our lives. My father, Claude, brother of Eustace, while acknowledging Uncle Bertie's existence and his generosity in providing me with a legacy dependent upon my bearing his name, was surprisingly reticent about the nature of their relationship and it is only after considerable effort on my part that the coincidences in our lives have come to light.

In this glorious period of the 1950s I find myself almost mirroring the old chap's life, not least in the appointment of the man who tends to my needs. Yes: I am aware that post-war unmarried men of my generation have almost without exception put their aristocratic noses to the proverbial grindstone with some alacrity and forgone the luxurious lives that once pertained. Bertram Wooster II, on the other hand (which makes me sound like the son of some American oil baron – which I am most certainly *not*), being blessed with the trust fund handed down by said great-uncle, is in a position to tiptoe gently towards the world of commerce rather than rushing headlong into the *mêlée* with little thought to the future. It is important, I would argue, to work out the precise nature of one's own talents before careering willy-nilly into the workplace, leaving a trail of devastation and disappointment in one's wake. There are abundant examples in the lives of my forebears to demonstrate the foolhardiness of this approach. I have only to mention the name of Monty Bodkin to those of my ancestor's acquaintance to be greeted by a sharp intake of breath, an involuntary shudder and a knowing nod.

But I digress. I was in the process of explaining my current situation which is, thanks to the nest egg of which I have already apprised you, that of a young man hovering on the brink of a career, but as yet, uncertain as to which of his considerable attributes would best be brought to bear in order to achieve some kind of success. I have reconciled myself to being what is called a 'late developer' and as such I am wary of being too hasty.

As to my domestic situation, rather than spend all hours of my day occupied with the intricacies of maintaining the apartment in Berkeley Mansions bequeathed to me by my aged relative, I had the great good fortune not only to find a gentleman's gentleman who was equal to the task, but — and here is the coincidence to top all coincidences — to actually bear the same name as the bod who attended to the wants of GUB (easier to say than Great-Uncle Bertie when one needs to find some kind of shorthand, in the interest of not wearying one's reader).

Reginald Jeeves (I know! Dashed coincidence, what?) is a nephew of GUB's gentleman's gentleman who, by all accounts, rescued him from many a scrape. You would be astonished, nay astounded, by the similarities between GUB's Jeeves and my Jeeves. Mind you, there are some similarities I could well do without. There are moments, I will be frank, when my Jeeves's disapproval of certain aspects of my wardrobe and even, on occasion, my actions is, to put it bluntly, inappropriate. In the 1950s life is different from the 1920s, I keep telling him. Should a chap wish to wear his hair after the fashion of someone in a skiffle group, or pull on trousers that cling closely to the pins, I reckon that he should be allowed to do so without the accompaniment of disparaging comments — however oblique — to the contrary.

But sartorial considerations are among the least of my worries, since, as my predecessor discovered, it is a truth universally acknowledged that a single man in possession of a good fortune will have the dickens of a job fending off the unwanted attentions of those determined to prove the veracity of Miss Austen's opening lines in *P and P*. Of which more in a mo.

So here I am on New Year's Eve with all the world before me and the prospect of a genial bash at my club, the Drones – an establishment founded back in the Gilded Age and still hanging on to its old members. (It is also still hanging on to a chef who should, long ago, have been pensioned off to a Lyons Corner House where his inabilities might have been regarded as the norm, but that's by the by . . .)

Within the hallowed portals of the Drones I can look forward to the company of like-minded souls who are, in many instances, as fortunate as myself in the financial stakes but still ever ready to pop a few quid on a sound tip from Salty Spicer, an old Stowe chum whose inside knowledge of the turf has seldom let us down in twenty years. His recommendation of a crisp fiver on the nose of Caughoo in the 1947 Grand National netted his school chums a welcome five hundred pounds apiece, coming in as it did at a hundred to one. (Rumour has it that old Spanker Courtney, the games master, retired on the proceeds, having wheedled the info out of Salty by threatening to expose his illicit behaviour to Chalky Bulstrode, the headmaster. Apparently, Spanker wagered his entire savings on the nag. The beatific expression on his face as he left the head's study having delivered the news of his departure was that of a clam at high tide.

But back to the party. 'Who else will be there?' I hear you ask. Oh, just the usual suspects: Arnold 'Squiffy' Benger (squat, short-sighted but a wizard on the stock exchange – another welcome source of help in these straitened times), C. D. 'Seedy' Potter-Pirbright (like me, scouring the horizon for an irresistible opportunity), Septimus 'Froggy' Fink-Nottle (dabbling in biology at the Natural History Museum, when he can be bothered to go in, but as a distant relative of his left the institution pots of money in his will, they don't seem to mind his inconsistencies), and Bedivere 'Bedsock' Threepwood, scion of the nobility whose family have a castle in Shropshire to which most of us will retire on New Year's Day – no doubt to lick our wounds and recover from the efforts of the previous evening.

I am lying beneath the fragrant Floris suds in my bath as I relate to you the story so far, waiting for Jeeves to . . . oh . . . the gentle tap on the door. He refrains from entering these hallowed portals while I am, as they used to say of the female of the species in the days of Botticelli and Titian, 'at my toilet', reserving his presence for the moment when I emerge in my silk dressing gown to dress for the evening. (Incidentally, the one I have recently acquired from New & Lingwood in Jermyn Street – a fetching pattern with the flowers of a pink lotus set off beautifully against a lime green background – seems to have caused him some discomfort, if the sour expression upon his face whenever he regards me thus attired is anything to go by. Be that as it may, I am particularly fond of said garment.)

'I have your evening dress laid out, sir.'

'Thank you, Jeeves.' I cannot see the disapproving expression on his face from this side of the door and that much at least is a blessing.

'Might I suggest a virgin Mary to see you on your way, sir? Bearing in mind the likelihood of an evening of some exertion, as far as alcohol is concerned.'

'Certainly not, Jeeves! A dry Martini. A strong one, if you please. With a twist. A chap needs a stiffener to face his chaps, if you get my meaning.'

'Indeed, sir.'

If I were not the sort of chap who is reluctant to take offence when a chap's chaps are impugned, even indirectly, I should bridle at the implied criticism. I rise above it.

It will not surprise you to discover that on emerging from said toilet I discover a somewhat staid array of garments lying on my bed in preparation for the evening's festivities: dark penguin suit, black bow tie, starch-fronted shirt, black socks and patent leather lace-up shoes. Even the cufflinks are those plain gold ones bearing the Wooster crest.

'Jeeves! It is New Year's Eve. I thought I might go for the mulberry smoking jacket and a contrasting bow tie.'

'Indeed, sir?' His eyebrows rise, and there is, I am certain, the merest hint of a smirk about the narrow-lipped mouth.

'Surely a chap can be a bit more raffish on New Year's Eve? The clothing here would be entirely suitable for the annual dinner of a reputable firm of provincial solicitors, but for New Year's Eve at the Drones?'

'As you wish, sir. I had rather assumed you might want to greet the year 1955 with a relative degree of sobriety, bearing in mind the proposed journey we are to make tomorrow and the need to keep, if not a clear head, then a vestige of dignity about our person.'

'Jeeves, you sound like your aged relative. Loosen up a bit. This is the 1950s.'

'Forgive me, sir. I had rather assumed that having reached the central year of the decade we might be wishing to take a more, should I say, level look ahead of us. Knowing that you are anxious to impress when we reach our destination in Shropshire, I thought it prudent perhaps to start as we mean to go on.'

Again, I ignore the implied slight.

'Yes, yes, I see what you mean, but we can "start as we mean to go on" tomorrow. Right now, I want to see out the old year – which has been, might I say it, singularly lacking in glorious incident and well peppered with the kind of near misses a chap heaves a sigh of relief at escaping – in such a way as to bid it a fond and hearty farewell. The sober rig you have laid out for me is hardly a reflection of my sentiments.'

'Very well, sir. The mulberry smoking jacket, you say? I will attend to its condition. I fear there may be one or two remnants from last month's . . . er . . . celebration, that I was unable to expunge at the time.'

Sometimes Jeeves talks as if he were a relic from a bygone age. He uses words like 'expunge' as though he were a guardian of the *OED*. But he means well.

'Oh, and I am in possession of a note, sir.'

'A note?'

'From Miss Pennyfather, sir.'

The old warning bells ring. 'Lavinia? What sort of note?'

'It is in an envelope, sir, and I was reluctant to open it lest the contents should be – as I am sure they are – of a personal nature.'

'Oh, glory! A note from Lavinia on New Year's Eve? I thought I had clarified my position in the Lavinia stakes. What can she want?'

'I might hazard a guess, sir, if you will forgive the impertinence.'

'Not impertinent at all, Jeeves. I think we both know what she has in mind. Lavinia is the nearest thing to a leech in human form.'

'Sir?'

'She hangs on and won't let go.'

'So it would appear, sir.'

'Go on then; bung me the note.'

'You will find it alongside your suit, sir, upon the counterpane.'

I don't mind telling you that next to putting one's entire monthly allowance on a horse that has not had the nod from Salty Spicer, the riskiest thing a chap can do is to give any encouragement whatsoever in the romantic stakes to a bird by the name of Lavinia Pennyfather. Oh, she's attractive enough – long-limbed, blonde-haired, blue-eyed – but in another life she could well have been a gamekeeper of the old school, determined to snare any form of human life that happens to cross her territory. You might think, on seeing her for the first time, that any chap with half a mind to take her on a date would be in for a good time. I can tell you from experience that anyone of *sound* mind would be well advised to run a mile. At first, she is simperingly attentive; hanging on a chap's every word and batting the eyelids with what she regards as an irresistible allure. But after a few dates one's native charm has clearly palled, and the simpering turns to criticism as she adopts the order of the wedding service. You know the sort of thing: Aisle, Altar, Hymn. Which when spoken out loud reveals its true meaning: 'I'll Alter Him.'

I thought I had managed to disengage myself from Lavinia, but the note revealed the extent of my misplaced optimism:

Dearest Bertie,
I'm sorry that we haven't seen each other for such a long while . . .

It has been a mere three weeks . . .

It seems ages since you took me to that delightful soirée at your club . . .

An evening of unbridled tedium, thanks to the lack of any chums making an appearance, and a particularly off night for the chef who must have been at the amontillado. The steak Diane would not have disgraced the portals of the Worshipful Company of Saddlers.

I have managed to break free of my commitments . . .

Lavinia's commitments amount to little more than appointments at her hairdresser's, her manicurist and her couturier. Not for her the 'off the peg' outfits beloved of the denizens of Derry & Toms and C&A, thanks to a mother who funds her daughter's clothing bill in the belief that the investment will pay dividends in ensnaring a suitable groom...

> *You'll be delighted to know that on New Year's Day I have been invited down to Shropshire courtesy of Bedivere Threepwood...*

'What! Horror upon horror!'

> *I gather from Bedi that you are also a house guest. How lucky are we?*

'Lucky?!!!'

> *So looking forward to seeing you at Blandings. Until then, Lots of love, as always, my angel,*
> *Lavinia x*

My angel? My foot!

'Jeeves! We have a problem! And not, I think, a slight one.'

The journey to Blandings Castle on that crisp New Year's Day was not one that I recall with unbridled affection. At the wheel of my treasured scarlet MG TC, Jeeves seemed determined to hit a bull's-eye on every bally pothole in the road by way of making his point about my rash approach to New Year's Eve. Even the effect of one of his patent hangover cures that morning, passed down, no doubt, by his considerate ancestor – involving the likes of raw egg and Worcestershire sauce – did little to ameliorate the feeling of nausea that pervaded the lower reaches of the torso and the upper reaches of the belfry.

The countryside might have been bathed in low-level golden sunshine, and the branches of the trees that lined the old Roman road from Londinium to Deva, now more concisely referred to by Her Majesty's Stationery Office and the Ordnance Survey as 'the A5', were rimed with the kind of hoar frost that would have gladdened the heart of the poet Wordsworth. He would have found it within his heart to wax lyrical about their luminescent charms, but to Bertram Wooster they were of little consequence when compared with the intestinal and cranial discomfort which seemed to banish all lyrical thoughts.

After some three and a half hours (which included a stop at a roadside café glorying in the name of Ye Olde Whistle Stoppe, where it was as much as I could do to imbibe half a pint of strong tea and a cheese sandwich so curled at the edges that it seemed to be laughing) we finally turned into the driveway of Blandings Castle. But for the sense of foreboding at the thought of a reunion with the tiresome Lavinia, my spirits did lift somewhat, not least at the prospect of what the poet calls 'hair of the dog'. I mean, what could *possibly* impair the joyful shedding of old ties and the prospect of freedom?

As the wheels of the trusty MG ground to a halt on the perfectly raked gravel – as artfully arranged as the aggregate in one of those Japanese gardens one reads about, where every pebble represents something of significance – I heaved a sigh of considerable relief. It was also a relief that Jeeves leaped nimbly from the driver's seat, replaced the bowler hat he had removed at the outset of our journey in the interests of retaining its ownership, and set-to hauling out my crumpled body from the passenger seat before attending to the luggage strapped securely to the boot. The problem with these old two-seaters is that they offer little room for the stowage of one's wardrobe when it is of the comprehensive nature necessary for the full enjoyment of a weekend in the country. You know, huntin', shootin', fishin' and the like – not that any of these pursuits offers yours truly much enjoyment, but one does at least like to *look* the part even if one's skills are rather lacking in the practical department. (Furthermore, Jeeves had baulked at the appearance of my new tweed Norfolk jacket purchased especially for this occasion. His mutterings included a reference to the suddenness of its check being similar to the one worn by my bookmaker. I had, again, ignored the intended slight.)

With a shiny crocodile leather suitcase in each hand (I always feel a pang of sympathy not only for the beast that donated its robust hide to the cause, but also for the staff who have to lug about such weighty valises) Jeeves offered me a nod and an indulgent smile and strode off in the direction of the servants' entrance whose location he seemed to know as if by telepathy.

I stood for a moment, gazing up at the noble parapets and marvelling at their sturdy countenance, battleship grey against a clear blue sky, already muting its tones as it doffed its proverbial cap to the evening.

I had little time to admire the verdant demesnes and messuages that lay on either side of Blandings Castle before a stout gentleman stepped from the majestic proportions of the front porch. He was of pretty majestic proportions himself and announced himself as Beach the butler.

'Oh!' I responded, keen to show an awareness of the castle and its history. 'I thought Beach had retired?'

'The old Beach has retired, sir. Sebastian Beach. I

am his nephew, sir, Arthur Beach; but you need not use my Christian name. Beach will suffice.'

I was about to explain to him this further coincidence of coincidences – my world seemed overflowing with them – but my explanation was rendered unnecessary since, with a degree of celerity that would have impressed his superannuated uncle, he turned on his heel and, showing little emotion about – or indeed, interest in – the fact that I had done my homework, walked up the steps of the imposing entrance. The sky darkened, and nightfall announced its impending arrival to the hills and valleys of Shropshire with the plangent contralto of a solitary blackbird.

Supper that evening was, to put it mildly, a trial. For a start, Squiffy Benger had chucked, citing 'unforeseen circumstances'. As Jeeves might have remarked while helping me into the mulberry smoking jacket (had his diplomatic propensities not got the better of him), there was nothing at all 'unforeseen' about Squiffy's absence, bearing in mind the quantity of amber fluid he had managed to sink the night before. This left yours truly struggling manfully to be the life and soul of the party; the aforementioned Lavinia, clearly on a mission to trap the unwary; Seedy Potter-Pirbright, still *sous-le-temps* but struggling manfully; and Froggy Fink-Nottle, taking yet another break from his naturally historic duties in Kensington and regaling the assembled company at every possible opportunity with the importance of sustainability in the wetlands of Somerset – a subject which, I think you will agree, is unlikely to set the world on fire. (Oh, rather neat that: wetlands setting the earth on fire . . .) As you were . . .

We four were joined by the Honourable Bedivere Threepwood. No sign of the excesses of the night before ever seemed in evidence with Bedsock, however hard he partied – something he inherited from his late Great-Uncle Galahad who had finally shuffled off his mortal coil when weaned from the amber fluid by an unsympathetic GP. Until then it seemed that alcohol had perfectly preserved his internal organs. Bedsock's grandfather Lord Emsworth sat silently for the most part at the head of the table, joining in the conversation rarely, and then almost exclusively to request the passing of some condiment that was out of reach. The noble Earl, now in his nineties, had inherited the title from his father half a century ago and was, by all accounts, every bit as vague as his predecessors. Funny, isn't it, how the nobility and gentry seem incapable of avoiding the passing on of their own idiosyncrasies and foibles to their successors. It happens much less frequently in the working classes where, I am told, quite run-of-the-mill parents can produce progeny of surprising intelligence. In my experience – and the circles in which I find myself moving – this happens but rarely. Show me a father who is dim, and I'll show you a son who is slow enough off the mark to give him a run for his money. Show me a wastrel and you can bet your bottom dollar that his dad taught him all he doesn't know. Mind you, this does not always follow with daughters. Bedsock's sister, Virginia, was seated next to me, directly opposite Lavinia.

Now, Virginia, I discovered, was a different kettle of fish altogether; sparky and attentive, dropping in the odd *mot juste* which showed just enough spirit to avoid being a smart Alec, if such a masculine simile can be employed when referring to the fairer sex. She had a neat, upturned nose, a short, dark bob of hair that glistened in the candlelight and an off-the-shoulder dress of deep blue that revealed a gently freckled pair of shoulders, set off by a single strand of pearls as white as her teeth. She was . . . well, you get my drift, everything that Lavinia was not, and I gazed at her in awe – a situation which clearly did not impress the latter named, who took to jabbing me under the table with the pointed toe of one of her stilettos whenever I gazed in Virginia's direction.

I could sense trouble ahead, not least thanks to the presence of the three imposing matriarchs who occupied the remaining places at table. On either side of the hunched, if lanky, form of Lord Emsworth were positioned, after the manner of a defence force, two of his numerous cousins: Lady Eugenia Bast, and Lady Philomena Carthage – the former a cottage loaf of a *grande dame* with an expansive bosom draped with sapphires and a portly dachshund at her feet, and the latter more conservatively attired in black bombazine. Lady Philomena bore a frightening resemblance to Lord Emsworth but lacked the moustache. Well, to be strictly accurate – and as my old form tutor used to say, 'Accuracy is the twin brother of honesty' – she did have a moustache, but one which was deficient in both the vigour and the density of that of her brother. And, whereas the Earl's appendage was a snowy white, Lady Philomena's was somewhat darker. You will forgive the apparent indelicacy of my remarking on this, but I do so only in the interests of giving you a full picture of these 'spectres at the feast' whose complement was completed by Lady Cecily Parsloe-Parsloe, the relict of Lord Emsworth's neighbour, a distant nephew of the late Sir Gregory Parsloe-Parsloe who had inherited his relative's stately home of Matchington Hall.

It became clear to me that Lady Cecily was regarded

as surplus to requirements by Lord Emsworth who was mostly concerned with ensuring that the book concealed beneath his napkin should not be discovered by the other members of the party. Bearing in mind the proximity of his cousins, such a situation was unlikely, but after years of being accustomed to his lack of application where domestic matters were concerned, they had learned, for the most part, to turn a blind eye to his addiction to *Fancy Fowl – A Practical Guide* by the Reverend Decimus Grippe, which spent much of its life hidden – more or less – upon his lap. At one time he was devoted to his pigs. The Empress of Blandings, whose portrait hung somewhat incongruously between those of the seventh and eighth Earls on the wall behind him, shuffled off her mortal coil some decades ago and the Earl, deeply mourning her passing on to styes above, had turned instead to poultry in the belief that when his birds flew aloft to meet their maker he would find the experience somewhat less traumatic.

The foregoing descriptions will hopefully have helped you to form a picture of the general atmosphere in the small dining room at Blandings Castle, upon whose dark oak panelling, along with the portrait of the prize porker, hung smaller images of all the previous Earls of Emsworth whose life-sized equivalents graced the state dining room. That vast mausoleum of a chamber was reserved for special occasions of which there had been only one in the last twenty years – the wake held in honour of His Majesty's Lord Lieutenant of Shropshire on 1st September 1939, mercifully cut short by the declaration of the outbreak of the Second World War which, at that time, seemed a somewhat trifling disagreement when compared with the mutual animosity displayed by two local Deputy Lieutenants clearly vying for the role vacated by the previous incumbent. It should be noted that the present Earl of Emsworth was, before his elevation to the peerage, pottering along happily in a house and garden in the far reaches of the estate. He looked at the ancestral pile which was to become his home, shrugged, explored the adjacent grounds and decided that if he could continue to devote himself to the rural pursuits which were the province of the gentleman farmer he could happily settle within its confines. In this aim he had evidently succeeded.

So, who do we have seated around the stately board? Two young ladies – one of whom I am growing fonder by the moment, and one in whom my interest long ago waned but who clearly still has hopes of getting her claws into the old Wooster flesh – three old biddies of uniformly terrifying mien; one ancient earl who, like as not, has hardly recognised the old Wooster presence; a trio of chums, one still *hors-de-sherbet* and the other waxing lyrical about wetlands; and one Bertram Wooster II, agog to discover the likely eventualities of a weekend spent in the embrace of jolly old Shropshire.

It did not take very long for the evening to show itself in its true colours, and for the fickle finger of fate to poke itself into the ribs of Bertram Wooster and make it quite clear that while he might finally have set eyes on a potential soulmate after years of dodging the talons of society's *femmes fatales*, the old FF of F had other ideas. This became abundantly clear when Lavinia Pennyfather put down her glass of chilled Chablis, cleared her throat and said in tones as clear and clarion as the Mediaeval trumpet, 'Has Bertie told you all of our future plans?'

The echoing silence that followed found all heads turned in the direction of yours truly, and the Wooster jaw as near to the Axminster as the undercarriage of Lady Eugenia Bast's dachshund. A glance at the incredulous face of the lovely Virginia caused my heart to sink and my tongue to cleave to the roof of my mouth.

What happened next, dear reader, I will vouchsafe to you the next time we meet. Until then, as a school-friend of mine by the name of Benson used to say, '*Au reservoir.*'

Jeeves Out-Jeeved

Jasper Fforde

ONE

Those of you who use the expression 'woke with a start' have simply no idea of the waking habits of the Wooster, which invariably begins with a stop – that is to say, a collapse back into the pillows with a winsome gurgle and a wholesale regret of whatever festivities the current pounding of the turnip might indicate. As I lay in bed attempting to piece together the shattered fragments of the night before, Jeeves hovered in as though borne along by a thin carpet of ball bearings. He simply hove into sight, laid the proffered cup of tea on the bedside, intoned a soft 'Good morning, sir, I shall not draw the curtains quite yet' and reversed out the door with no discernible movement of the lower extremities.

JEEVES AGAIN

I lay there for quite some time.

'Did the games conclude in a favourable manner, sir?' enquired Jeeves as I sat for breakfast a full hour later, washed and brushed and booted and now firing favourably on all cylinders. He was alluding, of course, to the reason my head was in an unusually enfeebled state: the Drones Annual Games Night.

'I would like to say it could have gone better but I cannot,' I replied. 'Jeeves, you are now looking at the Outright Winner of the LXXXVII *Droneimpiad*. No longer shall the name of Bertram Wooster be absent from the Games Trophy – and not before time.'

'My heartiest congratulations, sir.'

'Taken, dear fellow, taken. It's at times like this I feel as though I'd gone into the ring with Jack Dempsey, Sugar Ray *and* LaMotta and put their backs on the canvas before the bell's chime had faded. Invincible, Jeeves, *invincible*.'

'Akin to Achilles, no doubt, sir. Could I interest you in some bacon and eggs? As the gentleman once said, the chickens were involved but the pig was wholly committed.'

That's what I like about Jeeves. Always a pithy quote to raise one's spirits.

'Bring the e. and b. on with all due ceremony, Jeeves. This will be the breakfast of champions.

I'll have you know I was a little worried about the Games Night and its multi-disciplinary format, but Lady Luck was gazing fondly upon Bertram with the sunniest of smiles, and yes, 'tis true, I faltered mildly on the current affairs part of the games.'

'Indeed, sir?' said Jeeves, laying the breakfast in front of me.

'Yes,' I replied, 'while I know the Minister for Transport – we played fives together at Eton – I didn't know Spatchy *was* the Minister for Transport. I mean, who'd'a thought it? Little "Spatchcock" Fizzington, playing the big prawn over cars and trucks and whatnot. If the nation knew what I knew, they'd not put him in charge of a train set.'

'It's a very good thing that the general public are ignorant of such matters, sir.'

'I agree. But back to the Games: I came out top of the class in darts and swimming and first overall in designing the least drinkable cocktail with the fewest and most readily obtainable ingredients – a concoction of two parts absinthe to one part Optrex that I dubbed "Wilde about the eyes".'

'It sounds winningly frightful, sir.'

'Oh, it was, believe me. Even young Boko Fittleworth pushed it away, and he'd drink muddy water if it had a pretty label and smelled of bagpipes. I then won hands down getting around the smoking room without touching the floor, balancing a sherry glass on my forehead while at the same time singing the "Catalina Magdalena Hoopensteiner" song.'

'The games seem quite varied this year, if you don't mind me saying, sir.'

'I don't mind you saying it a bit, Jeeves. The problem lies with scheming Drones attempting to game the system by practising all year round at balancing a walnut on their nose or wallpapering themselves to a telephone box or some such. Won't do at all. No, the freestyle components of the games are announced on the night of the games themselves. Keeps us all on the tippiest of tippy toes.'

'We have a similar Games Night at the Junior Ganymede Club, sir, but of a more cerebral nature – oratory, chess, poetry reading and a game we call—'

'Yes, yes, all in the best of times, Jeeves, I was just getting to the choicest part. Before you could say "Pour me a G and T but hang back on the T", the finals were upon us and who were Last Men Standing but yours truly and the frightful Lord Sidcup.'

'I was not aware the former Mr Spode was a member of the Drones, sir. I understand he is a frequenter of the Demosthenes Club across the road.'

'Neither was I, and I'm not sure how he circumvented Convention Five of the club rules: "Feckless youth only, no exceptions." But there he was – my adversary for the night.'

'A most dangerous adversary, if I may say, sir.'

'Dangerous? I'll say. He's threatened to punch me into a jelly more times than Tuppy Glossop's had hot dinners. He's a bruiser of a man. The sort of chap that when the stork arrived to pour him into his romper, his mother forgot to say "when".'

'I wholeheartedly agree, sir. More coffee?'

'Oh yes, Jeeves, only Kenya's finest for the champions of champions. Where was I? Oh yes; the finals. This was to be a dash to Trafalgar Square by any route, a circuit of Nelson's C and then home again.'

'That seems hardly a challenge, sir.'

'Dressed as a pantomime horse?'

'Daring, sir,' intoned Jeeves, 'and a red flag to the local constabulary for whom the Drones Games Night is viewed, I believe, with some distaste and a mind for reprisals for previous indiscretions?'

'Couldn't have put it better myself, although for the life of me I can't see why those helmeted killjoys have such a downer on such harmless high jinks. But the first order of the day was to name our seconds as running solo isn't playing ball while dressed up as a panto dobbin. Spode chose Stilton Cheesewright to be his running mate as Tuppy had fallen off the map with the drink, and I tapped Gussie Fink-Nottle for the honour as he and I once paired up to play a Guernsey heifer at the Chuffnell Regis talent contest for the under-eights. And jolly good we were, too.'

'This pantomime horse, sir,' intoned Jeeves with a mischievous quiver of the eyebrow, 'were you the front or, *ahem*, the rear?'

'The front half, obviously. Someone responsible has to be at the helm. I think the world of Gussie, but his mind is too full of newts and romance to be good for anything other than the back half of a horse. Better minds have observed that he was likely dropped on his head as a child, and further, probably dropped on Boko Fittleworth's head. Two soft-headed loons for the price of one if you follow me. Anyway, we were given thirty minutes to plan our route and don our costumes while the clerk of the course posted a deputy at the square to see fair play and to witness a quick panto dance routine of comedy perfection before the charge home for fizz and medals.'

'And the side bets, sir? I presume that Team Wooster were the favourites?'

'I would have thought that too, but not a bit of it. Dash it all if poor Bertram here was seen as the hanger-on. The rank outsider. The unbroken colt. Say what you like about the Woosters but we don't shirk with the winning post in sight, and after myself and Spode had exchanged a few choice discourtesies the stakes were raised higher still. Viz. the loser has to pack his bags and join the Foreign Legion.'

'The *French* Foreign Legion, sir?'

'The very same.'

'That seems quite extreme, sir. And if I may be so bold, I do not believe the Legion would suit you, French or otherwise.'

'I should say not. Have you ever been to Aboukir? Hellish dusty, flies the size of biplanes and the nearest live cabaret forty miles to the north-west.'

'So I have heard, sir. *Most* inhospitable. I had an aunt based in Marrakech—'

'Never mind about your aunts, Jeeves. Is that the only thing on your mind with poor Bertram here about to sign on for twenty years being yelled at in French by a short man in a *kepi*? Have *you* ever been yelled at by a short Frenchman in a *kepi*, Jeeves?'

'I can imagine that might be an experience considerably less than optimal, sir. Did you stop to consider why his lordship might have suggested such a wager?'

I furrowed the old brow as Jeeves has a top-flight brain that were he behind gurgling retorts and a poster of the periodic whatnots instead of a trouser press and shoe polish, would most likely be waist deep in Nobel prizes. When he asks a question with a certain quizzical tilt to it, I always suspect he knows the answer but is willing Wooster here to divine it also.

'Good Lord, Jeeves,' I said, 'you think that rotter Spode was trying to get Wooster off to a dusty foreign coast for some nefarious reason?'

'The thought had occurred to me, sir. About a lady, perhaps?'

'Good gosh!' I said as a familiar face hove into memory. 'Spode has been all gooey over Madeline Bassett for months now, even to the point of writing poetry.'

'The last act of a desperate man, sir?'

'You could be right. That Bassett girl and I have been in and out of engagement so many times, doubtless he thinks me a fly in the old ointment, a shadow on his horizon, a hiccough on the path to marital bliss.'

I furrowed the old brow again.

'Jeeves, refresh the cells for me: am I currently engaged to Madeline?'

'Not at present, sir, but given past history, such an occurrence is not beyond the realms of likelihood.'

'And I aim to keep it that way. Beyond the realms of likelihood, I mean. Well, you can understand my predicament, and while Spode is an oaf of the highest order, he also played scrum half at Oxford and on a good day he could outrun Seabiscuit if he was having a bad day, so stakes were high and Gussie and I made our plans. Now, any old fool could have turned left out of the Drones and cantered down Piccadilly to peel right along Haymarket and straight on to Nelson's C.'

'Then that is what you did, sir?' asked Jeeves, taking my de-baconed plate to the sideboard.

'What? No. Knowing that the theatres would be emptying at about this hour Gussie and I shot out of the gate at the starter's flag and hoofed it down St James's, turned left into Pall Mall and then, taking advantage of an empty road, took to the asphalt and breezed into Trafalgar S. with barely a sweat. We then danced the 'Equestrian Gavotte' to the satisfaction of the appointed deputy as Spode & Co. arrived, huffing like a steam train as they had come to grief with the crowds leaving that evening's showing of *Spindrift*. With the win now so easily in the bag we turned back down Pall Mall at a jaunty trot only to take a detour through St James's Square to avoid the attentions of the constabulary, and – this is where the story takes a dark turn, Jeeves – we were waylaid by a group of ruffians without a neck amongst them and dressed in Black Shorts, armbands and the lick of pencil on the upper lip that purports to be a moustache with something to say – and none of it pleasant.'

'Ah,' said Jeeves, 'it seems that Lord Sidcup's flirtation with the fascist group known as the Saviours of Britain is not at an end.'

'You think right, Jeeves. That's the thing about amateur dictators. They just don't know when to give up the game. Show them a moving crowd and before you know it they'll jump to the front yelling, 'Follow me', and the next thing you know they're saluting flags and burning books and banging on about bunches of sticks and making up nonsense about people who never did us any harm.'

'In this, sir, I heartily agree. Quite reprehensible. I have it on good authority that his lordship struggles to keep staff, if you know what I mean.'

'Quite, Jeeves, quite. Anyhow, these four shaven gorillas told Gussie and I we were to stay with them for ten minutes to give Spode a chance to finish first, as it was well known that his comedic horse dance routines are rarely up to snuff. So there we stood, like an odds-on favourite at the Kentucky Derby who had romped home first, only to find they'd lost their rider straight out of the gate.'

'That sounds to me like a sorry state of affairs, sir, seeing as the evening had gone so well. I would venture, sir, that this might have been his lordship's plan all along, given his uncharacteristic attendance at a Drones event.'

'You could be right, Jeeves. What an absolute pip that man is. If only you had been there to keep me on the straight and narrow.'

'Yes, indeed, sir, if only I had.'

'Well, there was little we could do except wait, and already I could feel the hot scorch of the desert air singeing the back of my neck. What's that saying, "The something the obstacle, the more something the something"?'

'The greater the obstacle, sir, the more glory in overcoming it.'

'That's the one. So it was an angered and wronged Wooster who returned to the club fifteen minutes later. Spode had cheated me, but it's not the done thing to accuse another member of foul play, so I was going to have to take this one on the beak and look upon the bright side: an improvement to my French, likely a good claret over dinner, and little to no contact with Aunt Agatha.'

'I feel, sir,' said Jeeves after a pause, 'that there is more to this story, otherwise you would have already ordered me to pack your tropical suit, sent out to Christys' for appropriate headgear and to Foyle's for a copy of *Baedeker's Guide to Algeria.*'

'Spot on, Jeeves, never missing a trick. Well, here's the final act: blow me down but when I get back to the Drones I spy old Spode with a long face, and my chums are suddenly around me with all that "conquering hero returns" sort of guff and telling me I've won.'

'Won, sir?' intoned Jeeves without quite the sense of wonder my story deserved. 'I understood that you were waylaid by gentlemen of an unsporting temperament?'

'That's the rummy thing about this whole business, Jeeves. It soon transpired that an *identical* pantomime horse purporting to be yours truly had romped through the doors of the Drones Club a clear two minutes ahead of the field, then barked something about doing a victory lap around Berkeley Square and disappeared by way of the kitchens. When Gussie and I turned up as dejected souls ten minutes later we were as victors – and Spode could hardly accuse me of cheating while cheating himself. So that's where the matter rested. Long story short, drinks were had by all, and since Woosters are nothing if not the best of sports, I agreed to cancel the Foreign Legion wager on the basis that French Foreign Legioning is best left to the French and the French alone. But here's the best bit, Jeeves. As a *quid pro quo* for negating the wager I had Spode hand over a painting he'd bought that very afternoon at Sotheby's for ten guineas at the request of Sir Watkyn Bassett. He didn't like parting with it one bit, but an oath made unto Drones members is as good as written in blood, and it was either the painting, twenty years of French servitude or being blackballed from every club in London. The jolly canvas is over there and I'm sure you cannot have missed it.'

'I observed the work at first light,' said Jeeves, casting an expert eye upon the canvas. 'May I enquire as to the legal title, sir?'

'Of course, all above board. Spode bought it so he was the owner, and he signed it over to me. I have the receipt in my breast pocket.'

'Fascinating, sir, and I can understand why his lordship did not want to part with it, and why Sir Watkyn Bassett might want to have it, but not wish to be seen at the auction house.'

'Well, don't keep it all a big fat secret, Jeeves; spill the proverbials like a good fellow.'

'The canvas is named *The Madonna of the Shapely Shoulders*, sir, and has recently been in the news because it is currently considered "in the style of" but not "attributed to" Augustus Van Clunk, a Renaissance artist of some talent who lived between 1468 and 1516. The world is awash with Van Clunk copies, but originals fetch high prices at auction. The last authenticated canvas commanded, I believe, the sum of forty thousand guineas.'

'That's an eye popper of a sum, Jeeves, just for a bit of old paint, canvas and wood.'

'It is, sir, but only with expert attribution. It is my guess that Lord Sidcup's reluctance to part with the painting and Sir Watkyn Bassett's interest might suggest he is hoping to have it authenticated. In which case it might be worth considerably more than the ten guineas paid for it.'

'You mean forty thousand guineas, Jeeves?'

'I do, sir. I understand Sir Watkyn recently secured the services of Mr Lucius Pim, who is currently Professor of Renaissance Painting at the Royal Arts Academy of Arts.'

'Is he, by gum? Never trusted him. Married that Pendlebury girl as I recall.'

'He did, sir.'

'And he's now cosying up to Bassett?'

'So it appears, sir.'

This did not sound good at all.

'We shall have to be on our toes, Jeeves. I do not expect Spode or Bassett will be too happy with old Bertram here being the current legal owner of this *Madonna of the* er, er . . .'

'*Shapely Shoulders*, sir?''

'Those are them.'

'I agree wholeheartedly, sir.'

I took another restorative sip of coffee and once again mused over the previous evening's adventures.

'What I can't understand,' I said, 'is where that *other* panto horse came from and where it went. It's as though Bertie here had an equestrian guardian angel last night, keen and conscious to every machination of Spode's plans and ready and willing to step in when things went south. Ah, well,' I added, 'one of life's little mysteries. But enough about me, Jeeves, how did you spend the evening?'

Jeeves arched an eyebrow elegantly and gave me a look that would not be out of place between a stalwart uncle and his errant nephew.

'I assure you, sir, that I was not, like you, charging around central London dressed as a horse, but playing backgammon at the Junior Ganymede.'

'Fun had by all?'

'It was *most* diverting, sir.'

TWO

I consider myself an even-minded sort of chap, well used both to offering and accepting hospitality, so it was to Brinkley Court that I had hoped I would head for the weekend, there to rub noses with Aunt Dahlia and Uncle Tom, wave a racquet at some incoming and partake of the gastronomic delights of the chef, Anatole, a fellow who plays upon the taste buds as Paganini played upon the fiddle. Alas for Wooster and his taste buds, we were instead motoring towards Totleigh Towers, the country seat of the frightful Sir Watkyn Bassett, and I freely admit I felt like a cavalryman ordered to charge the guns at Balaklava without first being permitted a hot bath and a shave.

The events that had myself and Jeeves in the two-seater heading to the aforementioned with a shapely-shouldered *Madonna* wrapped in brown paper in the boot are soon explained. The morning after the panto horse escapade I was just popping out for a snifter and a rubber or two of bridge when a phone call from Aunt Dahlia brought me up short, and the convo went something like this:

'Ah! Bertie,' sayeth the aunt, 'are you sober, bright-eyed and bushy-tailed and ready to face the world?'

'Indeed, ancient relative, and yourself?'

'Top notch in mind but not in wallet, Bertie, and I'll get straight to the point: what's this I hear about you gallivanting around town dressed as a pantomime horse?'

'Indeed true, Aunt dearest. I showed a clean pair of hooves to Spode to win the Drones Games Night, although I have to report Gussie's dancing talents in the rear of a panto Dobbin have rusted somewhat through disuse.'

'Never mind that newt-nattering nitwit, Bertram. Congrats and "I-knew-you-had-it-in-you" and "Hoorah for the Woosters" and all that rot, but it's your Uncle Tom I'm worried about. He's made some unwise investments over some new railway company or other and the long and the short, beloved fathead, is that Uncle Tom has sold the family fund from beneath us. So if you don't do something to restore our fortunes and sharpish, Tom and I may have to let out the old pile and find paid employment. You don't want your aunt reduced to actually *working*, do you? Good. Now listen carefully: that viper Sir Watkyn Bassett has given up on all that silver cow-creamer nonsense and is now more interested in old masters, specifically Van Clunk, of which he has a copy entitled *Madonna of the Shapely Shoulders*.'

I glanced at my version of the painting.

'The plot thickens, Aunt dearest,' I said. 'Jeeves told me that Pim fellow has been engaged by Bassett.'

'Now you're getting it, numbskull. A small bird tells me you have in your hands a Van Clunk, is that so?'

'Indeed so, Auntie.'

'Perfect. So all you need to do is get down to Totleigh Towers *tout suite*, persuade that frightful Pim fellow to authenticate your *Shapely Shoulders* rather than Bassett's and then send the painting to us and we can have it in the sales by Thursday. Simplicity itself. Can you do that?'

'It depends. How will I persuade Pim to authenticate my painting and not his?'

'I always tended to favour blackmail in circumstances like this but failing that, use your initiative. Or, if as I suspect you have none, rely on Jeeves. He is going with you, I take it?'

'Of course, Aunt.'

'Jolly good. Don't let us down, Bertram my boy, or next time you see me I could be a charlady, whatever that is – or clearing tables at the Lyons Corner House, ditto previous comment. Well, pip-pip.'

And the telephone went dead. Despite Jeeves being in the next room, he doubtless heard the conversation as Aunt Dahlia has a voice so loud it could unseam leatherwork, and that's why we were here now, on a fresh day in spring, motoring towards Totleigh-in-the-Wold, Gloucestershire.

'You'd better educate me about this Van Clunk fella, Jeeves,' I said, 'and don't spare any details.'

'Details, sir, is what Van Clunk lacks. He painted mostly mundane subjects of little artistic merit, and posterity has been kindest for an altarpiece he painted in Utrecht. The triptych were all *Madonnas*, and each displayed the fleshy virtuousness that the then Bishop of Utrecht demanded. There is the *Madonna of the Curvy Calves*, the *Madonna of the Shapely Shoulders* and the *Madonna of the Ample Décolletage*. The latter is the only authenticated work, and was, I understand, something of a *cause célèbre* in the last war. It now resides in the Louvre. I took the liberty of making enquiries with a colleague at the Royal Arts Academy of Arts, and he tells me that the only copies of *Madonna of the Shapely Shoulders* currently in contention are yours, one held by Sir Watkyn Bassett and the other by person or persons unknown.'

'I see. And this attribution by Pim. He says it's real and it is?'

'Exactly so, sir. It is one of the peculiarities of the art world that if a short man wearing a pince-nez and equipped with an accent and incomprehensible speech patterns says that a banana nailed to a melon is art of the greatest value, then it is – and consequently worth a great deal of money.'

'A ludicrous state of affairs, Jeeves.'

'Anywhere but the art world it would be a matter of some mirth, sir.'

'So let me get this straight: Aunt Dahlia wants me somehow to persuade this Pim fellow – who is already in the pay of Sir Watkyn – to anoint my Van Clunk with the Midas?'

'Something like that, sir.'

'As I feared, Jeeves. As . . . I . . . feared. Do you have a plan?'

'Not as yet, sir, but I am hopeful that a way forward will reveal itself in the fullness of time.'

We motored on in silence and presently found ourselves, as the shadow of the evening drew on, at the melancholy Totleigh Towers, a huge pile of a house in the style of someone-or-other with additions and alterations by someone else. While Jeeves took the car to the rear to unload, I walked in through the front door which had been held obligingly open by Butterfield, to whom I nodded a greeting.

'The master is in the drawing room taking tea, Mr Wooster, sir. May I escort you there?'

'No, no,' I said. 'A Wooster's sense of direction is second only to that of the Siberian elk.'

'As you wish, sir.'

After finding myself by turns in the library, billiard room and a storage cupboard that smelled of furniture polish and soap, I eventually chanced upon the room in question.

'Ah, Bertram my boy,' said Sir Watkyn in a suspiciously friendly tone, our past differences seemingly forgotten. Bassett senior was smaller in real life than when behind the magistrate's bench, and it had been said that if anyone were to make an action figure from him, it could be done with a simple life cast.

'What ho,' I said genially, 'awfully pleasant to be invited and all that,' and then 'oo-er' as I recognised upon the shoulders of a human gorilla a screwed-up face that seemed to sing a song of silent Wooster strangulation.

'What ho, Spode.'

'Don't "what ho" me, Wooster. Return the painting that I bought for Mr Bassett or I'll have your lungs out.'

'Now, steady on, Spode,' I said with a sense of courage and fortitude that the recently wronged are apt to display, 'I don't owe you anything, and I need hardly point out that without the Wooster trademark disposition of spirit you would right now be steaming across the Bay of Biscay for a life of garlic-centric hardship to the strains of Maurice Chevalier.'

'You cheated, sir,' roared Spode, the veins standing out in his forehead. I had the distinct impression that when mankind was shuffling down from the trees to move ever forward, Old Spode just never got the memo.

'I think,' I said with considerable aplomb, 'that you were *counter-cheated* by person or persons unknown. I did nothing at all except saunter up after being detained by your neckless compatriots who were, I might add, of the lowest quality. I've seen better goose-stepping from a goose.'

At this Spode went very red indeed and I thought him likely to give a creditable impersonation of Mount Etna, but thankfully for the chintz wallpaper and floral-patterned Axminster, he did not. It was at this point in the proceedings that I noted a familiar painting displayed upon an easel near the bookcase, and recognised the painting instantly.

'Ah,' I said in the manner of an art expert, 'Van Clunk's *Madonna of the Shapely Shoulders*.'

'The *original*,' said Sir Watkyn, upon which statement Spode nodded his head like a toy dog that had made its home on the parcel shelf of a heavy Austin.

'How do you know this for sure, Sir Watkyn?' I asked in a breezy non-confrontational manner.

He did not answer, and instead said, 'You have brought your *Madonna*, Wooster?'

'I have.'

'Good. I expect the third copy to arrive quite soon and then no less a luminary than Prof. Lucius Pim of the Royal Arts Academy of Arts will cast his expert eye upon all three and give his stamp of approval. Let the best *Shoulders* win, eh?'

He then declared the meeting over, and that he would see me at dinner before the official authentication. Spode, sorely without a crowd, armband or Wagnerian marching band to support him, left the room also.

THREE

'Most enlightening, sir,' said Jeeves when I appraised him of the situation a few minutes later, outside at the stables. He had his jacket off for which he had apologised, and was conducting some maintenance on the car's inner gubbins, a series of cogs and wheels and oily parts that was likely indistinguishable from the contents of Gussie Fink-Nottle's head.

'Was Lucius Pim present during this conversation?' asked Jeeves.

'Well, no, Jeeves. He aims to arrive this evening. What's the plan of action? With Pim in Watkyn's pocket, he could authenticate a water stain on the ceiling as the One True Van Clunk.'

'As chance would have it, sir, I was conversing with Alan the footman who was previously acquainted with the Professor's maid Daisy, and she said that Lucius Pim has a weakness for the turf and currently owes an unsavoury character in White City named Roger 'the Horse' Bomperini a considerable sum. I understand that Professor Pim and Sir Watkyn aim to split the proceeds of the sale post authentication, something that would allow Professor Pim to repay a large chunk of monies owed, and while not completely in the clear, he would at least have breathing space.'

'I don't know this Roger "the Horse" Bomperini fellow, Jeeves.'

'You move in very different circles, sir. But I have it on good authority that *not* repaying Mr Bomperini may result in a future career as a tunnel support in the Northern Line extension. It was a fate that it is thought to have befallen "Stumpy" Fairweather who also had a weakness for ponies of a losing disposition.'

'I remember Stumpy well. What a come-down. He did *so* hate to travel any further north than Tufnell Park.'

'So I believe, sir.'

Jeeves finished what he was doing, pressed the starter to ensure the car was fully functioning and then donned his jacket. As he straightened his cuffs, the Wooster ear twitched to a friendly 'toot-toot' and I beheld the pale blue Bugatti that belonged to Roberta Wickham.

It was always fun to see Bobbie as she was a bright and amusing girl to whom the word 'bouncy' might have been coined, but this was never without careful planning and I glanced at Jeeves nervously. Usually the model of quiet dignity, Jeeves cast all propriety to the four winds when he encountered Watson, Bobbie Wickham's redoubtable gentlewoman's gentlewoman.

Personally I've had no issue with the old girl myself, and indeed, many people have commented upon how Watson is as crucial to Bobbie's well-being as Jeeves is to mine. But for reasons soon revealed, Watson and Jeeves shared a deep enmity that equalled the most intractable Corsican vendetta.

'Bertie!' yelled Bobbie as they drew up alongside. 'You old horse-face. How the devil have you been?'

I have to admit that Bobbie Wickham was about the closest to a Frightfully Splendid Chap that the female of the species was ever likely to see whelped. Full of sparkle and vim and fond of the highest high jinks. We'd known each other for yonks and had indeed once been engaged, but Jeeves had warned me off her, partly on account of her flaming auburn hair which he thought a dangerous and literal red flag, but chiefly, I have long suspected, because any union would place him far closer to Mrs Watson than he might have liked.

'How have I been?' I said. 'Up and down, old salt. Fourteen hours ago I was crowned Champion at the Drones Games Night, and this morning I'm trying to shore up Uncle Tom's finances armed with nothing but an aged sheet of canvas and a pot of ideas marked "empty".'

'I heard about the panto horse,' said Bobbie in admiration. 'What a lark. Millicent Cummings and I dressed as a llama once in the public gallery at the House of Commons for a bet.'

'Did you win?'

'Well, yes, obviously, you big potato. Oh dear. Bertie, look there.'

I swivelled the old swede to regard an unhappy spectacle: Watson and Jeeves were standing a couple of feet apart, hands resolutely on hips and each regarding the other with a glaring single eye that could only have looked more like a couple of organ stops if they'd had 'Vox Humana' written upon them.

'Gosh,' I said, 'do you think it will be the Rowcester Abbey incident all over again?'

This, alert reader, might be worth further explanation. If a valet's duty is to be there and not there at the same time, and a lady's maid's is to be similarly attendant and absent, then a quiet yet firm exchange of views while in the presence of employers with guests represents a monumental professional *faux pas* of the very worst sort, and a repetition of which was the chief reason why Bobbie and I ensure we always meet *sans* servant.

I will spare you the details, but Watson and Jeeves firmly locked antlers in the withdrawing room that night, and were quite naturally both mortified by the incident during the cool-down afterwards. Jeeves fully expected to be drummed out of the profession by the ceremonial snipping-off of buttons and Watson expected to have to hand in her hatpin and become a boarding house owner in Margate, as was the custom. That we retained both of them was due to some smart moves by Bobbie and me, where we explained it all away as an ill-advised rehearsal of the Junior Ganymede's Christmas Panto for the benefit of chambermaids who had fallen into distressing circumstances, a charity most earnestly and often anonymously supported by young men of the aristocracy.

But back to the present. It was a very good job indeed that we were all outside the stable block and any spectacle that Watson and Jeeves's meeting might precipitate would be witnessed only by Bobbie and me, a lazy-looking butcher's boy and a tabby cat with one ear.

'So,' said Watson in a cool voice, 'Mr Jeeves. Still quite stout, I see.'

'Mrs Watson,' intoned Jeeves in reply, 'how delightful. Tell me: if you are here, who is currently guarding the entrance to the underworld?'

'Hm,' she scoffed in reply, her tone of voice still of the politest, 'unoriginal as always. How does one press trousers with cloven hooves, by the way?'

Jeeves pursed his lips.

'Is that a question coming from a woman who

when junior housekeeper neglected sufficiently to rotate the linen, a singular act of incompetence that led to uneven wear upon the serviettes?'

'Clearly you listen only to ill-wagged tongues,' she answered, 'but I understand that a junior footman with a close resemblance to yourself closed the door without thinking in the face of the Prince of Wales.'

'A simple error blamed on the inexperience of youth,' replied Jeeves coolly, 'unlike a certain lady's maid who I understand was held at Holloway in connection with a missing necklace?'

Watson's eyes narrowed.

'Only to be released without charge, Mr Jeeves,' she said, still in an even tone but with an angry twitch of her eyelid, 'and exonerated fully. Which valet was it who stole the Earl of Basingstoke's second-best Hispano-Suiza in order to visit a showgirl in London?'

'It was his night off and the vehicle in question was in need of a service,' replied Jeeves, who then stared at Watson with the sort of look a millionaire reserves for his most dissolute grandchild.

'Mrs Watson,' he said with a polite bow, 'I suggest we leave off before my tongue is loosened into regretful impudence and makes reference to the story surrounding the Duke of Schleswig-Holstein's eldest daughter and a blacksmith.'

'Below-stairs tittle-tattle,' said Watson, 'nothing more. Quite unlike the incident involving ... *the langoustines.*'

There was a sudden deathly silence and I saw the minutest crack in Jeeves's usually indefatigable bearing.

'Is that the time?' said Watson, seizing on the sudden pause in the conversation to declare a *de facto* game, set and match. 'Good day, Mr Wooster, good day, Mr Jeeves. Will you have Mr Butterfield instruct William to bring Miss Wickham's luggage to her room? Miss Roberta, may I be dismissed?'

'Of course,' said Bobbie, and Watson bobbed politely to us all and departed.

'I too should wish to be dismissed, sir,' said Jeeves, 'back to London to await your presence. I will call a cab from the gatehouse.'

'No can do,' I told him. 'With Uncle Tom's finances up the river *sans* paddle, I need you here.'

'Very good, sir.'

And he bowed politely and was gone.

'Goodness,' said Bobbie. 'They *hate* one another. And to imagine it was once all tea dances, eggs and gammon at the Empire café and an engagement.'

'Yes, indeed,' I replied, 'but enough of them for now: what fair breeze brings your radiant disposition into Bertram's orbit? I thought you had tied the knot with Dan "Swoony" Palomino and were currently popping out Swoony Bobbinettes and making curtains and cakes and running up a Dickens & Jones charge account equal to the defence budget of Bolivia?'

Swoony, as his nickname suggests, was a ludicrously good-looking chap with a blond mane a lion would be proud of and a lantern jaw that, if nailed to the front of the *Titanic*, would have seen the ship safely reach port. Human catnip to the female of the species in fact, and marred in character only by the fact that he knew it.

'Did you not hear?' she said, her large soup-dish eyes brimming with tears. 'My dear betrothed Danny was part of the British Orinoco expedition and was eaten by a crocodile while on assignment – the only part of him they found was an Empire-brand sock suspender.'

'I'm so very sorry for your loss, old thing.'

'You are so very, very kind, Bertie dear – but then you always were. Do you remember when we first met at that house party in Deverill, when we were playing sardines?'

I remembered, of course, but at moments like this when a potentially loaded question comes sailing over from the female side of the fence it's always wise to sound a little foggy. We'd been eight years old and paired up inside a cupboard in the east wing and made the sort of small talk eight-year-olds generally make, something I recall about Perseus and Andromeda.

'I do seem to recall something about that,' I said vaguely, although truth to tell the thrill of her presence in the close of the cupboard was a recollection not easily unrecollected.

'You *must* remember, Bertie. We kissed an innocent kiss of childhood, my first – and I expect yours too?'

'Not so,' I said with a soft reminiscing sort of air about my voice and manner. 'Sophie was the first in line for Bertie to plant the smacker. Her lips were hot and sticky and tasted of chocolate drops, but the romance was short-lived: she caught rabies while ratting in the stable block the following year and had to be put down.'

Bobbie giggled her trademark giggle of wind chimes mixed with a welcome third glass of Pimm's, and punched me playfully on the arm.

'The course of romance never runs smooth, Bertie. But with dear Swoony now missing presumed digested in the Cameroons, I am free to marry and I think you and I would be a perfect match – unless you are engaged to Madeline Bassett, of course?'

I had to think for a moment. I'd discussed it earlier with Jeeves but couldn't for the life of me remember which side of the net the ball had fallen.

'Not as far as I know,' I replied, playing it safe. 'Wait a minute – how could Swoony be eaten in the Cameroons? The Orinoco's in Venezuela. Or was, the last I looked.'

'Easily explained,' she said. 'The Orinoco was so successful in Venezuela they opened another in Africa. Oh Bertie, could you love a woman like me?'

Her directness caught me a little off guard and I usually fall into a signature wobble when confronted with these matters.

'Oh, well, gosh – on a purely technical basis, I suppose – um – that is not beyond the realms of possibility, as I did once or twice before as you know, but whether I would fancy sharing some actual wedding cake—'

'That's all agreed then,' she said. 'Oh Bertie, what a joy: Mr and Mrs Wooster. We'll have three children, one of each. I've already prepared the banns. We can be married on Tuesday.'

I was still reeling from the news.

'Prepared the banns without me? How did you manage that?'

'Watson pretended to be you. She just said "Gosh" and "Frightfully good" and "Spiffing, d'you know, what?" and all that sort of stuff.'

'Is that how I talk?'

'Mostly, yes.'

'But how could she fool the registrar into thinking she was me?' I protested. 'Watson's a woman – and, well, Jamaican.'

'*And* a mistress of disguise. I'll have you know that to get my old school chum Flossie Baumgarten out of her less-than-desirable engagement with that odious fathead Archie McFarlane, Watson disguised herself as Stanley Baldwin, even so far as attending a meeting of the Board of Trade with no one the wiser. Don't fuss so, Bertie. I'll have my person call your person and arrange our relatives to meet and bless the union before we hoof it up the aisle.'

'Now listen here, Bobbie,' I said using my serious voice, 'I know you're an absolute topper of a girl and we go back awhile and you have an eighteen-carat sense of fun and can out-chap the most chappiest of chaps, but this is all frightfully sudden. Besides, I shall have to consult with Jeeves.'

'Jeeves?'

'Yes, Jeeves. It's a bally rotten state of affairs, but whenever I make a decision without him life tends to go a little squishy round the edges.'

'As you wish,' she said in an offhand 'that-won't-make-the-slightest-bit-of-difference' sort of manner that set the Wooster alarm bells jangling.

'Oh,' I said. 'Jolly good. By the way,' I added, 'what are you doing here at Totleigh Towers anyway?'

'That's easily explained,' she said brightly. 'Have you ever heard of a painter named Van Clunk?'

'I might have done.'

'Well, strictly between you and me, Swoony left me one thing and one thing only: the probably original and not at all fake *Madonna of the Shapely Shoulders*.'

'Let me guess,' I ventured. 'You've been invited up here by Sir Watkyn to have Professor Pim of the Royal Arts Academy of Arts cast his expert eye upon it?'

'Precisely so,' she said. 'However did you know?'

'Oh, just a wild stab in the dark. Well, toodle-oo for now.'

FOUR

'And that's about the tune of it, Jeeves,' I said, having relayed everything that had just transpired.

'Miss Wickham seems quite urgently to require a husband, sir.'

'Yes, I thought so too. Positively champing at the bit. Why ever do you think that might be?'

'Several possible scenarios spring to mind, sir, all of which indicate that a young lady in urgent need of a marriage is a young lady to whom "no" would not be an acceptable answer, and since Mrs Watson is a manipulator of the utmost talent, we must be on our guard. Might I suggest we adopt Emergency Protocol Delta where you do *absolutely nothing at all* without first consulting me?'

Emergency Protocol Delta was rarely invoked. Rarely even spoken about, in fact.

'You think me in danger, Jeeves?'

'I do not disapprove of marriage, sir. Indeed, it is an honourable estate that has brought much happiness to many. But I strongly feel it should be the union of two hearts beating as one, if you understand what I mean.'

'Very poetically put, Jeeves.'

'Thank you, sir. I have placed my resignation letter on the bureau and will work to the end of the week.'

'I must be getting hard of hearing, Jeeves, I thought you just said you were resigning.'

'I am, sir. To run a boarding house in Margate. I am not a salt-water fisherman by choice but can see myself adapting to circumstance. I will of course ensure a suitable replacement is found who can understand and complement your eccentricities.'

'Never mind all that, Jeeves. Resign? What's the meaning of this? Come on, out with it and spare nothing.'

Jeeves looked at me for a moment and his eyebrow quivered.

'While you were talking to Miss Wickham, sir, I was approached in the upstairs corridor by Mrs Watson who explained in no uncertain terms that yourself and Miss Roberta should be married, and since I had your ear and your confidence, I should support the union to the best of my ability.'

'You gave her the big fat no, I take it?'

'Indeed, sir. I replied that this was a matter entirely for you and Miss Roberta alone, and knowing that inducements of a monetary value would simply be insulting she threatened to reveal to the world the incident with . . . *the langoustines.*'

'The langoustines, Jeeves? Just how bad can that be?'

'You will recall the Hon. Galahad Threepwood's memoirs that Sir Gregory Parsloe-Parsloe attempted to spike on account of an incident involving prawns?'

'I had a gander at the manuscript. *Most* shocking. What of it?'

'A similar incident, sir – only bigger and with more snap.'

My eyes popped.

'Good God, man, what made you do it?'

'A youthful indiscretion, sir, that I thought long forgotten. I told Mrs Watson I would never induce my master to undertake anything against his will, so I told her she must do what she must do – but not reveal the secret for a week until I am away from your employ and unable to cause any embarrassment.'

'But this is frightful, Jeeves.'

'Not so, sir. You are still single, Mrs Watson has not yet triumphed, the Van Clunk is still unattributed, the incident with the langoustines is still secret, the weekend is long and if all else fails, the Totleigh Arms stocks a fifteen-per-cent proof real ale named "Get Thee Behind me Satan" which I understand to be a powerful anaesthetic.'

'But wait,' I said, 'you must have a plan, Jeeves?'

'Not yet, sir.'

'Well, best get the old noggin into overdrive, Jeeves. Bobbie told me she too has a *Madonna of the Shapely Shoulders* to drop into the mix.'

'Really? That does complicate matters, sir.'

At that moment there was a polite knock and the junior footman put his head round the door.

'Good evening, Mr Wooster and pardon the interruption, but may I speak to Mr Jeeves?'

'Go right ahead, William.'

'Thank you, sir. Begging your pardon, Mr Jeeves, but Mr Butterfield was wanting advice on the correct wine to be served with the beef this evening. Sir Watkyn generally prefers a Château Climens but when decanted just now it was found to be corked.'

'I understand the issue, William. Do you have any Château Latour 1915?'

'No, sir.'

'Lafitte '08?'

'No, sir.'

'Then I had better come down. Will you excuse me, sir?'

'Indeed I shall, Jeeves. The tactical choice of the grape takes precedence.'

So with Jeeves gone I took to pottering around the room, and even cocked another snook at the Van Clunk. I was just musing upon the astonishing shapeliness of the shoulders when there was another knock at the door. This time it was the housekeeper, a Mrs Stanhope.

'Pardon me for the intrusion, Mr Wooster, but Miss Wickham was wondering if you would go and see her on a matter regarding a daddy-long-legs that is fluttering against the pane? I would do it myself but I have an urgent meeting with the pantry staff. Her room is the third on the right. You can go straight in.'

'I've been removing *Nephrotoma appendiculata* from ladies' chambers since I was in short trousers,' I said with the gallantry of Hector. 'I shall go there directly.'

But Mrs Stanhope had been mistaken. There was no daddy-long-legs, and ten minutes later Jeeves found me back in my bedroom, sitting quietly upon a chair.

'Sir?' he intoned. 'You look somewhat... shocked.'

'I am, Jeeves. The thing is, I was sent on a heroic daddy-long-legs-removing mission, opened Bobbie's door as Hector might and there was Bobbie, completely in the buff, readying herself for her bath. What's more, Jeeves old man, I saw ... everything.'

'Everything, sir?'

'*Everything.*'

'This is most disconcerting, sir, and of the utmost seriousness: now that you have seen everything then by the rules of honour marriage is generally a given.'

'Even if by accident or deceit, Jeeves? Miss Stanhope must have been put up to it by that dratted Watson.'

'And the trip to the wine cellar, sir, to get me out of the way. Mrs Watson must have paid them both off, a trick that to my very great regret I did not divine. The conceit to which you fell prey is a desperate plan when all else has failed and in ladies' circles is known as "the Gygian Gambit".'

'I've never heard of it.'

'It is a secret well guarded, sir, based on the legend of Gyges of the Anatolian kingdom of Lydia, who chanced to see the Queen in an unrobed state, and she saw him and sent for him the following day and spake thus: "Either you must submit to death for gazing on that which you should not or else kill my husband and become King in his place."'

'What did this Gyges fellow do?'

'He killed the King, sir, married the Queen and became ruler of Lydia for thirty-eight years.'

'But hold on a sec, Jeeves. Swoony's long digested and there's no kingdom anywhere in sight.'

'The principle remains the same, sir. You did see *everything*?'

'Everything, Jeeves. And I can understand how Gyges felt. Sort of honour bound, really – although I'd not really stoop to the whole murder thing. Do you see a way out of this jam, Jeeves? Seems a little ticklish to me.'

'I have to admit that I am currently unable to think of a plan, sir.'

'Oh my goodness, gosh,' I said, suddenly realising what had happened. 'Jeeves, you've just been ... *out-Jeeved*.'

'I was thinking the same myself, sir.'

'What a turn-up. You must despise that Watson woman beyond loathing.'

'On the contrary, sir. Her skilled manipulation of events brings into my chest nothing less than a feeling of deep admiration. The fisherman does not treat the champion pike that eludes him with anything less than complete respect. Mrs Watson is a woman of formidable skill and intellect, and it was for this very reason that I once asked her to marry me. Shall I put out your things for dinner?'

There are times in the life of a Wooster when he has to stand up and take command, and that moment was now.

'No, Jeeves. If you're starting to use fish metaphors then the game's up. Come along, we're going to have words.'

'Do you think that's wise, sir? It might make matters worse.'

'How could they possibly get any worse, Jeeves?

Bobbie Wickham – usually a fair-minded lass – tempered to the extremity of the Gyges Gambit for reasons unknown, and Bertram here about to lose his valet to some hooks and mackerel in Margate when I know for a fact you're a trout and fly man. *Unthinkable*. I'm going to have to channel the inner Wyatt Earp and sort this out once and for all, O.K. Corral style. Only with no guns, cowboys, Morgans or a corral.'

'That leaves only the O.K. remaining, sir.'

'Precisely.'

FIVE

We found Bobbie and Watson in the upstairs hall, thankfully alone. We hailed them politely and after Jeeves had given a respectful nod to Watson – which I was gratified to see returned – we got down to business.

'Listen here, you two, gloves off and all above board and all that, but we're going to have to talk terms. This isn't an unconditional surrender, it's a . . . what is it, Jeeves?'

'An armistice, sir?'

'Exactly so.'

'Bertie,' said Bobbie. 'If I may? I'm so sorry for what we planned. It preyed upon your good and honourable nature, and I would not have done so without a pressing reason. But I do love you, ever since that silly game of sardines, the idle childish banter about Andromeda and Perseus and of course, that kiss. And all those times we've met since, I always felt that you and I were just about perfect for one another – the fruit in each other's Pimm's, the crackling log fire in each other's winters, the strawberries in each other's Wimbledon.'

She spoke in such a sincere manner that I felt some of the Earpness falling right out of me, but with the smell of Margate sands now sitting heavy up the hooter, I was not going to give an inch until I had made my case.

'That's as maybe,' I said, 'but an armistice is not without discussion, and here lie my terms: you, Bobbie, are a rum old fish and a friend most obviously in need. Woosters are not the sort to shirk duty when it calls, no matter what the circumstance, so I am prepared to make you *my* rum old fish so long as the langoustine issue is stricken from the record.'

'Watson?' said Bobbie.

'It shall never be spoken of again and the collected affidavits burned,' said Watson with a bow.

'Good. Second point: I shall keep Jeeves so long as he wishes to remain in my employ. And what say you, Mrs Watson, to that?'

Watson and Jeeves stared at one another, and something passed between them. Servants have a silent language that can convey great meaning across a crowded room. Something as subtle as a lifted eyebrow might mean: 'Mr Mulliner's wine glass needs refilling,' and a rub of the ear could be translated as: 'Ronnie Fish has probably had a skinful and needs to be removed lest he sparks a diplomatic incident.'

And that silent language passed between them now as Bobbie and I waited for several moments, breaths bated in unison.

'I'm sure,' said Mrs Watson slowly, 'we can move towards a workable solution so long as Miss Roberta's needs are met.'

'Jeeves?' said I.

'As Mrs Watson suggests, sir. A negotiated cessation of hostilities might bring forth a creditable merging of minds that would keep both your and Miss Roberta's friends out of trouble for the foreseeable future.'

And Mrs Watson nodded again, and I knew then that Margate was firmly off the table. There was little to do aside from officially propose to Bobbie who hugged me and kissed me happily on the neck while Watson and Jeeves offered their heartiest congratulations.

'Well,' I said, quite chipper at the way things had turned out, 'there it is then.'

'Not quite, sir,' said Jeeves after his trademark polite cough. 'There is still the matter of the Van Clunk. Without your version suitably authenticated by Professor Pim, your Aunt Dahlia and Uncle Tom may fall into a level of financial uncertainty incompatible with their social station.'

'By the deuce,' I said, 'I'd forgotten all about the *Madonna of the Shapely Shoulders*. Any ideas?'

Mrs Watson looked at Bobbie who nodded her agreement.

'While briefly detained in Holloway over that misunderstanding regarding the necklace,' said Watson, 'I made the acquaintance of a petty criminal by the name of Bessie Armstrong. I referred a lawyer friend to her plight, she was released without charge and I have retained her friendship to this day.'

'A charming tale of a fallen woman made good,' I said, 'but I am waiting for the epilogue?'

'Indeed, Mr Wooster. Bessie owes me a favour, and is usefully married to a gentleman who goes by the epithet Roger 'the Horse' Bomperini, he of the Northern Line Tunnel Support fame, and to whom Professor Pim owes a considerable amount of money. A word from me to Bessie and the debt is cancelled, and it was this leverage that was to have him authenticate Miss Roberta's painting as the one true Clunk.'

I looked at Jeeves, and Jeeves looked at me, then at Mrs Watson, and then I looked at Bobbie, and Bobbie looked at Mrs Watson and said, 'I think we know what must be done, Watson.'

Mrs Watson bowed and said, 'Given the positive outcome of this afternoon and my very great respect for Mr and Mrs Travers, I will happily instruct Professor Pim to authenticate Mr Wooster's painting in place of Miss Roberta's.'

And that's the end of the story, really. There was quite a lot more about Sir Watkyn's wailing and gnashing of teeth when Prof. Pim spoke the speak, and a paragraph or two about Spode's humiliation later that evening, but for another time, says I. Bobbie and I drove back to London Sunday morning in her Bugatti once I'd telegrammed Aunt Dahlia with the good news. Watson and Jeeves drove behind us in the two-seater, and we suggested they took lunch together in the Horse and Hounds at Beaconsfield, a suggestion they took up, and from indications, a very positive meeting it was too.

'Bobbie, old fruit,' I said as we motored into London on the Great West Road, 'may I ask you a question?'

'Anything, Bertie dear.'

'Was Swoony actually eaten by a crocodile?'

I could feel her eyes bore into me, and she laid a dainty hand on mine.

'Swoony,' she said slowly, 'despite appearances, was no gentleman and behaved poorly. There were several . . . regrettable incidents. Watson made a telephone call and he was relocated to an engineering position in the Northern Line extension.'

I swilled this around in the noggin for a few moments.

'Bobbie dearest,' I said at last, 'was it a ... permanent position?'

'It was.'

She laid her head on mine and squeezed my arm affectionately, and with, I think, a touch of melancholy. We never spoke of the matter again.

Jeeves by a Nose!

Ian Moore

I've always admired these writer chaps who, rather than let the reader get remotely comfortable, or focus the old eyes, set off at a dramatic lick – leaving said reader gasping, clinging on to the narrative for dear life, fingernails digging into the vellum, as it were. I'm sure you recognise the tactic: paragraph one, smoking gun, paragraph two, smoky-voiced *femme fatale* and barely any first-name terms to be had as yet. Good on them, I say. The calendar of a chap is wont to fill up like an overheated car radiator when lunches, cocktails and seasons shoulder up and shove their way through the door. One can't hang about, even when snatching a few minutes with the latest bestseller.

Other scribes set the drama bar high early on and get the mouth watering with one of those 'name change' wheezes. You've seen the sort, names changed to protect the innocent, when in fact few would have heard of the innocent anyway, names changed or not. The temptation lying more in the intrigue than in the reality. When venturing forth on one of these missives in the adventures of Bertram, I would normally favour the former stratagem: bait you and land you, so to speak. But the truth is that this shameful episode began in a fog, ventured into a mist and emerged in something of a vapour. A cliffhanger opening, it does not possess. It begins a little on the slow side — a touch of lollygaggery in the air, even. But as for names, I pull no punches. Let it never be said that we Woosters don't face down our enemies and smite them with the sword of justice, especially when — to put it bluntly — there's no one on board remotely deserving of the cloak of anonymity. Publish and be damned, I think the saying goes — just deserts and so on.

What I mean to say is, should a character emerge at some dramatic point in the piece and shoulder the name of (for example) Aunt Agatha, you can be bally sure I mean said aunt, and not Vlad the Impaler. A striking similarity in terms of bloodlust and barbaric tendencies there may be, but be sure I mean Lady Worplesdon, Agatha Gregson, *née* Wooster. The same goes for Bingo Little, a veritable typhoon of fatheadedness, leaving upturned trees of catastrophe in his wake where once was calm, and whose peerless ability to act the chump I blame for the whole sorry incident. There you have it: on this occasion, Bertram will take no prisoners.

It was with said Little that I promenaded through the dewy morning streets of Paris towards the Gare du Nord where we were to meet Jeeves, my manservant. Jeeves had stayed behind in London for the annual Junior Ganymede Club dinner, and we were to welcome him continent-side from the boat train. Bingo and I had biffed off early to *la belle France* accompanying Mrs Bingo – alias Rosie M. Banks, the novelist of such overwrought tomes as *Below Stairs, High in Our Hearts* and *Love, Is It Too Great a Distance?* – as she made a promotional tour of the local *bibliothèques*, or whatever they're called. How she was able to find said *bibliothèques* was something of a mystery to me, when even to this worldly *boulevardier* all the boulevards looked pretty much the same. I'm all for renovation and a little modernity, but the chap Haussmann – who had redesigned the city, according to Jeeves – had only the one idea in his mind about architecture and had run amok. Rues Rivoli and La Fayette could have been twins, the Champs-Élysées and Place du Carrousel separated at birth. All well and good and all that – just a bit one-eyed, like having dozens of the same portrait in the one gallery. I can look at the *Mona Lisa* all day if that's the requirement, but I do like a change of gear every now and then.

Relieved of our *bibliothèque* duties, we, that is Bingo and I, were struggling not only with the earliness of the hour – I fancy I heard a rather salty lark beg us to keep a lid on it – but also the backlash of an evening spent possibly too long at Harry's New York Bar. Harry's, having enjoyed a fine run of form in the production of cocktails, were keen to have their latest collection given the once-over by experts and we just happened to be available for work. And work us they did. To the bone. Harry, it seemed, has eschewed a previously well-earned reputation for cocktail quality and gone h. for l. in pursuit of quantity in its stead. Flavour and finesse had gone decidedly south for the winter and after a night's honest toil, both Bingo and I approached the new morrow, our heads replete with quarrelsome marching bands and mouths drier than algebraic theory. Of course cocktails were invented to cover the scandalous, tonsil-curling taste of illegal moonshine during the dark days of prohibition, but if these recent samples were what legality brought to the table, then I personally would welcome a return to the heady days of Coffin Varnish and Tarantula

Juice with open arms. In short, we were in need of soothing breakfast tea and lots of it. Now, I don't know if you've ever searched for a pot of tea among the early-morning boulevards of Paris; coffee there is by the gallon, but hunting down a cup of tea is, I suspect, a close cousin to water divination across the Sahara. The raw materials are there: there is tea, as such; there is milk; there are silver teapots; and no doubt someone of iron will and determination could even rustle up a cosy or two. It's finding all of these elements in the same place and in the hands of someone who knows the A to Z of production that's the thing, and the natives don't take too kindly to being told of the specifics of what any true-blooded Englishman is born with in the very marrow.

'*Thé?*' one of the apron-clad blisters demanded, as if I'd just asked permission to walk his sister around the Tuileries.

'*Oui, garçon,*' I replied with some haught, this being our fourth attempt. '*Thé.*' I knew immediately, by the necessary pronunciation, that what would emerge would be a fay, weak attempt at a morning cuppa, one that has seen the milk pass by, waving from a gilded carriage, but who has singularly failed to stop for any length of time and mingle. I wasn't wrong, and Bingo, taking it particularly hard, refused to cough up the coinage and sauntered off into the distance quivering at the outrage – leaving yours truly to negotiate with an irate waiter not exactly dripping in bonhomie. Eventually, the matter settled to mutual satisfaction, I took my leave, thinking, not for the first time, that had Napoleon taken a few more Parisian waiters to Waterloo, defeat might have been averted.

Jeeves then, was a sight for sore eyes. I don't want anyone to be of the opinion that we Woosters aren't about the most independent and self-contained of men – and there are scurrilous rumours floating about the salons of London that I, in particular, have the gait of a motherless fawn without his presence – but dash it all, the man breeds confidence. Add to which forty-eight hours in the presence of double Bingos leads one to seek solace where one can find it. Well, Jeeves ladles out consolation like hearty soup, and, what with my fragile physical state, I was glad to see the man.

'What ho, Jeeves!' I breezed, as well as I could muster, while Bingo made a noise like a hippopotamus who's taken on too much fluid.

'Good morning, sir. Good morning, Mr Little.' The man was oddly reticent and displaying a look that could only be described as askance. And not askance in a good way, if there is a good side to askance – quite the opposite, in fact. Frosty was the word. 'Have you developed partial sightedness, sir?' was his next utterance, which rendered me briefly baffled.

'Ah, I see what you mean, Jeeves,' I replied, removing a pair of sunglasses that I had quite forgotten I was wearing. 'Rather natty, don't you think?'

'They are perhaps tolerable in a resort, sir, but are wont to give the impression of shiftiness in a more urban setting.'

It was clear that a combination of overnight sea and rail travel had done nothing to dampen the man's crusade as to what he deemed right and proper, and though physically on the 'handle with care' side of things, I was in no mood to let it go. 'Oh, tosh and fie, Jeeves,' I offered with an indignant tone. 'These are Humboldt sunglasses, Jeeves, the last word in Hollywood chic, I'll have you know. They offer a conciliatory balm to one's beleaguered retinas.'

'Are your retinas beleaguered, sir?'

I admitted that they were indeed feeling the strain somewhat, and he produced a pewter hip flask and offered it to me.

'Jeeves,' I stammered, the mouth juices beginning to bubble, 'is that . . . ?'

'I took the precaution, sir . . .'

Jeeves held the specific ingredients of his world-beating restorative close to his chest, not inclined to revelation of any kind. Whatever the recipe, however, it proved, as always, just the ticket, and after a tumbler each of the liquid of the gods, we felt refreshed and ready to attack the day.

'I take it you passed a lively evening, sir?' he asked, now that both Bingo and I were capable of coherent interaction.

'Harry's New York Bar, Jeeves,' I answered, spritely. 'No doubt you've heard of it.'

'Indeed, sir. A popular, some say infamous, meeting place for visiting Americans of a creative bent.'

'Yes, I heard that too, though the place was light on Americans last night, Jeeves, and, I'm sad to report, quality in general. Not the finest hour in the world of cocktails or population.'

'No, sir?'

'No, Jeeves. Who was that scourge who wouldn't let you alone last night, Bingo, what was his name?'

'Sartre,' was my companion's reply, visibly re-approaching full fitness.

'That's right, Sartre. Very full of himself.'

'That would likely be Jean-Paul Sartre, sir.'

I stopped in my tracks. 'Do you know *everyone*, Jeeves?'

'I couldn't say, sir, but Monsieur Sartre recently published an essay entitled "*Transcendence de l'Ego*". It has led to much discussion.'

'Has it indeed? Not in my circles, Jeeves. What's the thrust?'

'It is a philosophical and phenomenological work, sir, dealing in the main with the idea of consciousness as a physical object and the intuitive apprehension of others.'

There was a brief moment when I thought about snatching back the controversial eyewear, such was the swift descent of a dense pea-souper on the old brain. 'Well, I couldn't offer comment, Jeeves,' I replied, attempting to head the conversation off at the pass. 'Though it seemed the blister certainly had an intuitive apprehension about paying for his own drinks.'

I will admit to briefly basking in these *bons mots* – I fancy I even saw a flicker of appreciation in Jeeves's own orbs – but my self-congratulation was tragically short-lived.

'BERTIE!'

Over the centuries the city of Paris has seen its fair share of bombardment, societal earthquakes and thunderous brouhaha, but an Aunt Agatha bellowing across the concourse of one of its main transport hubs was up there with the storming of the Bastille. Her voice reverberated off the ceiling-high iron girders, echoing from each of them as if there were not just one Aunt Agatha in the singular, but a whole battalion of Aunt Agathas. People scurried down below to the *Métro* for safety, newspaper sellers shed their wares and fled, croissants collapsed in fear. This ear-shattering bray, as though the Loch Ness Monster herself had woken late, and decided to tell the world that she had missed an important *rendezvous*, was inevitably backed by the solid, menacing physical embodiment of aforementioned aunt, and it was clear that it heralded no good for man or beast. There she stood, a look on her face that would have knocked Primo Carnera to the canvas and exactly the sort of merciless demeanour that catapulted Al Capone to the apex of the underworld. 'And what, pray, are you doing here?' she roared.

My usual reply when this threshing machine of a relative attempted communication was to pass word that I was out of town, and therefore unavailable. Yet here I was, out of town and very much available, being in the flesh, just inches from the woman. Nor, and this was definitely out of the question, could I respond with the truth that Bingo, Jeeves and I were on our way to the west of the metropolis, specifically Longchamp racecourse, to fulfil a long-standing appointment with the continent's richest, pre-eminent horse race, the Prix de l'Arc de Triomphe.

Bingo wasn't much use either. Attempting to use me as a shield from the glare of savage family, he hid to my rear.

'And who is that skulking behind you?' She ignored Jeeves entirely, deeming him of insufficient importance to warrant attention. 'I know you!' she barked at young Bingo who visibly wilted. 'You once tutored my son.'

She was correct on that score; Bingo had indeed once tutored her son, my cousin Thos, who, though still green, had readily accepted the inheritance of familial personality plague and was my aunt's willing accessory after the fact in all things bolshie and underhand. I was about to administer some sort of formal reintroduction between the two when once again speech was denied me. 'I suppose I should be pleased, Bertie. Finally you are in the company of someone with some level of education. Presumably — Mr Little, is it? — is giving you a tour of the museums of Paris. It is too late to save you, nephew, but I am encouraged that you are at last trying.'

'I say!' I exclaimed, wounded.

'Mr Little, I wish you to take my son Thomas with you on this tour.' Cousin Thos emerged sheepishly, or at least as sheepishly as a hyena can emerge, from behind his mother's skirts. 'I have business to attend to today and it will be easier if he is with you.'

'But . . .' This time it was Bingo who made a half-hearted attempt at pushing back the invasion, a futile if noble gesture.

'I particularly want him to see the Louvre. Now, I am already running somewhat behind schedule so be so good as to hail us a taxi-cab. I can escort you part-way to the museum.'

With that Bingo was marched unto distant battles, leaving Jeeves and myself looking with horror as the pestilence Thos grimaced in our direction. The day looked lost – not just for Bingo, who would now register as an absentee from the continental society event of the year, but Paris itself should also have been quaking at the knees. Take Thos anywhere near a museum of the standing of the Louvre and the *Venus de Milo* would likely be down several more limbs by close of play.

'It is a far, far better thing that I do, than I have ever done before,' Jeeves intoned with some solemnity.

'Self-sacrifice, you mean, Jeeves?'

'Precisely, sir.'

'Very apposite. One of yours?'

'Charles Dickens, sir. From *A Tale of Two Cities*. Sydney Carton goes to the guillotine in order that another might live.'

'Revolution, eh? Not a subject for morning conversation, Jeeves.'

'No, sir.'

'We're here to visit this fine city, but we'll be sure to depart before any of that kind of thing rubs off on us.'

While one was sorry to lose Bingo for the foreseeable, one had to consider the upside. That is, that while losing a Bingo we had not gained a Thos. One of those rare instances where a double negative, to wit two losses, turned into a positive. So while I'll never forget the look in Bingo's eye as he was led away – like the last rigid features of a man sinking to the briny depths – it was important to sally forth, even if just in memory of the old lad.

'So, Jeeves,' I asked in earnest. 'What news? You can't hide anything from the Wooster nose. The Junior Ganymede annual dinner mere hours before one of the biggest races of the calendar. You can't tell me it didn't crop up over the port and cigars.'

My excitement caused nary a flicker on the man's dial. 'You are correct in your assumption, sir. Conversation did gravitate somewhat heavily towards today's sporting spectacle; however, little conclusion was made, I fear.'

'No winged front runner, you mean? No Pegasus on which to throw one's hard-earned?'

'Quite the opposite, sir. It seems that there are few takers for anyone other than the filly Diable Rouge.

She has already won five major races this year, beginning with a win, of some considerable distance, in the Hardwicke Stakes at Ascot.'

'I remember her well, Jeeves, made the also-rans look lame by comparison.'

'Indeed, sir. It is difficult to see any stand-out challengers and, if I may say so, though she is French-owned, she is trained and ridden by two British gentlemen. A Mr Spencer Pyethorne and a Mr Charlie Banks respectively, the latter being a former champion jockey.'

'So it's the patriotic choice, you think?'

'In the absence of any serious competition, sir, I would say it was the wisest bet.'

'I'll take your word for it then, Jeeves. Diable Rouge it is. Shame old Bingo won't get to punt, but *c'est la vie* and *que sera sera*, what?'

'Very true, sir.' He coughed. It was that particular Jeeves cough signalling that, though there might be a lull in the current back-and-forth, he had further information to impart, and it was more than likely worth pinning the ears back for a good listen. 'There is one snippet of information that reached me, sir. More than likely it will have no bearing on the outcome of the race, but forewarned, forearmed; to be prepared is half the victory, as the writer Cervantes said.'

'Sounds intriguing, Jeeves, speak on.'

'Further down the card, sir, is a three-year-old mare by the name of Boadicea's Shield.'

'Another tip for the patriot, Jeeves? Let us not be blinded too much by love of country when considering the odds.'

'I agree, sir, and she has no form to speak of, it is more the identity of the owner that I wish to bring to your attention.' I wasn't keen on the man's tone. 'The Earl of Sidcup, sir, also known as Sir Roderick Spode.'

I started with some surprise at this revelation. I'd even go so far as to say that I felt a cold shiver play up and down the spine, causing one or two looks of wariness from the top hats and feather boas surrounding us in the tribune.

'Spode, Jeeves?' I asked, hoping I had misheard.

'I'm afraid so, sir.'

'And no doubt his brooding presence will be somewhere in the vicinity, striking fear into the hearts of men.' I sighed, fearing the worst. 'Have he and Madeline Bassett swapped "I do"s yet, Jeeves?'

'I believe that the nuptials are planned for next weekend, sir.'

I gulped in trepidation. Young Madeline Bassett, while having the profile of a mermaid capable of dragging sailors to the deep, also considered sentences like 'clouds are but the angels' hassocks' to be the last word in romantic thought. That she was wetter than a tureen of *bouillabaisse* was uncontested, but having had her hooks into me on a number of occasions, I knew that I would never be entirely in the clear until she was safely ensconced as Lady Sidcup – she still having it in her brain that I was slavering at the mouth to be her one and only. I shivered again.

'We must avoid the couple, Jeeves, at all costs.'

'I will endeavour to do precisely that, sir.'

I threw the man a dubious eye. 'I don't mean to hurt your feelings, Jeeves. Normally, as you know, I would be happy to confirm that your rod and your staff, they do comfort me and so on. But my faith is tested. First Bingo, now Madeline blasted Bassett. It is hard to ignore the portents and the gathering of clouds.'

'Indeed, sir.'

I decided to try and clear the head by strolling around the grounds. The pre-spectacle atmos is one of the things we sporting chaps live for, the low hum of expectation, like a rumbling stomach before a lavish nosh-up, the hushed tones like grace before same. The French do it differently, however, merrily slurping at the soup before nary a 'For what we are about to receive' has been uttered. Longchamp is no Ascot, no quiet contemplation of the card here, no scratching of heads re the odds, form and going. In point of fact, it seemed that some people were in celebratory mood already – just happy to be out, even. No wonder they were inclined to revolt at the drop of a *chapeau*. But dash it, it was infectious and the sound of cheery banter with the popping of champagne corks all acted to soothe the Wooster soul. That's one of the things I admire about our French cousins – and it may have been remarked upon before – their determination, above all else, and even under the most trying of circs, to feast constantly at the high table. It is their gift to the world. That they are given to fragile emotion is not in question. As a race they are combustible, but in the realm of comestibles they are way out in front with no sign of letting up. In short, my mooch among the great and the good was led by the keen Wooster nose and I found myself, laid almost semi-conscious by aroma, in the Fauchon marquee. Back in Blighty, of course, this would have been strictly Fortnum & Mason territory, but when in Rome and all that. It was a gourmet paradise, a picnic spread of Sun King proportions with hams, *pâtés, escargots, tartes Tatin*, cheese so ripe it could only be handled with gloves, and more varieties of wine than there are cobblestones in Yorkshire. I can't remember who said it, I made a mental note to ask Jeeves, but if food be thy medicine, let medicine be thy food. If this was to be Bertram's last meal on Death Row – by now my spirit had sunk well below the Plimsoll line – I was determined to get stuck in.

My reverie was determined not to last, however. There was a contretemps coming from the corner of the tent as a group of impassioned natives gathered around a table exhibiting much wailing and gnashing of teeth. We Woosters are curious by nature, and I edged closer to the mob to get a finer handle on proceedings. There was anger in the air. From the gist, it seemed that someone had wandered into this garden paradise, this Eden of the taste buds, and brought their own fare with them. One could understand the local dismay immediately. I mean to say, what kind of cold-hearted, emotionless wretch, exhibiting the insensitivity of an Easter Island statue, could perpetrate such calumny?

'Bertie! Don't skulk.'

To answer my own question – an Aunt Agatha, that's who, taking a sizeable bite from a very Anglo-Saxon Scotch egg. It was not a warm reunion. I managed to quell the rioters by displaying my own luncheon selection, chosen at random from the wares on offer, and they dispersed somewhat moodily.

'I thought you had business to attend to, Aunt Agatha?' I asked, slapping down an oyster as if it were my last.

'My business is here, Bertie, and kindly do not eat like an uncaged zoo exhibit in my presence.'

'Looking to invest in the turf?' I followed, scanning the table for a cheese knife.

She eyed me so coldly Medusa might have taken lessons from her. 'No, Bertie, I am investing in your future.'

Whichever way you sliced this dark sentence – and I mean sentence in all its definitions – this did not sound good. But in lieu of any strident defence or rebuttal I choked on an *éclair* instead. I considered it time well spent.

'Bertie! What are you doing here?' In the meantime, a shadow had thrown itself across the table. In hindsight, I assume the shadow was really that of Roderick Spode, who loomed above me like a malevolent airship, a dirigible of menace. To put it in contemporary terms, Spode stood approximately forty hands high and forty more wide, saw himself as a leader of men, and could have lifted me up and used me as a toothpick.

'Wooster!' he snorted without a scintilla of *bonhomie*.

The main shadow, though, came from the willowy figure of Madeline Bassett. It was a shadow of foreboding and far more damaging than any violence that Spode could mete out. I saw it all now, the scales fell from my eyes. Aunt Agatha, in her rampant determination to blight my existence, was working on a scheme, the end result of which would be that the Spode–Bassett fixture was to be scratched and a Bertram–Bassett union thrust in its place.

I staggered out, seeking clearer air.

'You really shouldn't have come, Bertie. It is too late for us now.' Madeline Bassett, as I have described, is a vision – and on the face of things, the perfect mate – but not for anyone in full possession of either hearing or critical thought. I ignored her entreaty and continued to choke while at the same time, I eventually realised, she was slapping my back with all the force of a butterfly landing on a rose petal. 'You see? Even the mere sight of Roderick and me together makes you unwell.'

My rate of choke increased at this point, no doubt a mixer of injustice adding to the issue, but I tried to right myself as I saw Spode approaching. Madeline's ineffectual back-patting was one thing, but if Spode decided to join in I might well end up briefly in Calais before skimming across the Channel like a smooth pebble. As it happened, Spode marched on and the coughing fit died down.

'Oh, Bertie!' Madeline clasped her hands together like a second-rate actress doing the role of Juliet a disservice. 'I fear for Roderick.'

'Really? He seems his usual self to me.'

'I don't like this world of horse racing, Bertie. It has changed him, he wants to conquer it and has drawn up plans to do so. He used to be so kind and considerate . . .'

I'll admit some confusion on my part. 'We are still talking about Roderick Spode?' She affected to wipe a tear from her eye. These were dangerous waters. 'Oh, come now, Madeline. This,' and I spread my arms wide, 'is a noble sport, the sport of kings, dontcha know? It has history and, and er, future. Drama! Emotion!' I was laying it on thick and she threw her big puppy-dog eyes in my direction. 'Not too much emotion obviously, just, just the right amount.'

'It is cruel, Bertie. What about the poor horsies bred solely to compete, to be whipped and pushed to exhaustion? They should be in the fields, gambolling with their playmates.'

'Yes, aren't you thinking more along the lines of spring ewes?'

'It breaks my heart, Bertie. I have asked Roderick to stop, but he is a man possessed. Do you know what happens if they lose, Bertie? Do you know what cruel fate lies in store for our dear, ancient friend, the horse?'

Apart from some ribald jibes about glue factories from a few music-hall wags, I have to admit I was short on detail, so I nodded along, trying not to upset her further. I thought taking a philosophical standpoint might help. The thing about philosophy, I always find, is that it gives one an air of gravitas while saying very little about anything. 'Such is life, Madeline, old thing. There are winners and there are losers. Destiny being a fickle mistress. A flip of the coin and you are either in a centrally heated stud farm with all the trimmings or reduced to paste and holding up practical signage along the lines of "EXIT, THIS WAY".'

I can get pretty wistful and deep dish at times, even when I don't mean to, and I noticed a dangerous twinkle in the Bassett eye.

'I knew you would understand, Bertie. We are like one soul joined, for ever tethered by our instinct and sensitivity.'

I hadn't the foggiest what she was on about and offered a non-committal 'Rather' in response.

'I shall offer Roderick an ultimatum. This will be his last race or we shall not marry, even if he wins — especially if he wins. I shall give back his ring and be yours, dear Bertie.'

As she toddled off, I felt as though I had stood in front of a twelve-strong field of Classics winners and they had all mowed me down at once. The knees buckled, the sweat seeped.

'May I be of assistance, sir?' Jeeves apparitioned from nowhere just in time, the young master in need of support. There was more to come, however.

'Hello, Bertie!' Bingo appeared where he shouldn't. 'You haven't seen that blasted cousin of yours, have you?'

Never let it be said that a Wooster has ever failed to rally round a friend in need – a bond is a bond, after all – but one couldn't help feeling that Bingo's timing was somewhat off.

'Why are you here?' I asked, trying to hide a severe case of exasperation. 'Shouldn't you be teaching young Thos the finer points of the Impressionists?'

A sick look came into his eye. 'I tried, Bertie, I really did, but we were ejected from the Louvre after that Beelzebub in short trousers tried to draw spectacles on the *Mona Lisa*.'

My shoulders slumped. 'And in desperation you thought that bringing the terrorist to Longchamp was the way forward, did you? That struck you as the wise and sensible choice, did it? Eschewing the quieter areas of the metropolis, you thought attending a heavily populated sporting event on which the eyes of the world's media rest, was the right and proper thing to do?'

'Bear with me, Bertie!' The chap practically leaped back, shocked by my end-of-tether indignation. 'I had a brainwave. Where, I thought, was the wisest place to take the boy where we most certainly would not bump into his mother, your Aunt Agatha? Here, Bertie! This den of top-hatted vipers and betting iniquity. Genius, don't you think?'

'No, Bingo, no. I do not think so at all. In fact, you have made a quite serious bloomer. My Aunt Agatha looms large in proceedings, Bingo. To be more precise, she is in the tent behind me, attempting to sever what remains of the *Entente Cordiale*!'

The colour drained from Bingo so suddenly that he went from a healthy and hearty complexion to lifeless aphid in seconds.

'B-b-but, Bertie, what if she finds Thos before we do?'

'We, Bingo? We? I'm in the soup up to my neck as it is, old fruit. My life hangs by a thread, and you talk of we! You fail to see the bigger picture, my lad. If Roderick Spode's horse, Boadicea's Shield, wins, then it's the marital version of 'for whom the bell tolls' for Bertram. Which poet was that, Jeeves?'

'It was the poet Donne, sir. "For I am involved in mankind. Therefore—"'

'Not now, Jeeves.'

'No, sir.'

'So you see, Bingo: you have your problems, I have mine.'

'But Bertie!'

'No, Bingo. It's every man for himself from this moment forth.'

'No, Bertie. It's you, you see, you who misses the bigger picture. Boadicea's Shield must win – I've put our house on it.'

It is not often that I let the world get me down, but while Bingo wittered on about talk from 'men in the know' re Boadicea's Shield and her being the one to watch, talk which Jeeves solemnly confirmed, my chin hit the Windsor knot. All looked lost.

Then I noticed Jeeves slyly retreat back into the tent, and remove a large fur coat that was on the cloak stand. This is it, I thought: the man's main valve has burst, and after a long-standing relationship in which his fish-fed brain has solved many a puzzle, he has taken to crime and is now fencing off stolen goods. I was lost for speech as he placed the coat on Bingo's shoulders and I almost jumped out of the Wooster skin and into orbit when an umbrella tapped on my shoulder.

'Bertie!' Aunt Agatha is not a tall woman, but that's really not the point. I have it on good authority that a good big 'un will always beat a good little 'un, but I doubt a good big 'un would fancy the job. 'Bertie!'

she repeated. 'I have spoken to Madeline and all is in hand. I think things will work out nicely.' She looked past my shoulder. 'And who, pray, is this?'

It is no exaggeration to say that my heart by this point rested somewhere near the socks, putting pressure on the leather uppers of my brogues, and I felt compelled to let it all out, before turning to see Bingo hidden under the fur coat and wearing my Ray-Bans.

'Allow me to make the introduction, ma'am.' Jeeves raised his head above the parapet with a timely interruption. 'This is Mr Rocco Mazzitelli, visiting from Chicago, Illinois.'

'How you doin', ma'am?' Bingo ventured in the worst American accent heard since the advent of talking pictures.

He was greeted with as much contempt as one physical human being can muster, his mere presence a strong reminder of everything that, in Aunt Agatha's opinion, was wrong with the world, including the loss of the colonies. But with lips pursed, nose in the air and steel in the eye she biffed off in search of fresh meat, much to the relief of all.

'Jeeves,' I asked, once Bingo and I had recovered. 'Do you have any contacts in the French Foreign Legion? I fancy there is little alternative.'

'I'm afraid not, sir.'

'Then what are we to do, Jeeves? If Spode's

wretched horse loses, then Bingo here is heading for the divorce courts and quite possibly debtors' prison. On the other hand, if Boadicea's Shield romps to victory, I am condemned to spend the rest of my life having buttercups held under my chin to see if I'm fond of butter.'

'Your image is a powerful one, sir. This is indeed a complicated issue.'

'Add to which,' I reminded him, 'Rocco Mazzitelli here has let loose the scourge that is Thos on an unsuspecting world, and who knows what mayhem will ensue.'

The effect of my words, though not instantaneous, hit home. The Jeeves nostrils flared, the chin protruded, and a look came into those dark eyes of his that spoke of a mastermind at work.

'I beg you, Jeeves, don't toy with me. Do you have a plan?'

'It is more the germ of an idea at present, sir.'

'Well, you couldn't water and nurture it with some haste, could you? The tape goes up in thirty minutes and my future is in your hands.'

'If I could borrow Mr Little for a period, sir, I will endeavour to do my best.'

'Borrow away, Jeeves, borrow away. Though I fail to see what this bootless pill can add to proceedings – and if the smooth road of my life is dependent upon his input, you'll forgive me if optimism doesn't immediately wrap its wings around my heart.'

'I say!' Bingo objected.

'Tcha!' I replied, and I meant for it to sting.

In one's darker moments, one's mind often wanders where angels fear to tread. The Prix de l'Arc de Triomphe, as I have intimated, is a social occasion *sans* comparison. The cognoscenti gather from far and wide, trading gossip and history, enjoying a snooter if one's on offer and generally relaxing in a world that, on the face of it, is the best of all possible worlds. However, this was not my overriding view of things as I wandered the paddocks and tribunes: a man condemned. Jeeves has fished me from despair on many an instance. The man is a marvel, unmatched in brainyness and *sang froid,* but I couldn't see him pulling this one out of the bag. If Spode's horse won, I lost. If Spode's horse lost, I won, but Bingo lost.

Fogged by my doldrums I failed to notice the cheer go up as the race started. I can't say that I had much stomach for the spectacle; too much was riding on it, so I decided to make my way to the paddock instead, and await my fate. At least the race is short and covered by highly trained thoroughbreds in less time than one would take to dunk toast soldiers into a boiled egg. The cheers went up with the hats, scattered, torn betting slips wafted on the breeze and I saw, from my position on the fence, the winner as she was led into the paddock.

We Woosters have, for generations, faced slings and arrows, triumph and disaster, good and ill. We fought in the crusades and have barely missed a combative fixture since, but when I saw Spode lead Boadicea's Shield through the applauding numbers, I nearly fell for good. The top lip didn't completely go, but it wavered. So be it, I thought. If this is to be your fate, Wooster, you shall face it down and get on with it. The milk may have been spilled, but I'll be damned if I'll shed a tear.

I felt a presence at my side. 'I don't want you to blame yourself, Jeeves,' I said, stoicism adding a certain stiffness. 'I am sure you did your best, but one can't win them all, as they say.'

'No, sir. It was a close-run thing, however.'

'Please, Jeeves, spare me the details. I shall take my medicine. Where's Bingo – off to collect his winnings, I suppose?'

'Indeed he is, sir. I advised him to recoup his money at the earliest opportunity. Before the controversy begins.'

'Controversy, Jeeves?'

'Ah, there is Mr Little now, sir. Would you excuse me a moment?'

Jeeves oozed off into the winning group's *mêlée*, where Spode held the shining trophy aloft and where I also saw Madeline off to one side, dabbing at her eye while being comforted by my Aunt Agatha, who led her away and towards the exit. All hope seemed lost as I watched Jeeves deep in conversation with the race officials. Whatever he said, the result was so many expansive displays of Gallic emotion, it might have been directed by Busby Berkeley himself. Then, as a finale, fingers were pointed at Spode, the trophy snatched back, and the jockey torn from his saddle.

'I think, sir, it would be advisable if we were to depart,' Jeeves said quietly on his return. 'I fear that it will take some time for proceedings to de-escalate and our train for the calming waters of Aix-les-Bains leaves in just under an hour.'

'Jeeves,' I said a few minutes later when we were safely in a taxi-cab. 'You don't have to tell me, of course, but what is going on? Am I to be for ever Adam to Madeline Bassett's Eve?'

'No, sir,' he replied, 'that particular circumstance is no longer a possibility, I am happy to report.'

'Not as happy as I am to hear it, Jeeves!' I breathed the air of a free man once more. 'What happened? Spare no detail.'

'Well, sir, it was important, in order to achieve a favourable outcome for both yourself and Mr Little, that there be two results. Boadicea's Shield must win, but also lose. It was not altogether a straightforward equation, but we had a little bit of luck.'

'Did we?'

'I found your cousin Thomas, sir, wandering the stable yards, and it was but the work of a moment to dress him as the jockey in Lord Sidcup's colours.' I fancy at this point in the explanation my mouth lay open like a halibut on ice. 'The original jockey was, erm, persuaded to sit out the race itself.'

'Persuaded, Jeeves? Persuaded how?'

'He was an American jockey, sir, of Italian descent, by the name of Enzo Maldini, one with a morbid fear of the black hand, sir. The mere presence at my shoulder of Mr Rocco Mazzitelli was enough to settle the matter.'

'So, let me see if I've got this straight, Jeeves. Diable Rouge is pipped at the post by Boadicea's Shield. Did you nobble her too? More Mazzitelli-style persuasion?' Jeeves nodded. 'So, Spode's horse is scratched from the race for fielding an underage jockey . . .'

'And Lord Sidcup will be banned from participating in any horse race in the future, sir. That was the suggested punishment.'

'Suggested by whom, Jeeves?'

'I may have had a hand in that, sir.'

I shook my head in wonder. 'So cousin Thos has won a Classic?'

'Yes, sir. The young man shows great promise in the pursuit and will stay quiet about his role in the affair because he does not wish to suffer the same fate as Lord Sidcup.'

'Banned, you mean? *Persona non grata* in the genteel world of equestrianism?'

'Precisely, sir.'

'And the Spode-and-Madeline union is back on full pelt?'

'I have no doubt of that, sir.'

I watched as the outskirts faded and the splendour of the city centre filled the eyes. 'Jeeves?'

'Sir?'

'*Allez-y*, Jeeves.'

Text Acknowledgements

The quoted extracts in 'The Age of Spode', though attributed to real people, have been edited or invented.

Page 93: Lyrics from 'Us Against the World' by Coldplay, written by Brian Eno, Chris Martin, Guy Berryman, Jonny Buckland and Will Champion.

About the Authors

Frank Skinner's career began in 1987 when he spent £400 of his last £435 booking a room at the Edinburgh Festival Fringe. Four years later he returned and took home comedy's most prestigious prize, the Perrier Award. Since then he has been awarded an MBE for services to entertainment, been inducted into the Radio Academy Hall of Fame, and has become a national treasure on television, on radio and on tour. As an author, his first autobiography spent forty-six weeks in the *Sunday Times* bestseller list and became the top-selling biography of 2002. He has penned four other books, most recently *A Comedian's Prayer Book*.

John Finnemore is a writer and comedian best known for his BBC Radio 4 shows *Cabin Pressure*, *John Finnemore's Souvenir Programme* and *John Finnemore's Double Acts*. His work has won many awards, including the Writers' Guild Award for Outstanding Contribution to Writing. He is also a puzzle-maker

ABOUT THE AUTHORS

and his complex narrative puzzle *The Researcher's First Murder* will appear in paperback soon.

Roddy Doyle is the author of thirteen novels, including *The Commitments, The Snapper, Paddy Clarke Ha Ha Ha*, for which he won the Booker Prize in 1993, *The Woman Who Walked into Doors*, and, most recently, *The Women Behind the Door*. He has also written three collections of short stories, eight books for children, and a memoir of his parents, *Rory and Ita*. He co-wrote *The Second Half* with Roy Keane, and *Kellie* with Kellie Harrington. He co-wrote the screenplay for *The Commitments*, and wrote the scripts for *The Snapper* and *The Van*. His most recent screen work was the script for *Rosie*, released in 2018. His four-part TV series, *Family*, was produced by the BBC in 1994. He has also written for stage, including the book of *The Commitments* musical. He lives in Dublin.

Dominic Sandbrook was born in 1974 and educated at Oxford, St Andrews and Cambridge. He is best known for his histories of Britain since the 1950s, most recently *Who Dares Wins*, as well as a series of history books for younger readers, Adventures in Time. He is a columnist for *The Times* and book critic for the *Sunday Times*. His podcast *The Rest is History* is the most popular history podcast in the world.

ABOUT THE AUTHORS

Deborah Frances-White is a comedian and writer best known as the host of the award-winning *Guilty Feminist* podcast. She is a *Sunday Times* bestselling author and is currently writing an animated feature film for Warner Brothers and Locksmith Animation. Her play, *Never Have I Ever*, has recently been produced by Chichester Festival Theatre, Melbourne Theatre Company and Black Swan State Theatre Company in Perth. Her new book, *Six Conversations We're Scared to Have*, has just been published by Virago Press. She has appeared on *QI*, *Have I Got News for You*, *Would I Lie to You* and *Question Time*. Deborah is a Writers' Guild Award winner and an Amnesty International ambassador. She is also a fizzing fan of P. G. Wodehouse.

Andrew Hunter Murray is a writer and broadcaster from London. He hosts BBC Radio 4's *The Naked Week* and the podcast *Page 94*, co-hosts the podcast *No Such Thing As A Fish*, and writes for *Private Eye* magazine. He has written three novels, the most recent of which is *A Beginner's Guide to Breaking and Entering*. His favourite Wodehouse character is Psmith.

Scarlett Curtis is the curator of the *Sunday Times* bestseller and National Book Award-winning *Feminists Don't Wear Pink (and other lies)* and *It's Not OK to Feel Blue*

ABOUT THE AUTHORS

Alan Titchmarsh CBE is a gardener, writer, novelist and television presenter. He is the author of more than seventy books and has broadcast on radio and television for almost fifty years. In collaboration with the composer Debbie Wiseman he has had two No. 1 classical albums featuring his poetry and lyrics. He has presented the *BBC Proms*, many concerts and hosts *Love Your Weekend* on ITV on Sunday mornings and the Saturday afternoon/evening programme on Classic FM. He is an ardent fan of P. G. Wodehouse.

Jasper Fforde has been writing in the Absurdist/Speculative Genre since 2001 when his novel *The Eyre Affair* debuted on the *New York Times* bestseller list. His eighteenth novel, *Dark Reading Matter*, will be the eighth in his Thursday Next series and is published in 2026. He counts his sales in millions and lives and works in his adopted nation of Wales.

Ian Moore has been a leading stand-up comedian for thirty years and is now a bestselling crime novelist. He lives in France with his wife, children and too many wilfully disobedient animals.

ABOUT THE AUTHORS

(and other lies). As a TV writer, Scarlett's credits include Amazon's *The Summer I Turned Pretty* and the upcoming *We Were Liars*. In 2017 Scarlett co-founded The Pink Protest, a feminist activist collective committed to helping young people take action. To date they have been a part of campaigns that have changed two laws. In November 2019 Scarlett was awarded the Changemaker Award for young activists presented by Equality Now and Gucci's Chime for Change. Scarlett also sits on the board of the Women's Prize. Scarlett is currently working on a new book and a scripted TV adaptation of *Feminists Don't Wear Pink (and other lies)*.

Fergus Craig is, as well as an author, a multi-award-winning actor, comedian and writer for television. *Murder at Crime Manor*, his second novel, was short-listed for the Bollinger Everyman Wodehouse Prize for Comic Fiction. His third novel, *I'm Not the Only Murderer in My Retirement Home*, will be released in 2026.

William Rayfet Hunter is a British-Jamaican author, poet and screenwriter from the north-west of England. They write about love, power and the delicate, messy parts of being alive. Their debut novel, *Sunstruck*, was published by #Merky Books in 2025.